COLIN D. PEEL

◆

CHERRY RED AND DANGEROUS

Complete and Unabridged

ULVERSCROFT
Leicester

First published in Great Britain in 1997 by
Robert Hale Limited
London

First Large Print Edition
published 1999
by arrangement with
Robert Hale Limited
London

The right of Colin D. Peel to be identified
as author of this work has been asserted
by him in accordance with the
Copyright, Designs and Patents Act 1988

Cover Artist: David Young

C403683160

Peel, Colin D. (Colin Dudley), 1936 –
Cherry red and dangerous.—Large print ed.—
Ulverscroft large print series: adventure & suspense
1. Suspense fiction
2. Large type books
I. Title
823.9'14 [F]

ISBN 0–7089–4103–6

Published by
F. A. Thorpe (Publishing) Ltd.
Anstey, Leicestershire

Set by Words & Graphics Ltd.
Anstey, Leicestershire
Printed and bound in Great Britain by
T. J. International Ltd., Padstow, Cornwall

This book is printed on acid-free paper

'Red mercury is real and it is terrifying. I think it is part of a terrorist weapon that potentially spells the end of organized society.'

Sam Cohen
Nuclear Weapons adviser to the
US Government
(*New Scientist* Vol 146)

1

At nearly thirty-five knots with the spray from the bow coming back at him in great sheets, Farrell pushed the *Stingray* into a turn, listening for any change in the roar from the diesels, keeping the throttles open until he was sure there was no trace of yesterday's vibration.

Spread out in front of him now, the coastline was a long, sweeping curve set against a backdrop of ochre-coloured mountains. To the north, stretching away to nowhere in a blast-furnace of heat, the Musandam Peninsula was shimmering in the morning haze while, to the south, he could just make out the Royal Palace, a white smudge floating between the shapes of the two old Portuguese forts guarding the entrance to Muscat.

It was all very beautiful, Farrell thought. And, at this time of year, so bloody hot that anyone in their right mind would get the hell out of it and leave Oman to the Omanis until the season changed.

His mood was souring, he realized, not because of the heat, and not just because he'd been up half the night. It was the pick-up, the prospect of another damn trip out into the Gulf tonight when there had been too many already this month. He made himself forget about it, centring the bow of the *Stingray* on the line of low, white buildings at Mutrah where he knew Tony Nelson would be getting anxious for a report on the vibration problem.

The *Stingray* was close to shore before Farrell noticed the Mercedes. Out of place among the Land Rovers and Toyotas collecting cargo from a row of beached fishing-boats, it was parked at the eastern edge of the spit where a crane was dumping rocks into the water.

The crane operator had seen the *Stingray*. Climbing on to the roof of his cab he pointed at the Mercedes and waved to show Farrell where he should tie up.

Farrell grinned at him, making a rude sign to show how he felt about being forced to use another mooring.

There was no driver sitting in the Mercedes, but on the far side of the spit, at the only place where the water was deep enough to take the *Stingray* at low tide, a young woman was standing on the rocks. She was a light-skinned Omani in her early twenties, dressed in a long-sleeved white blouse, jeans and cowboy boots. Over one arm she carried a folded, silk jacket. On her other arm she wore a cluster of expensive bracelets to match her ear-rings.

She watched Farrell drop the fenders over the side, but made no attempt to catch the rope he threw to her.

He ignored her, letting the diesels idle while he checked the new constant-velocity joint to see if it felt any hotter than the one on the port drive shaft.

He was still kneeling when he heard her shout.

'What?' Farrell straightened up and cut the engines.

'Are you the Englishman who works for Mr Nelson?'

'That's me.' He saw her look distastefully at his dirty hands and at the grease marks on his shirt.

'Can I come aboard?'

'No.' Jumping on to the rock beside her, Farrell searched for a place to secure the rope. He'd already decided he wanted nothing to do with her. Her attitude and her clothes gave her away. She would be like others of her kind — seriously rich, overeducated and westernized to the point where she was almost unrecognizable as an Omani.

³

'Nice boat,' she said.

Farrell finished knotting the rope around one of the larger boulders. Now he was back on dry land he could feel the heat. It was rising off the rocks in waves, and seeping through the soles of his shoes.

'I've been waiting for you.' She was holding an unlit cigarette. 'Do you have a light?'

'No.'

She produced a gold lighter and gave it to him. 'Now you do.'

Farrell looked at her carefully before letting it slip from his fingers. It bounced twice before disappearing into the water. 'Anything else I can help you with?' He turned up his collar to stop the sun biting into his neck.

'You don't know who I am, do you?'

'No.'

'I'm Almira Muammar.'

'Good for you.' Farrell tried to remember if he'd ever met her before.

'I want you to take me with you tonight.' She threw her cigarette away.

If he'd been uninterested before, now she had his attention. 'You'll have to excuse me,' he said. 'I've got things to do.'

She stepped in front of him. 'Stop pretending you don't know what I'm talking about.'

The situation was ironic, Farrell thought.

4

Unless she was fishing, she might have more information about the damn pick-up than he did. 'What exactly is it I'm supposed to know?' he said.

'You're collecting something for my father. He told me — emeralds. They'll be on a ship out at sea some time tonight.'

'What else did he tell you?'

'That he's paying Mr Nelson a lot of money for one night's work and that someone called John Farrell will be doing the job. That's you, isn't it?'

'And you want to go along for the ride,' Farrell said. 'Or is this daddy's idea?'

'My father doesn't know I'm here.'

'Well.' Farrell put his hands in his pockets. 'Suppose for a minute we pretend you're not making all this up, why would a nice girl like you want to spend a night being seasick out in the Gulf?'

'I don't get seasick.'

'Answer the question.'

'Because it would be — because I haven't done anything like it before.'

'For kicks, you mean?' Farrell knew his guess had been right. Except for being unusually pretty, she was no different to the rest — looking for any excitement she could find because she was bored out of her brain.

'Will you take me?'

5

'No.'

'I'll pay you a thousand American dollars.'

Moving her gently out of the way he began walking.

'Five thousand,' she called after him.

He turned round.

'I can make my father cancel his contract with Mr Nelson.' She was standing with one hand on her hip and her mouth was set.

'Don't push your luck.' Farrell studied her face. She had extraordinarily large eyes and, even with her lips clamped shut, there was something about her that he seemed to have missed before.

'Well?' she asked.

'Does Tony Nelson know about this?'

She shook her head.

'Do you know it might not be safe?'

'I don't see why. Collecting emeralds isn't dangerous — not compared with running guns. That's what you normally do, don't you?'

He disregarded the remark.

'Why should it be dangerous?'

'Ask your father.'

She adjusted the jacket over her arm. 'You haven't said if we have a deal.'

'I'll think about it.'

'What does it depend on?'

'Whether you're who you say you are, and

how I feel at the time.' Farrell was being more rude than he had intended to be. 'Look,' he said. 'If you want to hang around here at about six o'clock, I'll let you know then. No promises.'

'Oh.' Some of her confidence had gone and she was trying harder to be nice. 'What should I wear?'

'You're not coming on board in boots. Otherwise you can wear what the hell you like.'

'Six o'clock?' she said.

'Bring the money with you.' He paused. 'That doesn't mean I've made up my mind.'

'All right.' Glancing at him she walked past and headed for her Mercedes.

Farrell watched her go, wondering whether five grand was enough to take the risk, and whether he should mention the proposition to Nelson.

He had still not decided when he arrived at the office.

Tony Nelson was sitting on the windowsill, poking at his air-conditioning unit with a screwdriver. 'What's the temperature like in here?' he asked.

'Bloody freezing.' Farrell helped himself to a beer.

Nelson was Irish, a small, wiry man with a lined face and a tendency to speak too

7

quickly. Today, for some inexplicable reason, he was wearing a tie. 'How was the drive shaft?' he asked.

'Seems OK.' Farrell inspected the tie. 'Visitors?'

'Been and gone — the guy we're doing the pick-up for.'

'Who is he?'

'Ghassan Muammar — some kind of hot-shot trader in precious stones. Says he distributes right up through the Arab Emirates into Saudi.'

'Legally?'

Nelson shrugged. 'I didn't ask. Do you want to talk about tonight?'

Five minutes ago Farrell's shirt had been sticking to him. Now it was all but dry and he was shivering. 'What am I collecting?' he said.

'A whole bunch of emeralds — twenty kilogrammes of them. They're ex-Iran, southbound on a coastal freighter. She's due through the Straits of Hormuz early this afternoon so I've arranged for you to meet her between midnight and one a.m. The skipper's been told to anchor until you show up.'

'Anchor where?' Farrell found himself thinking about the girl.

'The co-ordinates are on there.' Nelson threw him a rolled-up chart. 'Mid-Gulf, off

Khabura. As long as the GPS doesn't screw up you won't be able to miss her.'

'Are you sure it's emeralds?'

'I did some checks. Muammar's pretty straight — no history of drugs. I told him you'd need to see what you're carrying.' Nelson paused. 'Are you OK? You look like hell.'

'Just tired. I could do without another night run.'

'Because you're worried about the competition?'

Farrell put down his beer can. 'It's those other bastards,' he said. 'They're out there every night. They've got it into their heads that any boat running without lights has to be loaded down with heroin.'

'Not a bad assumption if you're in their line of business. Look, John, if you don't want to do it, I'll go. It's probably my turn anyway.'

'No. It's OK. I got thirty-five knots this morning. That'll burn off anyone looking for an easy hit.' This was the time to raise the possibility of a passenger, Farrell decided. If he left it any longer it was going to sound all wrong.

'OK,' Nelson said. 'Now listen, this is important: as soon as you've got an idea of when you'll be back, call me on the radio so I can get Muammar here with the cash. I don't want his damned emeralds hanging around the office all day.'

'Meet me at the waterfront when I get in. Then you can hand them over right away.'

Nelson shook his head. 'I don't do business on the waterfront. There'll be too many people around. It'll only be a crate or a box or something. Just stick it in the truck and bring it here. Then we can all have a drink and find out how else we can help nice Mr Muammar spend his money.'

By now, as well as being so cold that he thought his teeth might start chattering, Farrell had abandoned the idea of mentioning the girl. 'I'm going home to take a shower and get some sleep,' he said. 'What's the name of the freighter?'

'The *Sarab*. I wrote it on the chart.'

'OK.' Farrell went to the door. 'You know, if you keep playing with your air-conditioning, you're going to have icicles hanging off the ceiling.'

Nelson grinned at him. 'Have a nice trip, and don't forget to radio.'

Outside, the heat hit Farrell like a wall, almost persuading him to go straight to his apartment. Instead, for no good reason he could think of, after making several phone calls he turned the truck on to the coast road and drove slowly down to Muscat.

10

He found the villa at once, a gracious home in the Qurm Heights, shaded by date palms overhanging the garden walls. Although there were at least half-a-dozen vehicles in the courtyard, it was easy to pick out the car he was looking for and easier still for him to identify the number plate on the Mercedes parked just inside the gates.

★ ★ ★

In the moonlight Farrell couldn't see her face properly. She had spent the last two hours sitting alone at the stern, and this was his first opportunity to find out if she was enjoying herself or whether the trip had turned out to be more boring than she'd expected.

'Here.' Taking her hands he placed them on the wheel. 'Hold it steady.'

'I don't know how to.' She sounded uncertain.

'Try.' Farrell poured himself a cup of coffee from the vacuum flask before he checked his course again. Despite the sea being almost flat and because he'd been keeping the speed down to conserve fuel, he was behind schedule and still travelling too close to the coast. Soon he would have to swing north, he thought, heading farther out where there would be more chop, and where he'd have to

11

be a lot more careful.

He was about to offer some coffee to his passenger when she glanced across at him. Dressed in jeans and a denim jacket, tonight she was barefoot and had dispensed with her jewellery.

'You don't like me, do you?' she said.

Farrell wasn't sure how to answer the question. 'Does it matter?' he said.

'No. Except it makes it awkward to ask you things.'

'Ask away. You're paying. What do you want to know?'

'Don't patronize me.' She spoke without turning her head.

'Look,' Farrell said. 'I'll tell you what: seeing as we're going to be stuck out here together all night, if you stop trying to score points, I'll promise not to be patronizing. How about that?'

'I haven't been trying to score points.'

He took the wheel again. 'You'd better help yourself to coffee,' he said. 'The sea's going to get rougher pretty soon.'

She fumbled with the flask. 'Will you show me where we have to go?'

'Sure. Right now we're about here.' He put his finger on the chart. 'And some time around 0100 hours we're due out where that red circle is.'

'How do we know when we're there?'

Farrell switched on the GPS. 'By using this,' he said. 'It's a Global Positioning System that lets us navigate by satellite signals. If the *Sarab* is where it's supposed to be, this little baby will take us right alongside. The *Sarab*'s the freighter we have to meet.'

'Oh.' She inspected another instrument. 'Is this thing a radio?'

'VHF. That other box you've got your hand on is a depth finder.'

'I don't understand why we're going up the coast instead of directly to where we want to go.'

'Because it's safer.' Farrell opened the throttles slightly.

'Why is it?'

'Well.' He paused. 'Most nights, once you get off-shore, there's a lot of traffic doing more or less what we're doing. Some of it's halfway legitimate, but the rest is as illegal as hell.'

'Drugs,' she said.

'Right. And whenever you have drugs being moved around, you're going to find people who've figured out how to short-cut the supply routes. There are boats out here which do nothing but run down the traffickers to steal their cargo.'

'Pirates.' She glanced at him. 'Is that what you mean?'

He nodded.

'What happens if one of them thinks we're carrying drugs? Do you have a gun or something?'

Farrell grinned. 'You don't mix it with these guys. There's a better way. Like this.' He pulled the throttle levers back to their stops, enjoying the surge of acceleration as the *Stingray*'s propellers began to bite.

A moment later he saw her put her hands over her ears and lean against the side of the cabin to steady herself.

Farrell kept the revs up, placing one hand on the engine cover, searching for any tell-tale buzzing with his fingertips. There was no vibration, just the sensation of power and the roar of the two big Volvo diesels doing their work.

When he eventually cut back to a more economical speed, the expression of his passenger had changed.

'What do you think?' he asked.

'I can't hear properly.' Despite being drenched in spray and having her hair plastered all over her face, she was clearly pleased.

Farrell handed her a life jacket. 'Time to put that on,' he said.

'I don't want to.'

'Just do it. Don't argue with me.'

'What about you?' She slipped the jacket over her head and fastened the straps.

'I've got one somewhere if I need it.' Swinging the bow of the *Stingray* north, he concentrated on his bearing while he started calculating the average speed he'd need to maintain from here on.

She interrupted him.

'What?' He finished drawing a line on the chart before seeing what she wanted.

'You may call me by my first name.'

Farrell was careful not to smile. In trying to be friendly she had managed to sound more condescending than usual.

'OK,' he said. 'It's Almira, isn't it?'

She nodded. 'And I shall call you Farrell. Is that all right?'

'Fine.' To prevent her from seeing his face he turned away. Although her English was all but perfect, it was difficult to know how to take some of her remarks. As a result, Farrell was still trying to decide whether his first impression of her had been right or wrong. Not that it mattered, he thought. By morning she'd have had her money's worth and that would be the end of things. Miss Muammar would have something to talk about next week when she met her rich friends over coffee, and he'd be out here again, delivering another load of gift-wrapped AK47s to some godforsaken Iranian beach where the nearest coffee shop would be 200 miles away.

He pushed the *Stingray* up to eighteen knots, staring out into the dark, looking for shadows and the give-away white streaks of wakes from other vessels. As well as the sea being rougher now, making it impossible to see anything low down, Farrell was starting to worry about the moon. It was nearly full, hanging in a cloudless sky and throwing a swathe of light across the water. Twice before on nights like this he'd learned the hard way, discovering that smaller boats had the advantage of being almost invisible until they were on top of you.

'Why are we going faster?' To counter the slamming of the hull, Almira was holding on to the cabin rail.

'So we get there on time, and to persuade anyone who's watching not to bother with us.'

'Do you think anyone is watching us?'

'I don't know.' Farrell pointed. 'There — off the starboard bow.'

'Oh my goodness.' She watched a school of dolphins skimming through the water ahead of the *Stingray*. 'I didn't realize you could see them at night.'

'Usually you can't. It's the moon.'

'Can I ask you some more questions?'

'Go ahead.'

'I just wondered why you do this. Do you get paid a lot?'

'It's a job,' Farrell said.

'But you've done other things before?'

He looked at her. 'You want a life history?'

'No. I didn't mean to sound rude.'

'I was making good money in Kuwait before the Iraqi invasion,' he said. 'My wife was working there too — teaching in one of the high schools. When the war started I moved down into Saudi and messed around there for a while. Since then I've sort of kept on going. Is that what you want to know?'

'Doesn't your wife mind you being out all night?'

'I don't think so. She went back to England seven years ago.'

'Oh. Is that why you came to Oman?' She stopped abruptly. 'I'm sorry.'

'It's OK. I knew Tony Nelson from Kuwait. We worked there together. He offered me a job in Mutrah. I took it. End of story.'

In the distance the shape of a tanker was looming. Like most of the others Farrell encountered at night, it was low in the water from a full load of oil and hogging the south-east shipping lane. He guessed there would be another one a mile or two behind it.

Now Almira had seen its lights she had fallen silent, watching the huge outline slide past in front of them like a moving wall of steel. She remained quiet for the next hour, either lost in her own thoughts or content to let Farrell busy himself with his navigation.

He had the *Stingray* within five miles of the pick-up point when she asked him how much farther they had to go.

'We're just about there.' He consulted the GPS. 'If the skipper's in the right place we should be able to see her anytime.'

'What are we looking for?' She peered into the darkness.

'Coastal freighter. Probably a small one.'

Farrell was wrong. By Gulf standards the *Sarab* was reasonably large. Streaked in rust and surrounded by floating garbage that had been thrown overboard, it was riding at anchor in a slick of fuel oil leaking from its hull. On the side of its bow the name *Sarab* was written in flaking white paint.

Keeping clear of the oil Farrell used his radio. '*Stingray* to *Sarab*,' he said. 'Please confirm you have cargo to transfer.'

There was a delay followed by a crackling noise before someone replied in unintelligible English.

'Repeat your message,' Farrell said.

'Here is the *Sarab*. By the light flashing you

will please to come along port side for the courier to board.'

'Over there.' Almira pointed to the superstructure where a flashlight was winking. 'Can you see it?'

Farrell didn't answer. Because this was the first he'd heard about a courier, the news had come as a surprise. He edged the *Stingray* closer, moving slowly through the mess of oil, plastic containers and floating bottles, until the bow nudged the side of the freighter. Where the light had been, two members of the *Sarab* crew were lowering a rope ladder.

Before Farrell could ask for clarification over the radio a man began climbing down the ladder. Hanging from a strap around his shoulder was what looked like a machine pistol.

'What's the matter?' Almira had sensed Farrell's disquiet.

'Take a look.' Backing the *Stingray* off a few feet he made it impossible for the man to jump the gap.

'You will please to come closer,' the man called out.

'Why the hell should I?' Farrell shone a flashlight on him.

'It is arranged.'

'Who by?' Farrell said.

'I accompany the consignment to collect

19

payment in Mutrah from Mr Muammar.'

Farrell was uncertain, wondering if he should call Nelson on the radio to see if he knew anything about an armed guard.

The man twisted himself around on the ladder. 'You will permit me to come on board,' he said. 'If not, then there will be no transfer.'

'OK, OK.' Farrell had decided. Out here it was his call and he knew Nelson would tell him so.

Moving the *Stingray* alongside to allow the man on deck, Farrell waited for a small steel box to be lowered from the *Sarab*'s rail before he went forward with his flashlight.

The courier was nervous, fingering his gun — an old model Uzi with a folding metal stock.

Farrell put his hand on it. 'Point that at me just once and you go over the side,' he said. 'Let me see the emeralds.'

The box was made from stainless steel, heavily reinforced with ribs. The lid too was reinforced, but distorted from having been forced open at some time. Welded crudely to it was a new hasp, secured to the original eye with a large padlock.

Kneeling down, the man unlocked it with a key that was chained to his wrist. He swung open the lid, but remained where he was, holding the padlock in one hand and clutching his gun in the other.

Farrell ignored him, flicking the beam of his flashlight over rows of chamois-leather pouches packed inside the box. The pouch he selected for inspection had the word MINATOM stencilled on the side. It contained what he estimated was about a kilogramme of large, uncut stones.

'OK.' He replaced the pouch and glanced at the courier. 'Bring your box with you.'

Farrell returned to the cabin where Almira was sitting on an engine cover fiddling with a strap on her life jacket.

'What were you looking for?' she asked.

'Heroin or cocaine.'

'My father doesn't deal in drugs.'

Farrell smiled at her. 'Nor do I.'

'Is it all right if I smoke a cigarette?'

'No. We're running without lights — remember?'

'I don't see why when the moon's so bright.' She moved aside to let the courier wedge the box alongside her feet. 'Are we going now?'

'Right now.' Instead of bothering to radio the *Sarab* to say goodbye, Farrell waved his flashlight to show he was leaving, easing the *Stingray* away from the shadow of the freighter before starting off on the long run home.

Beside him Almira was being careful to avoid the courier's eyes. Evidently surprised to discover her on board, he was a young Arab, badly dressed and smelling powerfully of sweat.

Almira waited until there was more noise from the engines before she spoke to Farrell again. 'I have to go to the toilet,' she said.

'Up front.' He handed her a bucket. 'Take that with you.'

Farrell found the situation amusing. Here she was, in the middle of the Gulf in the middle of the night, stuck with an Englishman she didn't like and a horny, Iranian courier with a gun — a larger slice of reality than she'd bargained for.

As soon as she came back he increased the engine revs, heading for the Omani coast at slightly more than twenty knots — an uncomfortable speed for the conditions, but one that Farrell knew was barely fast enough. If he adopted the same course he'd used on the way out it would be at least two and a half hours before he was off Khabura, with the prospect of another four hours after that if he hugged the coast on the final leg to Mutrah. By then the sun would be well up and Nelson would be getting scratchy.

He checked the gauges, wondering whether to risk burning up fuel on a straight, high

22

speed run when he was uncertain of the weather. In the end he decided to compromise, going a little faster and setting a course that gave him the option of slowing down if he hit a swell.

The *Stingray* was cutting through patches of milky phosphorescence now, pushing them aside as the throb from the diesels became deeper and the hull flattened out on the water.

If the courier was enjoying the ride he showed no sign of it. Eyes half closed, he was sitting on his box, the key to it dangling from the chain around his wrist. Almira too was silent, either because of the courier's presence or because she was tiring of her long night out.

For Farrell, the night had been routine. Having the girl on board had relieved some of the boredom, but because she seemed to have remained as disdainful as when he'd first met her, he was inclined to think it had been a mistake to bring her.

The *Stingray* was less than fifteen miles from the peninsula when Farrell made his next mistake. He saw two of them early, but nearly missed the third boat coming from behind. They were on converging courses, an attack pattern he'd encountered before, but never this close to the coast.

Almira had seen them too. 'Trouble?' she asked.

'Yeah.' Farrell strained his eyes, trying to see what kind of boats they were while he made an estimate of their speed. They were travelling fast, but not fast enough, and already they had lost the element of surprise.

Alerted by Almira, the courier was on his feet looking anxious.

Pushing him to one side, Farrell spun the wheel and hit the throttles, turning the *Stingray* south.

He had nearly completed the manoeuvre when the courier began to scramble forward over the deck.

Farrell shouted at Almira to stop him but changed his mind. At the bow the courier was struggling to his feet, bracing himself against the rail and levelling his gun.

Grabbing Almira by her belt, Farrell spun the wheel again.

He was too late.

Unbalanced but still standing, the courier opened fire.

The response was as immediate as it was predictable. Searchlights licked out at the *Stingray*, and above the noise of engines came the hammer of machine guns.

'Jesus fucking Christ.' Farrell held his breath. There were more muzzle flashes,

24

bright red bursts of colour from a launch less than a hundred yards away. It was closing on them, but the *Stingray* was nearly up to speed giving Farrell the few precious seconds he needed.

The courier stopped to fit a fresh magazine to his Uzi. It was the last thing he ever did.

Bullets smashed through the cabin wall, narrowly missing Almira. At the same time a line of splinters erupted along the deck.

The courier stood no chance. He staggered sideways, dropping his gun, before he collapsed with blood gushing from his mouth.

Ramming the girl into the space between the engine compartments, Farrell held her down with his knee while he put the *Stingray* into a series of wild turns to evade the searchlights and the bullets.

There was no more gunfire. Out of range, moving too swiftly for the attackers to follow, the *Stingray* was flying now, leaving the danger in its wake. Farrell kept the throttles wide open, cursing the dead courier and knowing how lucky they had been.

His relief was short-lived. There was the smell of fuel and the port engine began to miss. A moment later the other engine faltered.

A fountain of diesel spraying on to a bulkhead told him where to look. He searched quickly with his fingers, feeling ragged edges where a bullet had torn through both the fuel lines. The damage was worse than he'd expected — so bad it was impossible to plug the leak.

He hauled Almira to her feet. 'Now listen,' he said. 'Any minute our engines are going to die. That means we'll be boarded. Whatever they want, don't say anything — not a single thing. Open your mouth and we can wind up dead. Do you understand?'

She began to speak, but thought better of it, biting her lip instead.

Farrell had his shoe wedged against the fuel lines, forcing his foot sideways so hard that his ankle was aching. Even after the engines spluttered to a halt and the *Stingray* lost all headway, he kept his foot where it was as though it would somehow make a difference.

Except for waves slapping against the hull it was very quiet now and he could hear the sound of an approaching vessel.

Two or three minutes, he thought, maybe less. Long enough to use the radio, but not long enough for anything else.

He sent his message without waiting for acknowledgement, reading the co-ordinates of his position off the GPS and repeating each of them twice. Shortly after he'd finished a searchlight came on again. The source of the beam was close, no more than twenty or thirty yards away.

Farrell made Almira stand still. 'Nice and easy,' he said. 'Keep your hands in the open where they can see them.'

'What's going to happen?' she whispered.

'It'll be OK.' Farrell's throat was dry, and he could feel the sweat running down inside his shirt.

A slight bump announced the arrival of a launch alongside.

Two men came aboard. They were carrying automatic assault rifles and wore *khanjars* on their belts, the ceremonial daggers marking them both as Omanis.

One of them cast his eyes round the cabin. He was well built, unshaven and had several teeth missing. 'You have cocaine?' he said.

'No.' Farrell pointed to the box. 'Emeralds.'

After trying to open the lid the man looked at Farrell and made a twisting motion with his fingers.

'If you want the key, you'll have to get it,' Farrell said. 'It's up front on the guy you shot.'

The smaller of the two men clambered out on to the bow and started tugging at the courier's wrist, eventually resorting to his knife to free the chain. When he returned to unlock the box his hands were red and sticky.

Already Farrell knew what he was up against. These were men who preyed on the drug smugglers of the Gulf, hard men who cared little for the lives of the traffickers whose boats they plundered. Their attitude was one of indifference. All that mattered was what they could steal and how much they could sell it for. And when their work was done here, what then? Farrell wondered. Would they set the *Stingray* adrift? Or would the end come with a quick bullet to the head?

With the aid of Farrell's flashlight the well-built Omani was busy hauling emeralds from the box, checking the contents of each pouch before handing them to his companion for transfer to the launch.

When the last pouch had been removed the man tossed the empty box overboard and directed his attention to Farrell. 'The girl is virgin?' he asked.

'Leave her alone.' Farrell kept his voice level. 'She's my wife.'

'Ah.' The man said something to Almira in Arabic.

Responding hesitantly, she took off her life jacket and dropped it at her feet. Her face was without expression, but her hands were shaking.

She stood absolutely still while the Omani ripped open her jacket and cut through her blouse with his knife. But he had miscalculated. The instant he reached out to touch her breasts she spat in his face.

The man grinned at her. 'You are a little cat, yes? We shall dull the sharpness of your claws, I think. Please to go with my friend.'

Farrell started to move, but was forced backward by a rifle muzzle driven hard into his stomach. He was trying furiously to think, knowing that once Almira was taken away she'd be better off dead.

Slowly he reached into his pocket for the money. 'Five thousand American dollars for the girl,' he said.

The man took the notes, counting them with one eye on Almira.

Farrell was under no illusions. The chance of buying time was as slim as the chance of buying her safety and if he didn't act now, neither of them were going to remain alive for very long.

In the grip of the small man, Almira was being dragged over the side into the launch. She was kicking, shouting despairingly for Farrell as her feet left the *Stingray*'s deck.

Now, Farrell thought. In another second, she'd be gone.

Seizing the barrel of the rifle he twisted it, using all his strength to slam the Omani gunman against the bulkhead.

Half a second before Farrell reached Almira the first shots rang out behind him. But by then he was a moving target, tackling her in a headlong rush to break her free.

Unhurt he hit the water with his arms locked firmly round her waist.

'Under the hull,' he yelled. 'Dive.'

When she was slow to react he wound his fingers into her hair and pulled her down with him. No sooner had he done so than there was the awful sound of bullets zipping through the water.

Beneath the *Stingray* where it was darker, Farrell forced her toward the stern, knowing they would be shielded by the engines if bullets started coming straight down through the planking. But she was fighting him, already unable to hold her breath. Farrell too was running out of air.

He counted to ten, then helped her up, keeping her face pressed against the boat while she gulped and coughed.

Somewhere above him men were shouting. The shouts were followed by the sound of an engine and the noise of churning propellers.

Refusing to believe the launch was leaving, Farrell made Almira dive again. This time he held her hand, guiding it on to one of the drive shafts so she could maintain her position without his assistance.

The propellers were receding. Farrell was certain of it. And where before there had been a white glare from searchlights on the water, now the moon was casting a shadow from the *Stingray*. It was what he'd been hoping for — an indication that they still did have a chance.

While he was reaching for Almira's hand again, the first of the grenades went off inside the hull.

Shrapnel tore through his shoulder like a hot iron, and the shock of the detonation filled his lungs with water. The second explosion was worse, closer to the stern and igniting the *Stingray*'s leaking fuel.

His shoulder all but useless, Farrell kicked his way upward, towing Almira behind him.

On the surface the fire was taking hold. From one end to the other, the *Stingray* was ablaze, the reflection of the flames throwing a crimson glow out over the Gulf. For Farrell, his vision distorted by pain, it seemed as though the night itself was burning.

Trying unsuccessfully to breathe, he was able to give Almira one last shove before he started deciding whether or not to drown. He had not quite made up his mind when the blast from the third hand-grenade turned everything into a soft, enveloping blackness.

2

Both perfumes were familiar. They were from different places but, by trying hard, Farrell thought he had this one pegged. It came from an Arab village high in the mountains somewhere — a place he had once been. The image was of veiled women and young girls gathered around a smoking brazier. They were laughing, lifting their skirts to allow the fragrance of the smoke to permeate their underclothing. Farrell could remember the name of it now, and the village was much clearer in his mind. The perfume was *bakhour*, not unlike Omani frankincense, but more musky and more intoxicating.

The other perfume was equally intoxicating but it created images of England, memories of long summer nights when he'd been half crazy for Mary, and there was a more recent recollection too — of someone touching his face while he was asleep.

Sometimes the two perfumes overlapped. At other times they were faint as though whoever wore them was keeping their distance.

At the moment that was not the case.

32

There was no overlap, and the wearer was nearby — maybe even close enough for him to make contact.

Reaching out cautiously into the dark Farrell touched skin. His effort was rewarded by someone speaking his name and telling him to wake up.

He opened his eyes slowly to find a woman smiling down at him. She was a middle-aged Omani, beautifully dressed in a saffron-yellow shawl over a bodice embroidered with silver thread. Strings of coloured beads hung round her neck, her wrists were weighed down with bracelets and she wore heavy gold rings in both her ears.

'Good morning,' she said.

Farrell hadn't expected her to be a stranger. He hadn't expected to find himself in a strange bed either. He sat up, wincing at a stab of pain that shot through his left arm.

'It is good you no longer sleep,' the woman said. 'I shall telephone for the doctor.'

'Hold on.' Farrell used his other arm to push himself upright. 'I don't want a doctor. I'm OK.'

She laughed. 'Already the doctor has been to see you two times. But now you decide you have no need for him. Will you also decide there is no injury to your shoulder?'

Farrell was in no doubt about his shoulder.

As well as it hurting like hell, his arm was strapped to his chest. 'All right,' he said. 'Where am I? And who are you?'

'You are in the house of my brother where for more than two days you sleep. My name is Latifa. Does that tell you what you wish to know?'

'I don't think so.' Although he was reluctant to appear foolish, Farrell decided to guess. 'Almira,' he said. 'Is this her father's house in Muscat?'

'Yes, of course. I am Almira's — ' The woman searched for the correct word. 'I am the sister to her father.'

'You're her aunt?'

'Yes. It is good Almira is not here to make fun of my bad English.'

'Is she OK?'

'Very tired, but she is well, I think. She brings you here after you are both picked from the water by the coastguard.'

'And I've been here two days?' Farrell said.

'Yes.'

'Jesus.' The questions were coming faster now — so many of them that he didn't know which one to ask first. 'I have to make a phone call.' The vision of the *Stingray* burning was pushing everything else aside.

Swinging his legs off the bed Farrell stood

34

up, and immediately sat down again with his head spinning.

'If it is Mr Nelson you wish to call, I must tell you he has already made a visit. In the morning yesterday Miss Almira and my brother have spoken with him together.'

By keeping still, Farrell had stopped the room from going round. 'Could you phone him for me?' he said.

'I am to ask him to come?'

'Please.' Farrell hesitated. 'Have you been looking after me?'

'Sometimes.' The woman prepared to leave.

'*Bakhour*,' he said. 'Your perfume. It's from Yemen, isn't it?'

'Yes.' She turned smiling at the door. 'Please rest until I return.'

As soon as she'd gone Farrell experimented, holding on to the bedhead and moving much more slowly. He felt weak, but by keeping his eyes on a reference point he seemed to have overcome the risk of falling over.

The room was cool, overlooking the tiled courtyard he remembered seeing when he'd come to check out the Mercedes. Today there were no cars, just two dogs stretched out in the shade of a palm near the gate — salukis with light-brown coats and long, feathered tails.

Farther away, through some French doors on the opposite side of the courtyard, Farrell could see Aunt Latifa speaking into a telephone while above her, at an open window on the second floor, a maid was shaking a pillowcase.

He turned his attention to the room. As well as being light and airy it contained some of the most expensive furnishings that Farrell had ever seen. The floor was marble, Chagall lithographs hung on the walls, and in front of an eighteenth century French dresser filled with Islamic glass, stood a low table made in the form of a chess board. the chess pieces themselves were made of gold and enamel inlaid with precious stones, each piece being so highly polished that they appeared to be glowing.

Between the seven foot double bed and a curved leather sofa stood another table. On it lay Farrell's watch, his wallet and a silver bowl containing a pea-sized fragment of metal. He guessed what the fragment was — the shrapnel taken from his shoulder.

In the en-suite, he studied himself in the mirror. Apart from a large bruise on one side of his forehead and a cut across the bridge of his nose, there was little evidence of other damage. He decided against unwrapping the strapping from his chest, returning to the bedroom instead where he began to search for his clothes.

They were in the wardrobe, clean, dry and freshly pressed. His shoes were there too, one of them stained and smelling faintly of diesel fuel.

He attempted to dress, giving up the idea when he found it almost impossible with one arm out of action. There was no hurry, Farrell thought. And nowhere in particular he wanted to go.

Lying back down on the bed he let himself start thinking about what had happened, wondering if Almira had told her father about the emeralds and what the hell Nelson was going to say about the *Stingray*.

It was a little over an hour before Farrell was to discover his concern had been unnecessary.

A knock on the door was followed by Aunt Latifa entering the room with Tony Nelson close behind her. Nelson's expression was smug. He was grinning, evidently pleased to have received the phone call.

Before Farrell could say anything Aunt Latifa assumed control. 'Half an hour,' she said. 'Not one minute longer. If you still talk after that I shall arrange for your visitor to be removed.' She looked at Nelson. 'May I bring coffee for you?'

'No thanks.' Nelson sat down on the sofa.

'Very well.' She plumped up a pillow for Farrell before walking briskly from the room.

'Nice.' Nelson inspected Farrell's silk pyjamas. 'Very smart.'

'How much do you know?'

'All of it. Probably more than you do. You're a lucky bastard.'

'It doesn't feel like it,' Farrell said. 'What happened after you got my call on the radio?'

'You were over fifteen miles out and bloody near sixty miles from Mutrah. If you'd stayed afloat I figured you might have drifted in, but that it wasn't worth taking the risk.'

'So you called the coastguard,' Farrell said.

'Thought it'd give you the best chance. It still took the best part of four hours for them to find you. You know how they are.'

Farrell eased himself off the bed and went to stand at the window. 'And I was unconscious?'

'You ought to be dead. Somehow or other the girl threaded you into a life jacket, and got the water out of your lungs. She said the only thing left floating when the *Stingray* went down was one life jacket. It was all burned up in the fire so she had to work pretty hard to keep your head up. I don't know how the hell she did it.'

Her life jacket, Farrell thought, the one

he'd made her put on. 'None of it was her fault,' he said. 'I had a guy with a gun on board — a courier for the emeralds.'

'Yeah, I know. I've had the whole story.'

'Does the coastguard have the same story?'

Nelson shook his head. 'They don't know about the courier or the emeralds. It was just a fire at sea. Your girlfriend did a good job on them.'

'She's not my girlfriend. Look, I should've told you. She paid me five grand to take her along.'

'I heard.' Nelson grinned. 'Lucky you did, wasn't it? If she hadn't been on board you'd have been shark bait.'

'But that's not why you're so bloody cheerful, is it?' Farrell knew he was missing something. 'We're not even halfway through the contract from Sohar. There are another fifty crates of rifles sitting down there ready to go. How are you going to deliver them without a boat?'

'Don't you know?'

'No.'

'You don't know you're a big hero either?'

Farrell had no idea what he was talking about. 'How do you mean?' he said.

'According to Muammar's daughter, you saved her life. She says if you hadn't done what you did she'd have been raped and

39

killed. Her father's real grateful. Why else would you be here?'

Farrell didn't say anything.

'Muammar blames himself for the loss of the *Stingray*. You see, he wasn't exactly straight with me. I told him we only carry stuff that's pre-paid, but he hadn't paid a cent for those emeralds. His deal was for cash on delivery. That's why you got landed with a courier. Muammar knows if it hadn't been for your trigger-happy passenger you could've outrun the trouble. His daughter told him.'

'Did she tell him we're out of business too?' Farrell said.

Nelson removed the shrapnel from the bowl and rolled the piece of metal between his fingers. 'The *Stingray* was insured — through the UK. But it doesn't look as though that matters much, not now Mr Muammar's decided he wants to be sure we don't lose our share of the market. He's funding a replacement boat.'

'A whole new boat?' Farrell was astonished.

'And a once-a-month delivery run for him up through the Straits. He's having problems with his overland routes, and he doesn't fancy aircraft. Don't forget he hasn't lost money on the emeralds.' The grin was back on Nelson's face. 'He figures he owes us both a favour.'

'He doesn't owe me anything.'

40

'How about the five grand his daughter paid you? You haven't got that anymore, have you? She said you gave it away.'

'I didn't give it away,' Farrell grunted. 'And I don't want any favours from anyone.'

'You'd better tell your girlfriend then.' Nelson held up a hand. 'OK, OK, so she's not your girlfriend.' He paused. 'Have you thought she might be pretty grateful for what you did as well?'

Farrell wasn't thinking much about anything. Although his shoulder was aching and his head was full of cotton wool, he got up and went to stand at the window again. 'Was I really in the water for four hours?' he said.

'Sure. With concussion and a hole in your shoulder.' Nelson dropped the shrapnel back into the bowl. 'Did you hear what I just said?'

'Yeah.' Outside in the courtyard the dogs were no longer in the shade. They were panting, too lazy to change their position. Farrell watched them until they moved out of the sun, wondering if he could face another Omani summer and whether this would be a good time to tell Nelson. It depended, he thought; partly on how hot the summer would get, and partly on how false the image created by the other perfume might turn out to be.

* ★ ★

On odd occasions in Saudi Arabia Farrell had been inside the houses of the truly wealthy, large pretentious buildings combining Islamic and western themes in unsuccessful attempts to provide the best of both cultures. The Muammar residence was unlike any of them. Despite some of the furnishings being European, the architecture itself was distinctively Omani, the western influence so subdued that if it intruded at all it was only to add practicality in places like bathrooms and the service areas.

The room he was in now was the only one Aunt Latifa had not showed him in her afternoon tour of the villa. It had a soft-beige terrazzo floor and seemed to consist mainly of bookcases.

'Please, you will sit down.' Ghassan Muammar's English was better than his sister's, but not as good as his daughter's. He was a large man, significantly overweight, but with a bearing that allowed him to carry his weight to advantage. This evening, instead of the business suit he had worn at dinner, he was in traditional dress; a cashmere turban, white robe and expensive leather sandals.

Farrell chose a chair by the window. Over dinner Muammar had been the perfect host,

42

even coming to his guest's assistance when Farrell had been struggling with his one good arm. By now, though, because the conversation had been mostly small talk, Farrell was having trouble keeping his eyes open.

'This is my study.' Muammar waved a hand around the room. 'Here I learn what is happening in the world outside Oman. It is my sanctuary. No one else is permitted to enter.' He glanced at Farrell. 'My sister is angry because I have invited you to join me. She believes you are very ill.'

Farrell smiled. 'I'm fine. The doctor's told her, but she won't believe him. She's been clucking over me all day.'

'Yes. You will forgive her, please. I myself would not keep you from your bed but for the need to speak privately with you. Will you have more coffee?'

'No, thanks. I've had about two gallons since lunch.'

'Then allow me to say at once what I wish to say. It is this; I must apologize to you on behalf of my daughter.'

'For what?' Farrell said.

'For putting your life at risk. For your injuries.'

'It wasn't her fault. She doesn't have to apologize for anything. Nor do you. She kept me afloat while I was unconscious. Tony Nelson told me.'

'May I speak frankly to you?'

'Sure.'

'Mr Farrell, I am a very bad father. I have two children; my son Salim, and my daughter Almira. For both of them I have tried my best, but since the death of my wife it has been most difficult. For reasons that need not concern you I have paid many thousands of rial, not only to provide my daughter with the best education, but also to give her the widest possible exposure to the culture of America and other western countries. Yet despite my efforts — or quite possibly because of them — in the last year she has become extremely unhappy. She has also forgotten the ways of our people. I am told that, since you have regained your strength, she has not been to offer her thanks to you. For this reason I wish also to apologize for her behaviour.'

'It's OK,' Farrell said. 'I understand.'

'No, you do not. She believes you regard her as a poor, little rich girl who is searching for some kind of excitement. Because of this she is ashamed and embarrased.' Muammar inspected his finger-nails. 'Perhaps if you could find a way to show my daughter that she has misunderstood your opinion of her, it

44

will be easier for her to carry out my instructions.'

'Which are?' Farrell said.

'While you are recovering as a guest in my home, she will make sure you are comfortable. Until your shoulder is better she will drive you wherever you wish to go, and she will be happy to show you my stables, to accompany you to my beach house or to collect anything for which you have a need.'

Tough assignment, Farrell thought. And a tough father. 'I don't think that's a good idea,' he said. 'I've got a perfectly good apartment in Mutrah and I don't want to put her to any trouble.'

'Please. You will offend me if I cannot repay your kindness. It is the least I can do and certainly the least my daughter can do.'

'Suppose we see how things work out.' Farrell could already imagine what it was going to be like, but because any firmer form of refusal would be tantamount to an insult, he knew he had little, if any choice. 'You're being very generous to someone you don't know,' he said.

'I am a dealer in precious stones, Mr Farrell. That has made me an extremely cautious man. I would not invite a stranger into my house without first observing certain precautions. Now will you take whisky with

45

me? Or would you prefer to retire?'

'I'll turn in if you don't mind. It takes me half an hour to get dressed or undressed.'

Muammar smiled. 'Let us hope your bandages can come off tomorrow. I will see you in the morning perhaps.'

'Sure.' Farrell returned the smile. 'Goodnight.'

Outside in the hallway he leaned back against the wall for a moment, considering what precautions Muammar could have taken to make certain his house guest didn't steal the family jewels. Not that it mattered, Farrell thought, as long as whatever he had found out didn't make things with his daughter more complicated and confused than they already seemed to be.

★ ★ ★

For five days it had been like this, five difficult days during which Farrell's efforts had either fallen on deaf ears or been rejected so thoroughly that he had begun to believe he was wasting his time. As a result, and because this afternoon was already well on the way to becoming the same as all the other afternoons, he was nearing the end of his patience.

'Look, I can drive myself,' he said. 'You

don't have to take me. I'm not a bloody invalid.'

'You said your shoulder still hurts if you lift your arm too high.' Almira continued walking toward the Mercedes. 'Or do you feel awkward being driven around by women?'

'No, I don't feel awkward.' Farrell climbed into the passenger seat. 'Why not just let me borrow your car?'

'Because I want to see your apartment.' She smiled slightly. 'Is that all right?'

His answer was drowned out by the sound of squealing tyres as a red sports car swung into the courtyard and skidded to a halt alongside the Mercedes. The driver was a young man, smoking a cigarette and shirtless. He wound down his window and spoke to Almira in Arabic.

She interrupted him to introduce Farrell. 'This is my brother Salim,' she said. 'He lives here sometimes.'

Farrell reached across to shake hands through the window, conscious of his arm brushing against Almira's breasts.

'Hi.' The young man spoke without removing the cigarette from his mouth. 'You are the Englishman, yes?'

'Yes.'

'I look forward to talking with you.' Salim Muammar turned his attention to his sister.

'When do I get the cheque?'

'When I decide I'm ready to give it to you.' She started the Mercedes and had it moving before anything further could be said.

'Is that his Porsche?' Farrell asked.

'It's new. My brother likes fast cars — among other things.'

Farrell shut up, noticing the bright patch of colour on her cheek.

'You didn't answer me,' she said. 'About me seeing your apartment.'

'It's pretty ordinary. Do you want to go somewhere afterwards?'

She shook her head. 'We've been everywhere you've been able to think of, haven't we?'

'What about somewhere you can think of?'

She put her foot to the floor, threading the car in and out of the traffic. 'Shall we go to the beach?'

'No.' Farrell made his decision. 'It's about time we had a talk.'

'About what?'

'I'll tell you at my place — assuming we get there in one piece. Why don't you ease up a bit?'

'I don't want to.' She lit a cigarette. 'When we get to Mutrah you'll have to tell me where to go.'

Because Farrell had been resisting the

48

temptation to tell her where to go ever since he'd met her, he thought he could hang on for another half an hour. After that he imagined he'd know whether he had misread the signals or not.

In Mutrah, after she'd followed his directions and parked the car, she walked with him to the door of his apartment without saying anything.

He held the door open, allowing her to go in first.

'Thank you.' She waited while he checked his answering machine then followed him into the kitchen. 'Have you lived here long?' she asked.

'Eighteen months or so.' Farrell went to the fridge, 'Beer, fruit juice or coke?'

'Juice please — as long as it's not too cold.'

He poured some into a glass and gave it to her. 'Do you want to look around?' he asked.

'Not until I know what it is we're supposed to be discussing.'

Farrell searched for the right beginning, trying to keep his eyes off her, trying to understand how over the space of a few days this slender, arrogant Omani girl could have become so extraordinarily desirable that he could think of little else.

Today, to Farrell, she appeared to be more desirable than usual, partly he thought, because of the way she was dressed. She was wearing a yellow skirt drawn in at her waist with a white cord, her earrings were enormous and, in addition to the usual bangles and bracelets on her wrists, she had on more necklaces than he could count.

'We need to get a few things straight,' he said. 'First off, you don't owe me anything. What happened on the boat was my fault, not yours. I'm just sorry you got mixed up with it. I'm grateful to you and your father for what you've done, but from now on I'll be living back here so you don't have to carry on running me around. I know it hasn't been easy for you.'

'Is that some kind of speech you've been rehearsing?'

'I haven't finished.' Farrell drank from a beer can. 'Now I'm out of your hair, and you don't have to follow your father's instructions anymore, will you let me take you to dinner?'

'Why?' She met his eyes.

'You came to my room when I was unconscious, didn't you?'

'I might have done.'

'Chanel perfume,' Farrell said. 'You wear it all the time. I smelt it. You touched my face too.'

'I shaved you, and changed your dressing, that's all. Aunt Latifa wanted me to help her.

What's that got to do with you taking me out to dinner?'

'Nothing. I just figured it was a good idea.' He paused. 'I'd like us to have dinner together.'

She smiled. 'You don't understand, do you?'

'Understand what?'

'Remember on the *Stingray*, when you thought I was asking for your life history?'

'Yes.'

'Well, I never gave you mine. Do you want to hear it?'

'Sure. If you want to tell me.'

'In case you hadn't noticed, I'm an Omani. My mother was Lebanese, but I was born here in Oman. That means you and I are different. I've spent long enough in Europe and North America to know how people like you think about people like me.'

'That's crap,' Farrell said. 'You don't know the first damn thing about how I think.'

She sat down on a bar stool and crossed her legs. 'Let me tell you about my childhood. I was a very lucky person. To begin with I was born into a rich Muslim family — that's quite an advantage. Then, of course, because female circumcision isn't practised much in Oman, there was no suggestion of me having a clitoridectomy. And I was spared the

51

pleasure of becoming a child bride when I was eleven or twelve years old. You can't get much luckier than that, can you?'

Farrell waited.

'But when I was thirteen my luck started to change — after I ruptured my hymen riding a horse. You see, Farrell, when an Arab man gets married, as well as wanting a perfect woman, he expects blood and pain from his bride on her wedding night. Some of my friends who weren't virgins when they got married stuffed themselves with sheep's bladders full of blood to give the right effect. I wasn't given that option. I was sent away to a hospital in Saudi to have my hymen stitched up. I can still remember it. But that was OK — I was whole again — or at least until I reached fifteen I was.'

Farrell remained silent, conscious of gripping his beer can too tightly.

'I was going to a birthday party,' she said. 'Aunt Latifa's husband was driving the car — my uncle. My mother was in the front with him. I was in the back seat, all dressed up for the party. There was this big truck, a concrete truck. It hit us side on while we were crossing an intersection. My mother and my uncle were killed. I was thrown out on to the road. After that, and after I got over the accident, I went horse-riding bareback

52

every day for six months.'

'Why?'

'I'll show you.' She removed her blouse, folding it carefully on her lap. Beneath it she was wearing a brassiere of black lace.

Farrell wasn't looking at her brassiere. He was looking at her arm. It was twisted, terribly disfigured with lumps of what appeared to be plasticine skin bunched all along the outside of her forearm and around her elbow.

'What do you think?' she asked.

She was sitting in front of him, half naked, waiting for him to say something he couldn't say. Except for her right arm, her skin was like honey-coloured satin, blending into the swell of her breasts and the flawless curve of her neck. With the fragrance of her perfume all around him, it was all Farrell could do to stop himself from touching her.

'Put your damn clothes back on,' he said.

'You've seen me undressed before — when that man cut open my blouse on the *Stingray*. But you didn't know I looked like this, did you?'

'You look fine.'

'But not the kind of girl anyone would want to take out to dinner.' She slipped into her blouse. 'Especially if she was an Omani.'

'You've got things way out of proportion.'

53

Farrell said. 'You're hung up about your arm for no reason. One arm doesn't make any difference to anything.'

'It does to me. And it does to my family. That's why I've been sent all over the world — to make up for my being so scarred that I'll never be able to find a husband. No expense has been too much. Ask my brother — Salim hates me because he's missed out on all the money my father has spent on my education: English boarding-schools, Swiss finishing-schools, University of California, and vacations in Paris and New York. I'm even allowed to keep dogs at home — really something when the Koran prohibits it because dogs are supposed to be unclean.' She finished her drink and put down the glass. 'So you see, Farrell, I am what you think I am — a spoilt, little rich girl. You've wasted the best part of a week trying to find out if there's more to me than you think there is. Now you know there isn't, and now you've seen my arm, perhaps you'll leave me alone.'

'Maybe I don't want to leave you alone.'

'Because you'd like to take me to bed, you mean? Because I'd be the first deformed Omani girl to open her legs for you? I don't think so. Find yourself a nice, fresh English girl with two good arms.'

'Have you finished?' He was angry, partly

with himself, but mostly with her.

'Why?'

'Stand up.'

She remained seated.

'Look, if you don't stand up, I'll make you.'

She rose to her feet, her eyes steady and unblinking.

Farrell went to her, holding her wrists to keep them by her side while he kissed her gently on the mouth.

There was no response. She was still rigid, breathing quickly when he let her go.

'Thanks for saving my life,' she said. 'This is for the kiss.' She hit him hard, flat-handed across the side of his face, following the blow with another from her other hand that smacked into the bruise on his forehead.

By the time Farrell's eyes had stopped watering and the room had stabilized, the door had slammed and she was gone.

3

Farrell was tired of looking at new boats. This one was like the rest of them, sleek, fitted out with every conceivable extra and horribly underpowered. Only the hull made it worth considering — a steel hull with a deep vee that would perform well off-shore in a rough sea.

The American salesman stopped talking to Nelson and came over to see what Farrell was doing. 'Do you know about diesels?' he asked.

'A bit.' Farrell withdrew his head from the engine compartment.

'That baby will take you up over twenty knots, and she'll cruise all day at sixteen if you want her to.'

'It's a nice boat,' Farrell said.

'But not what you're after, right? Your partner said you need something with more grunt.'

'A lot more.' Farrell saw Nelson beckoning to him. 'Thanks anyway.'

'My pleasure.' The man was clearly disappointed. 'Let me know if you change your mind.'

Nelson's waving was becoming more

56

urgent. He was sitting in the truck now, and he had already started the engine.

Farrell hurried, getting in to face a blast of cold air from the airconditioner. 'What's the rush?' he said.

'I don't want to be late for this meeting.'

'What did Muammar say on the phone?'

'Not much. Only that he's got these two guys making noises about some kind of job. They're supposed to be at the office at five o'clock.'

While Nelson ground his way through the gearbox in an attempt to coax more speed from the Toyota, Farrell let his mind drift back to Almira. Because his efforts to forget her had been largely unsuccessful in the week since she'd flounced out of his apartment, the prospect of meeting her father again was not entirely welcome. Unless Muammar would be tactful enough to avoid the subject, Farrell thought, in which case everyone could pretend nothing had happened.

Nelson tried another gear. 'What did you think of the boat?'

'We're wasting our time. You'd be better off buying a hull, and letting me install the engines we want.'

'You haven't got any ideas of doing something else, then?'

'I don't know.' Farrell was cautious. 'It's

just that half the time I can't figure out what the hell I'm doing in Oman at all.'

'Having people throw hand-grenades at you warps your outlook. You probably need a break.' Nelson glanced across the cab. 'You're not thinking about the girl again, are you?'

'No. Why?'

'That'd be some break, don't you think? Have you ever imagined how she'd look with no clothes on?'

For several days Farrell had been deliberately avoiding any such thoughts, and he was unwilling to consider the possibility of seeing her again with or without clothes. He turned on the radio instead, closed his eyes and tried to listen to the music over the rattle of the engine.

He was nearly asleep when Nelson swung the truck into the carpark outside the office building. In the adjacent parking bay two men were sitting in the back of Muammar's Range Rover. They climbed out and waited for Muammar to introduce them.

'Sorry we're late.' Nelson slammed the door of the truck behind him. 'The traffic beat us as soon as we turned off the highway.'

'It is of no consequence.' Muammar stood aside. 'May I present Mr Anatoli Volchek and his colleague Mr Hasan Rajavi.'

'Hi.' Nelson shook hands first. 'I'm Tony

Nelson, this is John Farrell. Come on up. It'll be cooler inside.'

Muammar held back to speak with Farrell for a moment. 'Your shoulder is better?' he enquired.

'It's fine, thanks. Just a bit stiff.'

'I am pleased. I hope this afternoon you and Mr Nelson will do business with these gentlemen.' He accompanied Farrell into the office where Nelson was arranging chairs.

'OK,' Nelson said. 'If everyone likes to make themselves comfortable we can get things going here right away.'

Volchek sat down, placing the palms of his hands on the table. 'You will forgive me if I do the talking,' he said. 'As an Iranian, Mr Rajavi is fluent in many languages, but his spoken English is sometimes a little difficult to understand.'

Farrell was trying to pick the accent. Unlike Rajavi who was a sour-faced Arab, Volchek was European. He had a pale complexion and, for a well-built man, his hands and his features were unusually fine.

'May I begin?' Volchek said.

'Sure.' Nelson leaned back in his chair. 'What can we do for you?'

Volchek slid a business card across the table. 'I am the marketing director of a company called Intech,' he said. 'Mr Rajavi represents our business interests here in the Middle East. Intech was originally formed by the Russian Government to facilitate the export of technology — trading under the name of International Technology. Two years ago the company was reorganized and put under private ownership. We are based in Moscow and do business throughout the world.'

'What sort of business?' Nelson asked.

'I am sure you appreciate that the end of the Cold War has left my country with a substantial surplus of military equipment. There is also a great deal of technical expertise which we have developed over a long period of time. In the present political and economic climate, exporting this equipment and expertise is a valuable means for Russia to obtain hard currency.'

'What exactly is it you sell?' Nelson said.

'What would you like? I can offer you a good price on MiG-29 combat aircraft, or would you prefer fully equipped battle tanks? Alternatively, there are rare metals in which you may have an interest — zirconium perhaps? I am also authorized to accept bids for a new ground-to-air weapon system. This is selling particularly well to Middle East countries for less than five million US dollars per unit, including spares.'

'How about a minesweeper?' Nelson grinned. 'I'm in the market for a boat.'

Volchek smiled. 'I shall enquire. In the meantime, Intech has encountered a small problem that I believe you may be able to assist us with. It concerns one of our shipments, delivered a little over a month ago to the Iranian Government. Unfortunately, although the shipment was stored under close guard in a military warehouse, it subsequently went missing after the warehouse was raided by thieves.'

'Inside job?' Nelson said.

'I think so. The authorities in Tehran believe one of the guards was involved. The break-in was very unsophisticated. Only non-military items were stolen — the kind of things that have a ready market in Iran — clothing, tools, canned food and a quantity of precious stones.'

'Emeralds.' Farrell had already guessed. 'Did you ship emeralds to Iran?'

'Indeed we did, Mr Farrell. A large number of them.' Volchek fingered the end of his tie. 'I should perhaps say that they were not ordinary emeralds, but destined to become part of Iran's military laser development programme.'

'How the hell did you trace them to here?' Farrell asked.

61

'By casting a very wide net. Mr Rajavi has recently received information about emeralds being sold on the market in Oman for prices that I think even Mr Muammar would find suspicious.'

'You might be out of luck,' Farrell said. 'They'll be spread all over the Middle East by now.'

Volchek nodded. 'Mr Muammar has made that clear. Our investigations have, of course, put us in touch with Mr Muammar as one of the region's foremost dealers in precious stones. He has been kind enough to explain his own involvement and he has given us an account of how he came to arrange for the purchase of the emeralds from a private seller in Tehran.'

'Has he told you what happened after that?' Farrell asked.

'Yes. Which, of course, is how we learned of your remarkable survival at sea. Let me say that we are not in Oman to recover what almost certainly cannot be recovered. There is a quite different reason for our visit. May I ask you a question, Mr Farrell?'

'Sure.'

'To save us all time, and to avoid me having to compromise my company's position unnecessarily, would you tell me if you, yourself, ever saw the emeralds?'

'Yes. I saw them. I checked them.'

'In what were they contained?'

'Pouches,' Farrell said. 'Chamois-leather pouches.'

'And do you recall any marks of identification?'

'MINATOM,' Farrell said. 'It was stencilled on each pouch. I'm pretty sure that was the name.'

'I see. Doubtless the courier was carrying the pouches in a sack or a suitcase of some kind.'

'They were in a box. The lid was bent where it had been jemmied open by someone — probably by whoever broke into the warehouse in Tehran.'

'Yes. I am sure you are right.' Volchek's face was expressionless. 'After coming such a long way I am pleased to discover that Mr Rajavi's investigations have not led us up a blind alley.'

Rajavi cleared his throat, speaking at length to Volchek in Arabic until the Russian held up a hand to stop him.

'We would like to come straight to the point.' Volchek addressed himself to Nelson. 'Mr Rajavi has asked if you would offer your opinion on the feasibility of locating the box and lifting it from the sea bed.'

'The box?' Nelson said. 'The empty box?'

63

'Mr Muammar assures me that you have the expertise, and he is confident you know the approximate position in which to conduct a search.'

'What the hell's it made of?' Nelson asked. 'Solid gold?'

'It is made of stainless steel.' Volchek smiled. 'I have no intention of misleading you. We are all businessmen, I think. The box is double-skinned. Concealed in the sides and the ends are flasks of some valuable and rather rare material.'

'I suppose you don't just happen to be in the radioactive-material business?' Farrell said.

'Yes, of course we are, Mr Farrell. But in this instance I can guarantee that there is no radiation hazard — not because of shielding, but simply because the flasks do not house a nuclear product of any kind.'

'So the emeralds were a front,' Farrell said.

'Not entirely. As I have said, they were to be used for a laser weapon development. However, the Iranian Government wished to be discreet in regard to this other material, and we, ourselves, were unwilling to advertise what the inner skin of the box contains. For this reason we chose to combine two shipments into one — a foolish mistake as things have turned out. Had the box not held emeralds, I doubt if it would have been stolen.'

'I'll need to know more about what's in the flasks.' Nelson looked directly at Volchek.

'It would mean nothing to you. I am not interested in the stones Mr Muammar sells to his customers. He is equally disinterested in the armaments you handle. Why then should you question the products with which Intech carries out its business? May we instead discuss whether or not you are prepared to recover the box?'

'OK,' Nelson said. 'Let's discuss that. Are you in a hurry?'

'Of course.'

Nelson began scribbling on his blotter. 'We're talking about deep water,' he said, 'an uneven seabed and some pretty lousy tidal currents at this time of year. That means a lot of gear — maybe video cameras and underwater lights if we have trouble.'

Farrell was more amused than surprised. Nelson's attitude was one of serious concentration while he compiled his list of non-existent difficulties.

'Right.' Nelson put down his pen. 'Assuming a minimum of four days' work and at least six divers, the best we could do is seventy-five thousand US dollars all up. Fifty thousand up front to look. The other twenty-five thousand if we find the box.'

This time Farrell was impressed. The numbers were staggeringly high, more than triple what the job could possibly cost, but the quote had been volunteered so nonchalantly and with such authority that it almost sounded believable.

Volchek, though, was unconvinced. 'That is extremely expensive,' he said. 'I understand the Omani coastguard has the co-ordinates of where Mr Farrell was rescued. Perhaps it would be better if we were to approach them.'

'I'm sure it would.' Nelson smiled. 'Look, I'm real sorry, but diving always winds up costing a lot more than you expect, and we've got a couple of other contracts to finish over the next week. We're all behind because of John's accident with the boat. The coastguard's a good idea. They might even do it for nothing. I'll give you the name of a guy to see there.'

The lies were only half plausible, Farrell thought. And there were too many of them.

Rajavi spoke again in Arabic. He was animated, using his hands to emphasize the point he was making.

'Yes, yes.' Volchek turned back to Nelson. 'Two equal payments of thirty thousand dollars each,' he said. 'I am not prepared to

66

negotiate beyond that.'

'I don't know.' Nelson was visibly unhappy. 'Sixty grand might not cover the cost of the equipment, and I sure as hell can't afford to make a loss right at this minute. How soon could you get the money here?'

'Two, perhaps three days.'

'It'll have to be cash.' Nelson's expression was unchanged. 'Jesus, I don't know why I'm agreeing to this.'

'Because if you succeed you will make a very large amount of money,' Volchek said. 'You do not deceive me, Mr Nelson. However, in the circumstances, I think perhaps we can do business.'

'OK.' Nelson pushed his chair back and stood up. 'John and I can start getting things together right away — that's as long as you can guarantee there'll be no delay in the money arriving.'

'There will be no delay. Either Mr Rajavi or I will telephone you once we are ready to proceed.'

'Fine. In that case I think we're all done here, don't you?' Nelson shook hands with Volchek and prepared to escort the visitors from the room.

Until now, Muammar had been sitting quietly at the back of the office, listening, but being careful not to intrude. He remained behind to speak to Farrell.

'Mr Nelson is an Irishman?' he asked.

Farrell grinned. 'Did you check him out too?'

'Of course. This is good business you have negotiated here, I think. It has been my pleasure to make the introduction. You will excuse me leaving, but I must drive Mr Volchek and Mr Rajavi back to their hotel. Perhaps we could talk again one evening?'

'I'd like that.' For a second Farrell was tempted to ask about Almira, but the timing was inappropriate and Muammar was already hurrying off, car keys in his hand.

Nelson said goodbye to Muammar at the door, waiting until everyone had gone before allowing a huge grin to spread across his face. 'How about that, then?' he said.

'Luck,' Farrell grunted.

'Skill. Nice clean deal, don't you think?'

'As long as we find the box.'

'Find what's left of the *Stingray* and we find the box.'

'It wasn't on the *Stingray*,' Farrell said. 'Our friendly neighbourhood pirates heaved it over the side.'

'So it's twenty feet away — so what? The water's not too deep there. All we need to do is drive up the peninsula to Khabura, rent ourselves a boat and hire some of those

Shihuh pearl divers. We can use a hand-held GPS unit.'

'We'll be lucky to hire any Shihuh divers: there aren't any left.'

'Yes there are. Stop being so bloody pessimistic, will you? We just have to know who to ask.'

'And how to ask.' Farrell recalled the last occasion he'd tried to communicate with tribesmen on the peninsula. 'What do you figure Volchek's got inside that double skin?'

'God knows — except Intech doesn't deal in peanuts. Even if it's plutonium, Volchek isn't going to admit it. These guys are only in Oman because that box is worth one hell of a lot of money. All we can be sure of is that Volchek doesn't want anyone else sticking their fingers in it. Did you see how he backed away from the coastguard idea?'

'One of these days you're going to bullshit yourself out of business,' Farrell said. 'Why take the job if you think it could be plutonium?'

'I let other people decide what's right or wrong. For sixty grand I'll run anything except drugs and slaves. You know I wouldn't pass up an opportunity like this.' Nelson stretched. 'I think things have turned out pretty damn well. Do you want to hang around and have a drink? I've got a new bottle of scotch somewhere.'

Farrell shook his head. 'No thanks. I'll celebrate at home. I'll see you in the morning.'

'OK.' Nelson handed him a pencil. 'Draw me a picture of what we're looking for in case you get run over.'

Farrell sketched the box on the blotter, adding approximate dimensions and showing how the lid had been distorted. It was easy to remember, he thought. As easy as it was to remember the rest of the night on the *Stingray* when his passenger had been the girl with big eyes and the honey-coloured skin.

* * *

The illustration in the airline brochure showed a Mediterranean beach somewhere off the coast of Greece. Bikini-clad models were sprinkled against a background of rocks and what could be a distant olive grove. Farrell had studied the picture before with much the same reaction — the feeling that if Greece rated seven out of ten as a place to make a living, Oman would always be struggling to get on the scale at all. He poured more brandy into his glass, wondering how hot it got in Greece and whether Nelson knew anyone there.

The idea was a fantasy, Farrell realized, the same old pretence, the familiar urge to go on searching for whatever it was he had once imagined he could find. He swallowed the brandy quickly, waiting for its warmth to spread through him while he turned the pages of the brochure, discovering that the pictures had become meaningless because his mind was already back out in the Gulf somewhere.

At the office this afternoon he'd been able to believe the search for an empty box was nothing more than a way for Nelson to make a few more thousand dollars. Now, though, back home in his apartment with the brandy running through him, Farrell was less certain. The whole thing was suspect, he thought, another damn contract, this one to recover something that would probably be better off staying where it was. The notion was vaguely unsettling, but by the time he was ready for bed the alcohol had done its work and Farrell had ceased to care.

Leaving his glass on the counter he switched off the kitchen light and was heading for the bathroom when the front-door buzzer sounded.

He opened the door expecting to find Nelson outside. Instead it was Almira, standing awkwardly on the step holding

71

something in her hand.

'You don't have to look so surprised.' She forced a smile.

'What are you doing here?'

'I've been visiting a friend in Mutrah so I decided to call by. You don't mind, do you?'

Farrell straightened his thoughts. 'What time is it?' he asked.

'I know it's late. I didn't mean to disturb you.'

'It's OK. I'm sorry. Come in, please.'

'I've brought you these.' She gave him a twist of coloured paper. 'That's from Aunt Latifa. This envelope is from me.'

The coloured paper contained the piece of shrapnel; the envelope contained a cheque for US$5,000.

'It's the money you lost on the *Stingray*,' she explained. 'When you tried to buy me — remember?'

Farrell slid the cheque back into the envelope. 'I don't want your money,' he said. 'You already paid me once.'

'Well now I've paid you twice.' She went into the lounge and picked up the bottle of brandy. 'Are you going to offer me some of this?'

He could smell her Chanel. She'd used too much of it, either because she'd recently put more on, or perhaps because the friend she'd

72

been visiting liked her that way.

'I should have come before.' She took the glass he offered. 'To apologize, I mean. You know — for hitting you. I don't usually do things like that.'

'Next time take your bracelets off.' Farrell smiled at her. 'You wear too much hardware.'

'My father says your shoulder's better.'

'It's OK. Why don't you sit down?'

'Because I don't want to.'

He'd heard the answer often enough to recognize the warning. She was endeavouring to be assertive — looking for the right opening, trying to pretend this was a spur-of-the-moment visit. He watched her light a cigarette and blow a stream of smoke out into the room.

'We had a family dinner this evening,' she said. 'My brother was home. My father was too. He says you're going to search for that box.'

'Did your father tell you the whole story — about these guys from Intech?'

She nodded. 'Salim knows some people who could do the diving for you.'

'Get him to talk to Nelson.'

'Why should I, when I've just told you?'

'Jesus.' Farrell was exasperated. 'I've never met anyone like you before. You're hard work,

73

do you know that? Why not just say what you're really doing here?'

'I can help you in Khabura — if you'll let me. I won't be any trouble, and it wouldn't be anything like last time, would it?'

'Is that what the envelope's for?'

Her eyes flashed. 'No. Why won't you ever give me a chance — just once would be nice? I wasn't offering you money.'

'You didn't come for any other reason, then?'

'No, not exactly. Except that I had a long talk with Aunt Latifa this evening. But I'm still not sure.' She dropped her cigarette into her glass. 'I'm embarrassed too.'

'About what?'

'I don't know how to do this.' She paused. 'Not after the other day.'

'Look,' Farrell said. 'I'm too full of brandy to play games. If you've got something on your mind, wouldn't it be easier just to come right out with it?'

'All right.' Standing on tiptoe she put her arms around his neck and kissed him hesitantly on the lips.

For Farrell the experience was extraordinary. Lightheaded, uncertain if it was really happening, he was slow to react, just managing to grab her when she drew back. He stopped her from talking, pulling her hair

74

away from her face before he returned her kiss.

She started melting, leaning against him, kissing him open-mouthed with her tongue flickering against his lips, squirming to push her body closer to his. With her arms round his neck again she began whispering, telling him how she had lain awake for the last three nights imagining what this would be like, and how Aunt Latifa had instructed her to ask Allah for guidance before she'd made her decision to come here.

When she unbuttoned her blouse and forced his hand down to her breasts Farrell couldn't stand it. On fire, so eager for her that he was frightened of what he might do if she resisted, he slipped a hand down over her stomach, hearing her gasp as she slowly opened her legs for him.

Only by making an enormous effort was he able to come to his senses and stop himself.

Almira was wide-eyed, breathing too quickly to speak.

'Easy.' He placed a finger on her lips.

'You don't have to stop,' she whispered.

'I know.' Farrell picked her up and carried her to the sofa. 'Do you have any idea what you're doing?'

She shook her head.

'I don't want to mess this up,' he said. 'Really I don't.'

'It's not my arm, is it?'

'No,' Farrell said gently. 'It's not your arm.'

'Oh.' She sat up. 'You do want to make love to me, though, don't you?'

'I just want you to be sure, that's all.'

'I am. What do you think I spoke to Aunt Latifa about?' She began undoing his shirt. 'Of course, mainly I have to be sure you'll take me with you to Khabura.'

'Blackmail,' Farrell said. 'I should have guessed.'

'Mmm.' She smiled as she removed her ear-rings and kicked off her shoes. 'The five thousand dollars was supposed to be enough. I hadn't planned this second part very well.'

'Lies.' Farrell pushed her off the sofa and on to the floor. 'Tell me you don't have to go home tonight,' he said.

'No, I can stay. I want to stay. My aunt said I'd be silly not to take advantage of you while I had the chance.'

This time when Farrell kissed her she fastened her mouth to his, arching her back while she helped him to remove her clothes. But soon her hands were busy elsewhere, sharing in the searching and touching until Farrell became so lost in the exquisite pleasure of exploring her body, that when she

76

finally guided him inside her, his need for release was as great and as urgent as her own.

He held her through her shudders, his face buried in her hair, his thoughts no longer of distant summer nights in England, but of now, of the Omani girl in his arms, and of some half-imagined fresh new future.

4

Sitting fifteen miles out to sea on an afternoon like this, Farrell could understand why the Jebel Akhdar was called the backbone of Oman. The mountains were immense, towering to over 10,000 feet in places, a gigantic and forbidding wall of rock rising up from the Batina coastal plain that had been built up by the outwash from the wadis. There were late shadows on the mountains too, colourless patches of nothing where the sunlight was retreating from the ravines.

For the last two days the view had been less spectacular, softened and distorted by a heat-haze that was nowhere in evidence this afternoon. Because of the breeze, the air was much clearer than it had been, and Farrell could sense the drop in humidity that was making conditions more tolerable on board the fishing boat.

At the bow, Nelson was again shouting at the two young men in the dinghy. They were sixty or seventy yards away, still paying out their heavily weighted drag-line.

Almira was annoyed. 'They don't understand what he's saying,' she said. 'Do you think I should tell him?'

'It won't make any difference.' Farrell grinned at her. 'He's only yelling to let off steam. He gets like this when he's worried.'

'I don't see why he has to be so angry.'

'You're not Nelson. He's uptight because so far he's got everything wrong. The water's twice as deep as he expected and, after spending half of Saturday going round Khabura trying to hire a boat, he wasted nearly all of yesterday looking for pearl divers who don't exist.'

'It's a good job, isn't it?'

'What is?' Farrell said.

'For us, I mean. If there were still pearl divers working up here, you wouldn't have needed me. When I asked Tony if I could help he said I'd be a distraction. He only let me come today because I arranged for proper divers with scuba gear.'

'You didn't arrange anything. You'd never met those two guys in the dinghy before this morning. They're friends of your brother.'

'So what?' She slipped her hand into his. 'I'm not a distraction, am I?'

Her question was unanswerable, he thought. Since they had first made love, his preoccupation with her had increased to the point where she was almost continuously on his mind. In the last six days, twice they had slept together in the comfort of her father's beach house, and twice Farrell had awoken in the morning to discover he was still unable to resist her. On other occasions they had spent long self-indulgent evenings at his apartment, or gone out only to be overcome with the need to return so they could again seek pleasure in each other. For Farrell the days and the nights had been a reminder of how he had felt many years ago — a rekindling of something he had almost forgotten. Now, even out here in the Gulf on board a run-down fishing boat in the company of Nelson and the two young Arab divers, he still found her presence disconcerting.

His thoughts were interrupted by Nelson who came clambering aft over the mess of ropes and fishing nets.

'We're going round in bloody circles.' He wiped the sweat out of his eyes. 'Have you got any ideas, or are you just going to sit there getting sunburned?'

'What did you tell Volchek when you phoned him last night?' Farrell asked.

'I said we'd got divers and a boat and that we'd have it done either today or tomorrow. I wish I hadn't told him anything the way things are going. Are you sure we're in the right place?'

'Yeah, I'm sure.' Farrell pointed to the

yellow buoy off the starboard bow. 'I checked our position a dozen times before I chucked that over this morning.'

'How do you know the anchor's holding? Suppose it's dragging?'

'It isn't,' Farrell said. 'I checked again ten minutes ago. The GPS unit says we're right on top of the *Stingray*.'

'So where the hell is it?'

'I don't know.'

'I do.' Almira stood up. 'The *Stingray* isn't here.'

'Where do you think it is?' Nelson grunted.

'Well.' She put her hands on her hips. 'It's obvious, isn't it? You've been using the co-ordinates from our radio message — the one we sent on the night the *Stingray* sank. But it didn't sink right away. Those men who came on board went through all the emerald pouches before they threw the box into the water. The *Stingray* could have drifted a long way before they did that.' She paused. 'There was a breeze too. I remember how the flames and smoke kept blowing sideways — afterwards, when I was trying to swim away.'

'Where was the breeze coming from?' Nelson asked.

She pointed out to sea. 'More or less the same as today, I think.'

'OK.' He picked up a piece of cork and

tossed it into the water. 'Let's see, shall we? Five minutes?'

'Maybe more,' Farrell said. 'Give it seven.'

Nelson glanced at his watch. 'I'll tell the guys in the dinghy we're moving position.'

'I'll do it.' Almira smiled. 'I don't think they understand your English very well.' She left Farrell's side and began making her way forwards, waving to show the divers that they should pull in the drag-line.

'If we're not careful we're going to run out of daylight.' Farrell had been studying the mountains where the shadows in the valleys and ravines were noticeably deeper.

Nelson was staring too. 'I don't care if we're here until after dark,' he said. 'I don't mind spending more time looking for the box, but we need to find the bloody boat today. Is the lovely Miss Muammar staying in Khabura overnight with the divers?'

'No. I thought she could go back with us in the truck. She can sleep at my place so she doesn't have to drive up from Muscat tomorrow morning.'

'I'll explain that to her, shall I? In case she gets the wrong idea.' Nelson grinned. 'You want to be careful. That smart-arse brother of hers might not like what you're doing to his sister as much as she does.'

'How much of a smart-arse is he?' Farrell

attempted to redirect the conversation.

'Hard to tell. I only saw him for ten minutes — when he came to the office to talk about his diving friends. He got pissed off when I told him he wanted too much money.'

'Did he want a finder's fee just to introduce these guys with the scuba gear?'

'Yeah. I suppose he figured it was worth a try. I gave him half of what he was asking.' Nelson was watching the cork bobbing on the water.

Already it was nearly fifty yards away from the yellow buoy, surprising Farrell by the speed at which it was moving. 'Almira's right,' he said.

'Looks like it.' Nelson pushed a button on his watch. 'That's seven minutes. See if you can manoeuvre us over there. I'll winch up the anchor.'

With some reservation, Farrell turned his attention to the boat's power plant, priming the carburettor before he cranked the engine over. It was worn out and temperamental, an old single cylinder stationary engine that had been converted to marine use by someone who believed a welding torch was the answer to every engineering problem.

On his third attempt the engine coughed, spluttered and then settled into an uneven idle, pushing the boat into a curve around the buoy. Fifty yards away, the divers had secured the drag-line to the bow of their dinghy, allowing themselves to be towed into the new position.

'OK,' Nelson shouted. 'Chuck another marker over and we'll have a go right here.'

It took some minutes for the divers to start their outboard motor and pay out the weighted line again, but soon dinghy and boat were travelling southwards together in another slow trawl of the seabed.

This time success came quickly. They had just commenced the second leg of their search pattern when the divers began yelling and Farrell saw the line tighten. He cut the engine at once, recording his position before going to join Nelson and Almira at the bow.

Nelson was letting the anchor rope run through his hands. 'Still pretty bloody deep,' he said. 'Tell the divers they'd better get ready.'

There was no need for Almira to translate. Alerted by the tautness of the line, one of them was already in the water, mask on, mouthpiece in place. The other diver waved briefly, flipped himself backwards over the side of the dinghy and headed downwards.

'How deep do you think it is?' Almira asked.

Nelson's frustration had given way to

concern. 'I'm not too sure. Might be nearly a hundred feet. I hope these cowboy friends of yours know what they're doing.'

'They're not cowboys and they're not friends of mine. They're divers who do this for a living. Don't you believe what my brother told you?'

'Sure. I believe everything people tell me.' Just as Nelson was careful to defuse his remark by smiling, so was Farrell careful not to show his amusement.

Either because of her upbringing, or as a result of the wall she'd built around herself because of her arm, since yesterday Almira's attitude towards Nelson had been as cool as it was predictable, and she had made little or no effort to be friendly. It was part of who she was, Farrell realized. Only when she was alone with him did she seem to feel secure enough to let the other side of her emerge — the private Almira, still self-assured in her own way, but captivating and so possessive that it was often hard to reconcile how different her two personalities could be.

Unaware of his attention, she was balancing herself on a pile of nets, shielding her eyes from the sun, evidently anxious for the divers to reappear.

Farrell too was apprehensive, knowing that if this was a false alarm, finding the *Stingray*

85

might prove to be impossible. If the divers came up empty handed this time, from here on, without a change in the way their luck was running, the search would be as good as over.

His doubts were short-lived. Sixty feet away, close to the dinghy, a splash was followed by a glint of sunlight on a mask as one of the men surfaced.

Kicking with his fins the diver swam over to the boat, and reached up to hand Almira something. It was a gun, the courier's Uzi, dripping water from its muzzle and already red with rust.

'Right on target,' she said. 'I told you.' Leaning over the bow she spoke quickly to the young man in Arabic.

He removed his mouthpiece and spat before replying and pointing to his wrist.

'What's he saying?' Nelson asked.

'He says it's dark down there and that he's worried about sharks.' Almira hesitated for a moment. 'The courier's body's tangled up in the front rail. It's all bloated and sharks have bitten off one of the hands.'

'Forget about sharks,' Farrell said. 'That was a knife. Tell him not to bother with the *Stingray*. He has to look off the starboard side — level with the cabin. Even if it's murky down there the box should show up pretty

86

well because it's shiny.'

'All right.' She relayed the instructions, talking to the diver for several seconds.

'Now what the hell's the matter?' Nelson asked her.

'He says everything's charred and that there isn't a cabin — just metal things like the propellers, the drive shafts and the engines. And he wants to know if he can keep the gun.'

'Jesus Christ.' Nelson's patience was running out. 'Tell him he can have a brand new Kalashnikov if he brings up the goddamn box.'

The diver had understood the message. 'I go back,' he said. 'While there is light still.' Pushing himself away from the hull he vanished suddenly, leaving only a circle of bubbles to show where he had been.

'How much daylight do we have?' Almira asked.

'Maybe a couple of hours.' Nelson squinted over his shoulder at the mountains. 'The angle of the sun might be a problem if they have to hunt through a lot of weed and stuff down there. We don't know how far the *Stingray* drifted after the box hit bottom either.'

'They're allowing for that.' Almira smiled pleasantly at him. 'There's always tomorrow.'

'That's what I told our customer yesterday. I don't want Volchek and Rajavi breathing down our necks.'

'They won't be,' Farrell said. 'Look.'

Some distance away the other diver had surfaced, recognizable by his white tanks and green fins. A second later his companion bobbed up beside him. Both men spat out their mouthpieces and began to shout.

'They're not still worried about bloody sharks, are they?' Nelson said.

'I don't think so.' Almira kept a straight face. 'Would you like me to translate?'

'Don't be cute. Just tell me if they've got it.'

Her reply was unnecessary. The divers combined forces to lift the box above their heads.

'For Christ's sake don't drop it!' Nelson yelled. 'Get it over here.'

The two men splashed their way over to the boat, supporting the box between them, letting Farrell take it from them before Nelson grabbed their arms to help them climb on board.

'Is the thing in one piece?' Nelson asked.

'Fine.' Farrell was surprised by the weight of it. 'Feels like there might be some water trapped between the two skins, but that's all. We'll have a look once we get it back to the office.'

88

The divers were clearly pleased with themselves, chattering to Almira while they stripped off their equipment.

'They want to know why they've been searching for an empty box,' she said. 'What shall I tell them?'

Nelson went to explain. 'It's made from a special silver alloy,' he said, 'worth many American dollars. Do you understand?'

Both divers nodded.

'Right then,' Nelson grunted. 'That's us done. Let's get organized so we can get the hell out of here.'

Although it took nearly a quarter of an hour to free the dragline and another ten minutes for Farrell to coax the engine back to life, by the time they were ready to leave, tension on board had eased considerably.

With Nelson stretched out on the fishing nets with his eyes closed, Farrell took the dinghy in tow and turned the bow of the boat towards the coast, opening the throttle cautiously until the engine settled into its normal, wheezing rhythm.

Beside him at the wheel, Almira too was a good deal more relaxed now.

'Are you really being paid sixty thousand dollars for doing this?' she asked.

'Nelson is. I get fifteen per cent of what's left after expenses. Pretty good for a few days' work don't you think?'

'Especially if you add on another five thousand from me.'

'You've had your money's worth.' Farrell grinned at her.

'No I haven't. Not yet. Stolen emeralds, pirates and sunken treasure doesn't mean I've had my money's worth.'

'I'll try harder,' Farrell said.

'Would Tony let you sneak some time off? You know, like a whole week?'

'If you call Nelson, Tony, why won't you call me John?'

'Because I don't want — ' Her answer was cut short by Farrell clamping his hand over her mouth.

She wriggled away from him laughing. 'We ought to go away somewhere, just for a little while. It'd be nice.'

Farrell hesitated before he answered. 'Have you ever been to Greece?' he said.

She raised her eyebrows. 'Greece?'

'Why not?'

She fell silent, holding his hand while together they watched the sky change colour over the Jebel Akhdar where the sun was going down.

Ahead of them, flying fish were appearing in greater numbers, occasionally exploding from the water in their attempts to evade the dark-blue, bullet-shaped bonito which were leaping to catch them in mid-air. There were dolphins too, dozens of them, feeding on the other fish as they kept pace with the fishing boat.

For Farrell, the leisurely journey back to Khabura was an opportunity to recall another trip — the early morning test run in the *Stingray* three weeks ago. Then he'd been worried about the vibration problem and conscious of his dissatisfaction with what he was doing. Now, suddenly, everything was different.

The dissatisfaction was gone, and most of the memories he'd been carrying around with him for the past seven years seemed to have gone as well. Had it happened too quickly? he wondered. Could the girl beside him really have brought about the change in such a short time?

Like some of her questions, this one had no answer either, but the need to think it through continued to occupy him until they finally reached the wooden jetty at the Khabura waterfront where the boat owner was waiting for them. He was an elderly Omani gentleman who had been most concerned, he explained, not only because of the lateness of the hour, but because in recent weeks Allah had chosen not to confer his usual blessing on the engine.

To guard against a recurrence of the problem, Nelson paid him a bonus, leaving Farrell and Almira to unload the box and carry it along the jetty to the truck.

'Are you serious about Greece?' she asked.

'I don't know.' Farrell stowed the box on the floor inside the cab.

'If I ask you what it depends on you'll say how you happen to feel at the time, won't you?' She put her arms round his neck.

'You'll get us arrested,' he said. 'You're not a tourist in down-town Muscat. This is Khabura and you're supposed to be a nice Muslim girl.'

She let him go. 'Where's Tony?'

'Paying off the divers.'

'They're not going back to Muscat until Wednesday,' she said. 'One of them told me they saw pearl oysters growing on some of the rocks.'

'That's not why they're staying here. They'll be hoping to salvage stuff off the *Stingray*. The engines will still be OK if they can find a way to get them up.'

'Oh.' She smiled ruefully. 'Everyone has an angle, haven't they? My father always says that.'

'He's a businessman.'

'Who is?' Nelson came to join the conversation.

'Almira's father,' Farrell said.

'Sure. When did you last meet an Omani who isn't out to make a deal?'

Because Farrell could see that Almira had taken exception to the remark, he bundled her into the truck with him before she could respond.

'Just sit,' he said. 'Don't spoil things.'

'Am I driving?' Nelson climbed behind the wheel.

'We're taking care of the box,' Farrell said. 'You don't want to sit this side if it's full of plutonium, do you?'

Nelson grinned. 'If that's what's in it, I think we all might be in trouble.'

★ ★ ★

Trouble of a more tangible kind was waiting for them in Mutrah. Although it was dark when they reached the office, the sight of a white car parked beside Almira's Mercedes outside the building was enough to make Nelson jam on his brakes. In the truck headlights the OISS logo on the car door was unmistakable — the letters and the insignia of the Omani Internal Security Service.

Nelson began swearing under his breath

93

while he looked for somewhere else to park. 'All we bloody need,' he said. 'We should've thought of this.'

'How about leaving the box here in the truck?' Farrell said.

'Yeah.' Nelson got out. 'You head off home. I'll handle this.'

'Be easier if we both front up,' Farrell said. 'You don't know what you have to handle yet. Just hang on a second while I say goodbye to Almira.'

He accompanied her to the Mercedes, told her to drive carefully and stood watching the tail lights of the car disappear into the darkness.

'You ready?' Nelson asked.

Farrell nodded. 'What do you think?'

'Christ knows. Let's go and find out.'

The outer door of the building was unlocked. So was the one inside. It was wide open, and all of the office lights were on.

A man sitting at Nelson's desk stood up as they entered the room. He was a European or an American with a small, well-trimmed moustache and rimless glasses.

'Good evening,' he said. 'My name is Travers — Richard E. Travers.'

'What the hell do you think you're doing?' Nelson slammed the door shut.

'There's a recorded message on your

94

answering machine saying you'd be back this evening.' Travers opened a thin, leather briefcase before he stepped out from behind the desk. 'And here you are. I presume you're Tony Nelson?'

'Presume what you bloody want. I don't much like people breaking into my office.'

Travers' face was impassive. 'I don't think you'll find any damage,' he said. 'Perhaps before you get any more excited you should both see these.' Reaching into his case he withdrew three sheets of paper and tossed them on the table.

The first was a letter, a terse written statement in both English and Arabic, typed on official OISS stationery, bearing the signature, seal and name of the Omani Chief of Staff.

The statement on the second sheet was equally terse, but signed by the Head of the Ministry of Information.

Because the third sheet bore the letterhead of the Royal Oman Police, Farrell didn't bother to read it. The message was already clear. Whoever Travers was, he had what amounted to a blanket authority to do whatever he wanted to do, anywhere in Oman, to anyone.

'This is my card.' Travers handed one to Farrell and another to Nelson. 'Not as

95

impressive as the business card from Mr Volchek that I found on your blotter, I'm afraid. But, of course, I represent different people so I enjoy different advantages. As you can see, I work for the US National Security Council. You're at liberty to telephone the red number at the bottom right-hand corner of my card to obtain clarification of my authority. The same call will provide you with profile information allowing you to identify me as being who I say I am.' He offered the telephone to Nelson. 'Go ahead.'

'I'll skip it, thanks.' Nelson put the phone down. 'You're a long way from home, aren't you?'

'We all are, don't you think, Mr Nelson?'

'What I think is that you'd better tell us what the hell's going on.'

Pushing the papers aside, Nelson slid up some chairs before he reclaimed his own and slumped down in it. 'I don't need to introduce John Farrell, do I?' he said. 'Because you already know all about him, right?'

Travers ignored the question. He joined Farrell at the desk and carefully gathered up his papers. 'If you want to know what's going on, I'll tell you. Before I do, though, you should be aware that for the purpose of this meeting I represent the joint interests of the

96

United States, the British Government and his Royal Highness Sultan Qaboos Bin Said Al Said of Oman. Is that clear?'

'Yeah, that's clear,' Nelson said. 'So what?'

'Well, let's see, shall we?' Travers began to read from a notebook. 'July 12th, Mr Anatoli Volchek and his colleague Mr Hasan Rajavi are admitted into Oman ex flight 473 from Tehran. Three days later they visit the home of Mr Ghassan Muammar prior to attending a meeting here in your office on the following afternoon. That would seem to be July 16th if this information is correct.' He glanced up. 'If you're wondering where the information comes from you might like to know that Omani immigration have had the names of Volchek and Rajavi on their files for some time now.'

'Why?' Farrell asked.

'Because for the last two years Volchek's Russian-based company has been attracting the attention of western intelligence. A number of other governments around the world are interested in Intech as well. Even to people like you and Nelson the reason for this must be obvious. Any country or any individual who sets up an international organization to sell weapon systems on the world market is going to come under scrutiny sooner or later.' Travers coughed into a handkerchief. 'The real problem, of course, is that Intech will sell any damn thing to anyone. They don't discriminate between legal democratic governments and terrorist organizations.'

'But that doesn't mean their business is illegal, does it?' Nelson said.

'It depends on your viewpoint. If you're Saddam Hussein or the leader of some rabid Islamic fundamentalist group, buying equipment from Intech makes good sense. If you're American or British, you might feel a bit uncomfortable about Intech selling weapons-grade uranium to unstable countries who are hell bent on developing nuclear warheads.'

'So your job is to keep an eye on Intech,' Farrell said. 'And you think we're involved with them somehow.'

'No, Mr Farrell. I know you are. I've already spoken to Mr Muammar. As you can imagine, he was reluctant to have the Omani authorities investigating the details of his day-to-day business and he very sensibly decided it was best to explain the events of the last two or three weeks.' Travers paused. 'Did you recover the box today?'

'No,' Nelson answered. 'It's pretty deep water out there. Looks like we've found part of the boat, but there's no sign of the bloody box anywhere.'

'It's not outside in your truck, then?'

'What do you want it for?'

'You're jumping to conclusions.' Travers smiled. 'There's no suggestion of you forfeiting or losing the second half of your payment from Volchek: it doesn't work that way. We're not interested in confiscating whatever it is that the Iranian Government has contracted to buy from Intech. Take it away and the Iranians will just buy more.'

'So what are you interested in?' Nelson said.

'We need to find out what kind of material the box contains and where it's going. Once we know that we'll have a fix on how advanced the Iranians are with their weapon development programmes, and we'll know where their development is being carried out.'

'Which allows the West to bomb shit out of it later on if they have to.' Nelson grunted. 'Let me make sure I've got this right. You just want to have a look at what's inside this box and then follow Volchek when he takes it back with him to Iran — to where it was supposed to be going before some poor bastard stole it from the Tehran warehouse.'

'Yes. I'm sure you can see this is an opportunity for the West — one we can't afford to miss. If Intech hadn't packed emeralds in the same box it would probably never have gone missing, and we'd know nothing about it. As it happens, though, because our friends here in Oman have kept their eyes and ears open, we seem to be ahead of the game for a change.'

'Some game,' Nelson said. 'What's it worth to you if we do find the box?'

Travers' expression changed. 'You don't understand your position Mr Nelson. You and Farrell are both working and living in this country under No Objection Certificates issued by Omani immigration. I can have these withdrawn in twenty-four hours. It'll take one phone call. Does that answer your question?'

Nelson began to speak, but changed his mind.

'Perhaps you'd better get the box from your truck now,' Travers said.

'How do you know it's there?'

Travers closed his brief-case. 'Shall we go and see?'

'It's OK.' Farrell stood up. 'I'll fetch it. I don't think we should put Mr Travers to any trouble.'

Outside in the car-park Farrell stood for a moment in the dark, while he endeavoured to pinpoint the reason for his unease. There was no reason, he thought. With hindsight, after everything else that had happened, this was predictable — another twist to add to the others. He stayed where he was for a few more minutes, then retrieved the box, carried it back to the office and placed in unopened on the desk.

'It's got a double skin,' Nelson explained. 'Volchek said the stuff is in the sides and the ends — packed in some kind of flasks.'

'Did you ask him what's inside the flasks?' Travers opened the lid and started running his fingers around the rim.

'Yeah, I asked. He told me to mind my own business.'

'Got it.' Travers tipped the box on to its side to show what he had found.

Half an inch from the top of the inner panels, rows of tiny screws showed how the liner was held in place. Like the box itself, the screws too were made of stainless steel, some of them leaking sea water from around their heads.

Nelson produced a screwdriver from his drawer. 'Do we just open it up?'

'Only if you're careful,' Travers said. 'No scratches on the panels and no burring of the screw heads. I don't want anyone getting suspicious.'

'OK.' Nelson began work, removing one screw after another and holding them between his lips.

Showing no emotion, Travers watched over the top of his glasses, apparently unwilling to assist or offer advice.

'What are you expecting?' Farrell asked.

'Probably not plutonium or uranium unless the quantities are very small. There's not sufficient room for shielding. My guess is Osmium 187 or Boron 10. It might be anything. I'm not an expert.'

'Volchek said the stuff isn't radioactive.' Nelson spoke through a mouthful of screws.

'Did he?' Travers smiled. 'We might never know unless we open up the flasks and I doubt we'll be able to do that without breaking seals or leaving witness marks behind.'

Nelson had finished. He transferred the screws to an ashtray. 'This thing isn't likely to be booby-trapped, is it?'

'Only if Intech were intending to blow up some Iranian scientists.' Travers took off his glasses and polished them carefully with his handkerchief before putting them back on. 'I'll let you do the honours.'

Cautiously Nelson removed the liner. It slid out easily, spilling three or four cupfuls of water on to the floor as it cleared the outer casing. All four sides of the liner were fitted with moulded polystyrene chambers supporting what appeared to be rows of

102

innocent-looking metal rods.

Travers extracted one and stood it up on end. It was unimpressive, about an inch in diameter and a little over a foot long, manufactured from a dull grey material. A knurled cap screwed on to one end was the only indication that the rod was not a rod but a tubular container.

Farrell counted them. 'Sixteen altogether,' he said. 'All the same.'

By now Travers was looking worried. He lay a flask on its side and began rolling it backward and forward over the desk top.

'What's the matter?' Nelson asked.

'I'm not sure.' The American pointed to the word MINATOM engraved on the cap. 'That tells us where the flasks came from. MINATOM is the controlling body for the Russian nuclear industry. But I haven't seen anything like this before.' He rubbed his fingertips over some writing stencilled along the length of the flask.

In two places, KRASNOYARSK 27 was followed by the chemical symbol $Hg_2 Sb_2 O_7$ and the numbers 20:20.

'Hg is mercury,' Nelson said. 'And O is oxygen. What the hell is Sb?'

'Antimony.' Farrell was surprised he could remember. 'It's a metal, mostly used to make alloys for batteries and things. What do you get by combining mercury, antimony and oxygen?'

'Some kind of poison,' Nelson said. 'Or maybe a nerve gas.'

Travers shook his head. 'MINATOM aren't in the poison or nerve-gas business.' He withdrew more flasks, inspecting each one closely before he slid out the next. Not until all sixteen were lying on the desk did he seem satisfied.

'Well?' Nelson said.

'I don't know.' Travers frowned. 'I'll have to phone Washington to see if they've come across this stuff before. Volchek doesn't know you found the box today, does he?'

'No. He's waiting for me to call him at his hotel.'

'You'd better do that then. Say you're confident you'll have the box here by late tomorrow. That gives me time to make arrangements to have him followed after he's come to collect it, and I'll be able to get the airports covered properly by then as well.'

'Our Russian friend is going to be pissed off,' Nelson said. 'He's an impatient bastard.'

'I don't care how impatient he is,' Travers pushed the phone across the desk. 'Do it now.'

Nelson dialled the number and began speaking immediately, launching into a detailed description of how the *Stingray* had been successfully located, but explaining that poor light had forced a postponement in the search for the box itself. He finished the call by suggesting that Volchek should bring the second $30,000 payment with him at six o'clock tomorrow evening.

'Problems?' Travers enquired.

'No. He said he'd be here tomorrow.'

'Right. You and Farrell meet me here in the morning at eight o'clock. I'll have heard back from Washington by then, and I'll have people with me to wire your office in case we can pick up something from Volchek when he comes.'

'You're not wiring up my office,' Nelson grunted. 'And I'll tell you right now, you're not tapping my damn phone either.'

'Your phone's been tapped since twelve o'clock today, and if I want to fill your office with recording equipment, I will. You don't have a choice, do you?' Travers collected his brief-case and went to the door. 'Welcome to the real world gentlemen. I'll see you in the morning.'

Nelson waited for the sound of the car pulling away before he spoke again. 'More like welcome to one big fucking headache,' he said. 'If the ISS have been sniffing around, what do you bet they've tripped over

105

our Sohar contract?'

'The ISS don't care about guns going out of the country,' Farrell said. 'They only worry when it's the other way round.' He picked up one of the flasks, intending to slip it back into the liner.

'Don't do that.' Nelson started gathering the others together and wrapped some tape around the bundle. 'I don't want these things hanging around the office all night. Take them home with you.' He grinned. 'If they glow in the dark, you can put them under your bed or stick them in the fridge.'

During his drive back to the apartment, as far as Farrell could make out, the flasks showed no signs of glowing. Instead they lay in darkness beside him on the seat of the truck, an innocuous bundle of sixteen metal tubes that he guessed were worth a hundred times more than the emeralds had ever been. Except that making money out of them would even be beyond Nelson, he thought. Which, in the circumstances, was probably just as well.

Almira greeted him at the door. This evening, having decided to abandon her western clothes for some reason, she was dressed more traditionally in a dark purple *abaya* and a thin silk headband — an alternative to the conventional *lahfa* head veil she occasionally wore. She was also wearing her favourite ear-rings. They were hand-carved from solid silver, large and beautiful with three diamonds set into the pendant section of each one.

Farrell had seen her like this before — in her father's home where she seemed to be in a perpetual jewellery competition with her aunt. He was accustomed to seeing Omani women weighed down with bracelets, neck-laces, anklets and ear-rings, but the way Almira wore hers was noticeably different. He found it attractive, so much so that when she kissed him to say hello, and he felt her bracelets warm against his neck, the effect was peculiarly sensual. Her perfume too was sensual, the fragrance that identified her as who she was and coloured his thoughts of her whenever she was in the same room. Tonight, the cool and abrasive Almira was nowhere in sight. This was the other version of Almira, but one that was not very well disguised.

'What happened? What did the ISS want?' she asked.

'I'll tell you in a minute.' He took the flasks to the kitchen with him and rinsed his hands under the tap, wondering if the water might somehow wash away any radioactive contami-nation.

'Come and look at what I've done.' She

called from the other room.

After dropping the flasks into an empty cornflakes packet, he rinsed his hands again then went to see what she wanted.

The room was lit by two candles standing on a table piled high with food. Where Almira was in the shadows at the end of the table the candlelight was reflecting off her ear-rings making them sparkle against her skin.

'Surprise,' she said.

He inspected the dishes, discovering fresh salad, dates, bananas, cooked fish on a mound of rice, savoury kebabs of baked goat meat and mutton, wafer thin slices of bread and two bowls of *halawa*, the Omani sweetmeat made from ghee, starch and sugar, and wonderfully flavoured with cardamom and honey. There was also the inevitable cup of hot, sweet coffee waiting for him.

'Where did you get all this?' he asked.

'I bought some of it yesterday. And I phoned Aunt Latifa and had her send some things over from home. You didn't know I could cook, did you?'

Farrell shook his head.

'I can do a lot of other things too.' She sat down at the table. 'But you never ask me about them.'

He helped himself to salad and began stacking his plate with some of the fish. She

108

was the surprise, he thought, not the meal. Or was she just trying harder than usual to catch him off balance?

'I want to hear about the ISS,' she said.

Farrell told her while he ate, first explaining who Travers was before describing how Volchek and Rajavi had led the ISS to her father and subsequently to Nelson. When she made no attempt to ask questions, he carried on, giving her a brief outline of why the Americans and the British were interested in the flasks and how Travers was arranging to have Volchek followed tomorrow when the Russian arrived to collect them.

'Why are the flasks important to this man Travers if he doesn't know what's inside them?' she asked.

'He's supposed to be finding out — by phoning someone in Washington tonight.'

'Oh. But you're sure he won't stop Volchek giving Tony the money.'

'Sounds like no one gives a damn how much Volchek's paying us,' Farrell said. 'All the West cares about is what's in the flasks and where they're going to end up.'

'So Britain and America can find out what kind of weapon Iran is trying to develop. Is that what you mean?'

Farrell nodded. 'And whereabouts in Iran it's being developed.'

'But Tony's still getting the second thirty thousand?'

He smiled at her. 'Why are you so worried about the money?'

'Why shouldn't I be?'

'I don't see why it's so important, that's all.'

'Greece,' she said. 'Or was that just a throw-away remark?'

'If you carry on trying to bribe me with candlelit dinners, I might decide to take someone else.'

'Someone like Mary?'

Farrell was completely unprepared for the remark. 'What do you know about her?'

'You kept whispering her name one night when we were making love at the beach house.'

Now he was embarrassed. 'Look, I'm sorry,' he said. 'I really am. Mary was my wife. I told you about her once — remember?'

'Mm. I remember.' She suddenly burst out laughing. 'It's all right. Stop looking so upset. You didn't really whisper her name. I asked Tony about her.'

'Why?'

'I thought he'd be able to tell me what she was like and why you're still married to her.'

'Does it matter?' Farrell said.

'To a nice Omani girl like me, you mean?

110

Why shouldn't it? Under Islamic Sharia law a man can legally end his marriage by saying I divorce you three times to his wife. You could always do that, couldn't you?'

'What for?'

'So I can be sure your intentions are honourable. That's what you said you wanted.' Leaving the table she came to sit on his lap. 'Promise we'll go to Greece. I want to hear you say it.'

'I promise,' Farrell said.

'Now thank me properly for dinner.' She slid her hands inside his shirt.

'What happened to the nice Omani girl?'

'She spent two years in a Swiss finishing-school. You'd be amazed what I learned from nice American girls and from all those nice French and Latin American girls.'

She was wrong, Farrell thought. He had stopped being amazed some days ago. He also knew this was a prelude to a repeat of the last three nights. The adrenalin was starting to run and he was acutely conscious of everything about her. 'You'll need a head start to take off all those bangles and beads,' he said.

'I can't undo some of the clips by myself — on the ones Aunt Latifa told me to wear. She said we'd enjoy ourselves more because you'd have to take them off for me.'

If the idea was intended to be provocative it was working, as provocative as her perfume and the way she was kissing him — so much so that by the time he had carried her wriggling to the bedroom his plans for Greece had been forgotten and he had ceased to wonder at the extraordinary foresight of her aunt.

* * *

Normally he would have heard the phone much earlier. As it was, because the ringing seemed to be part of a dream, Farrell was not only slow to wake up, but clumsy enough to drop the receiver when he did.

Retrieving it from the floor he endeavoured to clear his head before he said hello.

'This is Travers. Were you asleep?'

'Of course I was bloody well asleep.' Farrell looked at his watch.

'How soon can you be at Nelson's office?'

'Ten or fifteen minutes. Why? What's going on?'

'I'll meet you there.' There was a click and the line went dead.

Almira switched on the bedside lamp. 'Who was that?' she asked.

'Travers. I have to meet him at the office.'

'Oh. What time is it?'

'Just after four o'clock.'

'Do you know what he wants?'

'Not yet.' Farrell climbed out of bed and started searching for his clothes. 'I won't be long, though.'

'Suppose Tony wants you to stay while you talk to Travers?'

'Then I'll call you. If I do, remember Nelson's phone's tapped. Don't say anything too personal.'

She sat up to kiss him goodbye. 'Take my car if you like. The keys are in the hall.'

'OK.' He smiled at her. 'Curl up and go back to sleep. Keep the bed warm for me.'

Picking his way through the bracelets and anklets on the floor he collected her keys from the dresser and let himself quietly out of the apartment.

In contrast to the reek of engine oil and exhaust fumes in the truck, the Mercedes smelt of leather upholstery and Chanel perfume. It was also a good deal more powerful than the truck, allowing Farrell to take advantage of the empty streets. With his thoughts half on Almira and half on the unexpected call from Travers, he made good time, swinging into the car-park shortly before 4.30.

Three vehicles were outside the building: the white Nissan that had been parked here last night and two police cars.

He was getting out of the Mercedes when he saw Travers standing in the doorway. The American's face was grim and he made no attempt to say hello.

Farrell's concern turned to alarm. 'What the hell is it?' he asked.

'You'd better come with me.' Turning his back, Travers led the way into the office, and stepped aside.

The whole room was strewn with paper, upturned drawers, empty files and the gutted remains of the air-conditioning unit. Even a portion of the ceiling had been smashed open to expose the joints in the roof cavity. And beneath the hole, lying on the floor among the debris, was the lifeless body of Tony Nelson.

In addition to the bruising on his face, cigarette burns disfigured both his cheeks and his eyes were wide open as though he had been looking upward into the roof at the moment of his death. His mouth was open too, still leaking blood into the puddle that had formed beneath the gaping wound across his throat.

Unable to move, Farrell was clenching and unclenching his fists, staring at the body while he fought the urge to look away.

'Nasty, isn't it?' Using the toe of his shoe,

Travers turned over the empty liner of the box. It was near the desk, surrounded by the remains of the polystyrene chambers which had been levered from its sides.

'I can't handle this,' Farrell muttered.

'Nor could the poor bastard who comes in to clean the building. He didn't like it much either. Still, at least he phoned the police.' Travers removed his glasses. 'Of course what makes it worse is that it's my fault. I should have contacted Washington right away, or taken the flasks with me last night. Now we've lost the lot.'

'What?' Farrell hadn't been listening.

'The flasks. I found out what that stuff is inside them. But now they're gone. Volchek's got the damn things back — all sixteen of them. I wish I could figure out how the hell he knew they were here, and why the son of a bitch had to do this.'

'Christ.' In Farrell's head warning bells were ringing. He groped for the car keys, knowing suddenly that he was in the wrong place.

'Where do you think you're going?' Travers blocked the doorway. 'I didn't get you over here just to see this mess.'

'Get out of my way.' Farrell spat the words out. 'Try and stop me and I swear to God I'll kill you.'

115

For a second the American wavered. Then he moved back.

Farrell didn't hesitate, running for the car, starting it and ramming it into gear before he'd even slammed the door.

He reversed violently, swinging the Mercedes into a slide to align it with the exit of the car-park before accelerating straight out on to the road with the rear tyres smoking. Foot hard down he was soon travelling at nearly seventy miles an hour, using all the road to save a few more precious seconds. Only the lack of traffic was keeping the Mercedes in one piece — at any other time of day his drive would have ended in disaster. Twice he missed approaching cars by the narrowest of margins, and on three occasions the Mercedes climbed the kerb when Farrell underestimated the sharpness of a corner. He was counting seconds under his breath, willing the car to go faster because, until he reached the apartment, speed was all he had.

It took him eight minutes, a wild drive across town that had either brought him back quickly enough, or a futile trip because he had been too slow.

The apartment was in darkness. The absence of light at the bedroom window and the still-drawn curtains told him nothing, but ten feet from the front door the impact of his

116

blunder hit him like a hammer.

The door was ajar, but not for Almira to welcome him home. Already he knew what he would find before he walked inside, just as he knew with awful certainly that she too would be dead.

Like the office, the apartment was all but ruined. Walls were smashed, the contents of every drawer and cupboard littered the floor from the hallway to the lounge, and in the bedroom, the mattress and the pillows had been ripped to shreds.

Farrell was numb, unable to come to terms with what had happened and incapable of investigating further. In less than an hour, an early summer morning in Oman had become a nightmare of such proportions that for a moment his courage had deserted him.

He made himself go on, walking slowly into the bathroom with his heart pounding. Her toothbrush was on the vanity alongside her ear-rings, but there were no bloodstains, no signs of a struggle and no body.

The answer was in the kitchen, not the evidence he feared, but something entirely unexpected.

By the side of the sink, dangerously close to the cornflakes packet, lay three photographs.

Farrell couldn't bring himself to look at them. Instead he checked the packet, using his fingers to search for the bundle of flasks inside. They were still there, cool to his touch, as innocent as ever, offering him the first few strands of hope, and allowing him to guess what purpose the photographs might serve.

They were colour polaroids, two of them taken yesterday at Khabura. One showed Almira helping him load the box into the truck at the end of the jetty. The other was a picture of her with her arms round his neck. Both had been shot from the same place, some distance from the jetty, but close enough for him to see the happiness on her face.

In the third photograph her expression was one of terror. This was a picture which had been taken less than half an hour ago here in the apartment bedroom. She was naked, facing the camera, kneeling on the bed in the grip of a man behind her who was holding a knife blade to her throat.

That she was alive was more than Farrell had hoped. That she had been torn from her bed when he should have been here was unthinkable. But it was what she was doing in the third photograph that told him how thoroughly and how terribly he had failed her.

She was holding a sheet in front of her — struggling not to cover her breasts, but to hide the twisted scarring of her arm.

5

There had been little opportunity for Farrell to confront the horror of Nelson's death. Now, the sound of a car drawing up outside gave him even less chance to accept what had happened to Almira.

He reached the apartment window in time to see Travers walking purposefully to the front door.

Dropping the photos into the cornflakes packet alongside the flasks, Farrell went to meet the American in the hall.

'Well I never.' Travers inspected the damaged walls and the litter with surprise.

Farrell said nothing.

'Isn't it funny how things turn out?' Travers smiled. 'Do you know, I actually thought Volchek had found the flasks? I suppose I should have figured it out before. They weren't at the office at all, were they? They were here.'

By forcing himself to think, in the last few seconds Farrell had decided on a strategy. It was thin enough — relying partly on truth and partly on Travers overlooking the cornflakes packet just as Volchek had done.

'Where exactly were they?' Travers asked.

'Nelson didn't like leaving stuff at the office overnight. I brought them come with me and stuck them in the fridge.'

'I see. And of course they're not there any longer.' Travers went to the kitchen, opened the fridge and peered inside. 'So you'd like me to believe we're back where we started.'

'Nelson's dead for Christ's sake,' Farrell said. 'Someone cut his throat. That's not being back where anyone started. If you've got people at the airports you can tell them this isn't about a bunch of steel tubes anymore; this is about some mad bastard with a knife who's just killed a friend of mine. You'd better locate Volchek and Rajavi in a hurry too, because if I find them first I'm going to rip their hearts out.'

'You don't understand,' Travers said. 'I wouldn't bother making threats if I were you. Not when you're as far out of your depth as you are.'

'What don't I understand?'

'Why Intech were so anxious to get their shipment back. Why Nelson had cigarettes burned into his face until he told Volchek and Rajavi where to find their flasks. Why your apartment looks like a trash heap. You see, Farrell, you don't know what's behind all this. I do.'

To make certain his eyes didn't stray near the sink, Farrell was staring at the floor. 'Why the hell would I care?' he said. 'People like you make me sick. You get off a plane in Oman and start poking around as though working for the NSC gives you some God-given right to fuck up people's lives and get them killed. I'm going to make sure half the newspapers along the Gulf find out about this.'

'No you're not. And getting angry won't help either of us.' Travers left the kitchen, and began wandering around the rest of the apartment. 'Were you here alone last night?'

'Most of the time.' Farrell prepared himself for the inevitable question.

It came as soon as Travers entered the bedroom and saw the mess. He glanced first at the rips in the mattress then at the clothing and jewellery scattered on the carpet. 'Whose are these?'

'I had a friend over,' Farrell said. 'She left about eleven.'

'Who did?'

'What does it matter?'

'You don't really need me to answer that, do you?' Travers picked up a lace brassiere and a pair of panties. 'In fifteen minutes I can find out where these were bought, how much they cost and where your friend keeps them.

Now tell me her name.'

'Almira Muammar. She's the daughter of Ghassan Muammar.'

'Of course.' Travers retrieved an anklet from under the bed. 'I should've realized. Must be nice to have an Omani girlfriend whose father is in the jewellery business. Did you run her home?'

Farrell nodded.

'In her Mercedes? The one outside? All the way to Muscat?'

'Yes.'

'Why go in her car? Doesn't that mean you have to return it to her?'

'She didn't want to go in the truck.' Farrell knew he was losing ground. 'I'm supposed to be taking it back some time today.'

Travers sat down on the bed and began toying with the clip on the anklet. 'If you or I had been searching for the flasks we'd have looked in the fridge right away, don't you think?'

'I'm not in the mood to think,' Farrell said. 'And you can stop being tricky. You don't have to pretend you're stupid. You know you're not, and I know you're not. I'm not interested in your fucking flasks, Travers. Go and find Volchek, follow him to wherever he's going and leave me and Almira out of it.'

'I'm afraid the game's changed, Farrell. No

one's interested in what you want — particularly now we know what we're dealing with. Overnight this whole matter has become rather more important.' Travers paused. 'Which is why I have no intention of believing what you've just told me.'

'Believe what the hell you like,' Farrell said. 'Why should things be more important than they were yesterday?'

'Before I answer that I'm going to explain something — and I suggest you listen very carefully, because if you don't you could be facing a charge of treason. Let's go over what happened here in your apartment while you were out, shall we? First, it's pretty clear that somehow or other Volchek knew you'd brought back the box from Khabura yesterday. So when he got Nelson's phone call last night he must have guessed things were going badly wrong. When he didn't find the flasks at Nelson's office he came here looking for them — he could even have been hanging around outside because he was expecting you to leave. What matters is that he tripped over your girlfriend. She hadn't gone home. She was here, half asleep, waiting for you to come back. Why else would you have been in such a hurry to leave the office this morning? Now, either she wouldn't tell him where you'd hidden the flasks, or she didn't know. So

Volchek tears the place apart, but he can't find them. That leaves him with only one choice. He needs a lever — a big stick or a carrot. And, as luck would have it, all tucked up comfortably in your bed is just what he wants.'

'If you think he took Almira with him, you're wrong,' Farrell said quietly.

'Where is she then?'

'I told you. She went home. I took her home. The flasks were in the fridge when I left here to meet you at the office. When I got back the door was open, the place was like this and the flasks were gone.'

'You're lying.' Travers polished his glasses.

'Why would I lie, for Christ's sake?'

'Because Volchek has something you want. You're expecting him to offer you a deal — an exchange — you give him the flasks, he returns the girl.'

'You're making this up as you go along,' Farrell said. 'It's a lot of crap. Nothing becomes this important overnight. What's so special about the flasks?'

'Changed your mind, have you? All of a sudden you want to know?'

'Yes,' Hard though it was to keep his mind off Almira, Farrell recognized the danger of letting his concentration slip. Without more information, he had no leads and no proper

124

idea of how to handle what Volchek and Travers wanted from him.

'Have you ever come across the term ballotechnic?' Travers asked.

Farrell shook his head.

'Nor had I until a few hours ago. It describes a very new and very unusual product — a cherry-red, semi-liquid gel that's supposed not to exist. Rumours about it have been coming out of South Africa, Germany and Britain for a couple of years now, but no one had any real evidence to support the suspicions.' Travers paused for a moment. 'This ballotechnic gel is unlike anything anyone has ever heard of before. It's an explosive, a chemical explosive so powerful that it can be used to fuse tritium atoms to generate a thermonuclear reaction.'

'And that's what's in the flasks?' Farrell said. 'This gel stuff.'

'The stuff, as you call it, is a substance called red mercury. It's a compound of pure mercury combined with mercury antimony oxide. Apparently the Russians developed the oxide in their chemical research laboratory at Yekaterinburg last year. Since then they've had scientists working in their nuclear research centres at Dubna and Krasnoyarsk on techniques to chemically bind the oxide to pure mercury by irradiating the compound in a nuclear reactor.'

'What makes it better than any other explosive?' Farrell said.

'I've already told you. Red mercury isn't just an explosive. It's off the scale — in a class of its own. This is a material that produces a staggering amount of chemical energy — thousands of times more energy than TNT. Some of the people I spoke to last night are real frightened. They believe red mercury could be a more critical development than nuclear fission.'

'That has to be bullshit,' Farrell said. 'You don't mean thousands of times more powerful than TNT.'

Travers took a slip of paper from his pocket. 'This is a fax from the Pentagon. Part of it's an extract of a statement made by a guy called Cohen — he's a scientist in the States — one of the people who worked on the Manhattan Project to build the first atomic bomb. He was a senior nuclear weapons adviser to the US Government for thirty years. Cohen's on record as saying that red mercury is a material having the potential to spell the end of organized society.'

Farrell's scepticism had begun to disappear, and the reason for the events of the last few hours was becoming clearer by the minute.

'So there you are,' Travers said. 'You have to understand that it's not only the explosive energy people are worried about; it's what red mercury can be used for. Cohen claims that for the first time it'll be possible to make a compact neutron bomb — something around the size of a baseball that can kill anything and everything over a radius of more than half a kilometre.'

'What's red mercury got to do with neutron bombs?' Farrell said.

'It's a trigger. You contain a small quantity of tritium and deuterium inside a thin shell of red mercury. Then all you need is a detonator and some ordinary high explosive packed around the outside. The detonator sets off the explosive which ignites the red mercury. When that blows, the pressure is so enormous that it initiates a fusion reaction in the core. Have you got the idea?'

Farrell nodded.

'It gets worse,' Travers said. 'The Pentagon thinks the Russians might even be able to launch one of these miniature neutron bombs out of a 240 millimetre mortar. If it's true, society is facing something no one has ever contemplated before — a completely new category of weapon — what every damn terrorist in the world has wet dreams about.'

'Or what Iran's been having wet dreams

about. Is that what they're developing?'

'We don't know.' Travers stood up and began pacing round the bedroom. 'Whatever it is we're going to make damn sure we stop them. Now maybe you understand why Intech had to recover their flasks. We're talking about millions and millions of dollars, and one of the biggest strategic threats the West has come up against in the last twenty years.'

'We're talking about Intech killing Nelson,' Farrell said. 'But you don't care, do you?'

'I've got a job to finish. Volcheck and Rajavi are minor players. They can wait. I have to find those flasks — before they go missing again. Military Intelligence are already screaming for action because they haven't got any red mercury to analyse, and because if they can't analyse it, they can't decide what the hell to do next.'

Farrell wasn't listening anymore, and his thoughts of Almira were giving way to a bitterness he could almost taste. If he'd ever needed confirmation, he knew now why Nelson had been killed and why Almira had been abducted. Nelson had died in a misguided attempt to keep the location of the flasks secret, and Almira had become precisely what Travers thought she had become — a pawn, a bargaining chip in a

128

game between international power brokers.

Travers had found Almira's cigarettes. He checked inside the packet before he carried on with his pacing, stopping occasionally to pick up other pieces of her jewellery as though the collection of necklaces and beads would somehow jolt Farrell into being more co-operative.

The American was wrong. Because Almira's jewellery was reminding Farrell of last night, the sight of it was having the opposite affect, not only making the notion of co-operation unthinkable, but making him realize how his bitterness could best be used. Already his despair was easing. Instead he felt detached and unemotional, conscious of what he had to do.

Travers sensed the change. Depositing the jewellery on a pillow he left the room and went to the kitchen.

Farrell followed him, aware that the longer Travers spent in the apartment the greater was the danger of him looking in the cornflakes packet.

'OK,' Travers said. 'One last time. Where are the flasks?'

'Christ. How often do we have to go through this?' Farrell wrenched open the fridge door so hard that he hurt his shoulder.

'They were in there.'

'Like hell they were. You carry on the way you are and I'll have you arrested. You're a British citizen. In two days I can have you extradited from Oman and under interrogation in London. I don't think that'll help your pretty girlfriend much, and it sure as hell won't do you any good.'

'She's at home,' Farrell said. 'Do you want to telephone her, or shall I do it?'

'She's nowhere you or I are going to find her, Farrell. Volchek's made sure of it. The only way you'll ever see her again is by handing over sixteen flasks of red mercury. And the minute you do that, you're dead meat. If Volchek doesn't stick a knife in you to clear up the loose ends, I promise I'll have you locked up for the rest of your life.'

Farrell said nothing.

'What's the matter with you?' Travers slammed the fridge door. 'Don't you understand what you're doing? What happens six months from now when some crazy terrorist launches a nuclear mortar shell into the centre of a major city? How are you going to feel then?'

'You get paid to stop that sort of thing,' Farrell said. 'Go and do it. For all you know, Volchek and Rajavi are down on the waterfront right this minute trying to get hold of a boat to take them down the coast to the

130

Yemen. You're wasting your time talking to me. I can't help you.'

Travers scooped up a handful of cutlery from the floor. 'In that case I can't help you either, Farrell. Don't make any mistakes, and don't try leaving Oman. One wrong move and I'll have your balls in a vice.'

'Is that it?' Farrell asked. 'Have you finished?'

'Yes, I've finished. If you happen to decide that Miss Muammar might stand a better chance if you were working with me instead of against me, give me a call.'

'I will,' Farrell said. 'Let me know if the flasks turn up.'

The American didn't answer, placing the knives and forks in a neat row along the edge of the sink before he turned to leave. He made no attempt to say goodbye.

★ ★ ★

An ISS car had come to join the surveillance team. From his vantage point at the apartment window, Farrell could see the driver talking to the three men who an hour ago had taken up residence on the lawn across the street. They were exchanging cigarettes and laughing, one of them using a pair of binoculars to scan the adjacent buildings.

The message was clear, as clear as the clicks on the phone had been when he'd lifted the receiver to see if someone was trying to get through. Travers was taking no chances, Farrell thought. Which meant that Volchek had a problem if he wanted to make contact.

Leaving the window, Farrell checked that the front door was locked for the second time then returned to the kitchen where he sat down to consider his position.

On the table in front of him lay the bundle of flasks and the three polaroid photographs of Almira. More than anything else it was the photos that generated the sense of coldness. Whenever he looked at them it was the same, a feeling of loss followed by rage, before the determination took over. He used the feeling now, making himself forget what he'd seen at the office so he could concentrate on the job ahead.

The flasks were no more impressive than they had ever been. But already he was seeing them in a different light. Not sixteen innocent steel tubes, but sixteen steel flasks having the power of 16,000 sticks of dynamite, a tiny quantity of explosive that was capable of producing so much destructive energy that it defied imagination.

Red fucking mercury, Farrell thought. The new ultimate explosive for which Nelson had died and the reason why Almira had been taken prisoner — victims in the bright new world of neutron bombs and military supremacy where all that mattered was power and the race to get hold of the technology first.

He studied the photographs again, trying unsuccessfully to ignore the out-of-focus background of the two pictures taken at Khabura. In each of them, parked some distance away from the jetty and partly obscured by trees, cars were dotted along the beach front. There were half a dozen of them, indistinct smudges of colour, almost unrecognizable as cars except for their general outline. Two of the smudges were green, while three were white or off-white. But it was one sandwiched between them that kept attracting his attention — a red blur, smaller than the others, but slightly clearer.

Wondering if he was being stupid he put the two Khabura pictures aside and looked instead at the single picture of Almira kneeling on the bed.

The man holding the knife to her throat was an Arab, a stranger, his face impassive as though he had been deliberately posing for the camera, or perhaps because Almira's life was no more important to him than Nelson's had been.

Farrell continued looking, absorbing the detail until he was sure there was nothing else to learn from the photograph. Then, slowly, he began to make his preparations.

It took him nearly half an hour to discover that taping the flasks directly to his skin was an unreliable method of holding them in place. Realizing he needed to experiment, he attacked the handles of two brooms with a serrated bread knife in order to saw them into a number of one foot lengths before using more tape to assemble them in a girdle around his waist.

Although the dummy girdle was uncomfortable and dug into his chest if he leaned forwards too far, it seemed secure enough when he walked round the apartment. He was also relieved to find that with his shirt on, apart from an increase in the size of his waist and stomach, there was little to indicate what he was wearing underneath.

He went to check in the bathroom mirror, wondering how much heavier the real flasks would feel when the time came, and endeavouring to persuade himself that the men outside were not there to prevent him leaving or to search him if he did.

To find out, shortly before ten o'clock, with his dummy girdle on and the flasks of red mercury once again concealed in the cornflakes packet, Farrell opened his front door and walked out into the oppressive heat of another Omani morning.

The response from the men was unhurried. They stopped talking but showed no interest in crossing the street, apparently unconcerned by his appearance.

Conscious of the girdle, he continued walking, keeping in the sunlight to allow the men to build a picture of him in their minds — a picture of a thickset Englishman with a slight paunch, the man he hoped they'd been told to watch and follow, but not necessarily apprehend.

The truck was unlocked — not because Farrell had forgotten to lock it, but because Volchek and his men had been through it. Like the apartment and the office, the Toyota had been taken apart. The glove box had been torn out of the instrument panel, the seats had been slashed and all the carpets had been ripped up.

Farrell kicked the carpets into a heap on the passenger side, got in and waited to see what would happen when he turned the key in the ignition. The normal grinding from the starter was followed by the clatter of the Toyota's engine coming to life. The noise was reassuring — one of the few things that was unchanged in an environment that had suddenly become hostile and unfamiliar.

He drove with one eye on the rear-view mirror, taking the direct route to the Mutrah waterfront where he parked on the west side of the spit. Twenty yards away the same crane was at work, dropping more rocks into the water in the place where the *Stingray* had once been moored. It too was reassuring — a reminder — this time one Farrell had deliberately set out to find.

Behind the spit on the coast road, the car that had followed him had drawn up, a dark-blue Nissan, strategically positioned to make sure he couldn't leave without the driver knowing. Farrell could feel the binoculars on him as he climbed out of the truck and began searching for the rock.

It was partly covered by the incoming tide but unmistakable — the rock on which a light-skinned Omani girl in jeans and cowboy boots had stood while she asked him to light her cigarette. He could see her still, as arrogant and assertive as anyone he'd ever met, but with the benefit of hindsight, achingly beautiful, mocking him with her eyes while she offered him her lighter. He could see the *Stingray* too, returning in the moonlight from its rendezvous with the *Sarab*, the emeralds safely on board, but with the courier at the bow beginning to raise his gun.

The memories were vivid, exaggerated by his will to recall them. There was the glow of searchlights turning the water white while he held Almira under the hull, explosions, the sense of drowning and then surprise at finding Aunt Latifa bending over him when he woke up. And interleaved with all the images were the memories of Almira herself, how she would sit cross-legged on the floor with her skirt pulled down between her thighs, her perfume, her jewellery, her clothes, and how she insisted on keeping her arm beneath the sheets whenever she was in bed with him.

Farrell made himself go on, knowing it was important to finish the exercise if he was to prevent a repeat of what had happened to him seven years ago. Then, for a whole summer, the loss of Mary had coloured and distorted almost everything until he'd discovered that remembering was more effective than trying to forget. He had learned the lesson well enough to take his time now, reviewing the last few weeks, unconscious of the waves lapping at his feet while he let the memories of Almira wash over him — conjuring up each one until there were no more of them, and only then allowing his thoughts to return to the present and inevitably to the flasks.

Yesterday the flasks had been a way to buy two tickets for a holiday in Greece — a way for Tony Nelson to outfit the new boat he was about to buy. Today the same flasks were the instruments of Nelson's death and the only thing they were ever going to buy was Almira's freedom or her life.

For the next forty-five minutes Farrell remained where he was, standing out in the heat on the spit, watching the tide creep in, waiting until he was sure it was time to go.

He drove home as slowly as he'd come, not bothering to watch for the blue Nissan because it made no difference whether it was following or not. Nothing mattered very much anymore, Farrell had decided; except for one thing — contact with either Volchek or Rajavi.

In the apartment he stripped off the girdle to examine the chafe marks on his chest. Although in several places his skin had been rubbed raw and sweat had been making his shirt stick to several individual lengths of broomstick, the idea seemed to have proved itself. Whether it would work equally well when it became necessary for him to substitute the flasks for pieces of wood was more doubtful — a question that could only be answered after he'd received instructions or demands from Intech.

He retrieved his toaster from the floor, and found half a loaf of bread in the fridge. Then, for the first time since his candlelit dinner of last night, Farrell began to eat.

He was buttering his third piece of toast when the phone rang. Wondering if Volchek would guess the line was tapped, he answered it cautiously, only to hear the much deeper voice of Ghassan Muammar.

'Ah, Mr Farrell. It is good you are home now.'

'Did you call me earlier?' Farrell could think of no way to warn him.

'Indeed. But it is unimportant. I am telephoning to say that I have this morning received the dreadful news about Mr Nelson. You have my greatest sympathy and my sincere wishes that whoever has done this thing will be brought to justice very quickly.'

Nothing about his daughter, Farrell thought. Not a single word.

'Mr Farrell, you are there?' Muammar enquired.

'Yeah, I'm here.'

'I am sure you have other friends with who you can share your grief. Nevertheless, if you would care to visit my family this evening, we would be most pleased to offer you whatever support we can. My sister believes it is frequently good to talk such things through.

She has asked me to explain this to you.'

Whether or not it was a message, Farrell couldn't tell. Muammar's voice was perfectly controlled, but by avoiding any mention of his daughter perhaps he was being too careful.

'I'd like to come,' Farrell said. 'Thank you. I'll bring Almira's car back.'

'Then it is settled. I shall receive you not at my home, however, but at my beach house. You know where it is, I think.'

'Yes, I know. What time?'

There was a short delay before Muammar answered. 'My sister is saying you will please come to dinner if eight o'clock is convenient for you.'

'That's fine. Tell her I'll be there.' He said goodbye and replaced the receiver, unable to decide whether it was foolish to consider going when he had still not heard from Volchek.

To pass the time in case the Russian elected to risk a phone call, Farrell spent the afternoon writing a letter that he should never have started. As well as taking the best part of four hours, when he'd finished and read it through for the tenth time, the urge to throw it away was as strong as ever.

He resisted the temptation, quickly writing the words Mary Farrell on the envelope and

140

adding her address as if to prove to himself that it was too late to try again.

In the hour that remained he busied himself by making a half-hearted attempt to clear up the apartment before embarking on his final preparations.

By 7.30, having received no communication of any kind from Volchek, Farrell was as ready as he ever would be.

Strapped around his waist now were the sixteen flasks of red mercury. Although they were heavy enough to have made him reinforce the girdle with more tape, and cool enough to make him aware of the steel against his skin, once he'd put on a clean shirt, they were no more detectable than the broomstick dummies had been and, after a check in the mirror, he found his confidence was growing.

The three other things he took with him were easier to conceal. He put Almira's ear-rings and the photos of her into his pocket along with the letter to Mary. Then, gripping the shrapnel fragment in one hand for luck, and dangling the keys to the Mercedes from his other, Farrell let himself out of the apartment.

Again there was little reaction from the men across the street. One of them went to the car to use the radio or a telephone, but the other three remained where they were, sitting on the lawn.

He opened the door of the Mercedes, more conscious of the flasks than he had been earlier, but certain the surveillance team would report that he was empty-handed when he left.

Now the trick was to maintain confidence, Farrell thought. Pretend this wasn't a wild-goose chase, and hope like hell that none of his guesses had been wrong.

★ ★ ★

The Nissan was less than a hundred yards behind him when he turned the Mercedes into the driveway leading to the beach house. This was an older and more modest residence than the Muammar villa in Muscat, but the sea views from the upstairs balconies were wonderful, and, on the occasions when Farrell had been here with Almira, he'd spent hours wandering around the grounds with her. Besides being a very private place surrounded by trees and bushes, it had the advantage of being difficult to observe from the road.

He parked behind Muammar's Range Rover and sat for a moment, waiting to see if the tail car had followed him down the drive.

But there was no sign of it, no sound of gravel crunching under tyres and no figures moving in the shadows near the gate.

'Mr Farrell.' It was Aunt Latifa, outside the car, tapping on the window. 'You are all right?'

'I'm OK.' He climbed out and tried to remember the questions he'd rehearsed. 'You know Almira's not with me, don't you?' he said. 'You do know what's happened?'

'Yes. It is very horrible, I think. Please to come inside where my brother is waiting.'

Farrell walked with her to the house, relieved that he would not have to break the news.

Ghassan Muammar met him at the door. Salim was there too, smoking his usual cigarette while he held Almira's two Salukis on leashes. Now they recognized their visitor they were wagging their tails, eager to lick Farrell's hand.

He said hello to Muammar and Salim then bent down to quieten the dogs.

'Mr Farrell, I am pleased you are here,' Muammar said. 'With the help of my son whose English is much better than mine I have searched for the correct words, but I cannot find how to fully express my dismay at Mr Nelson's death.'

'Was it Travers who told you?'

143

'Yes. With two men from the ISS he came this morning. First he tells me that last night in a brutal murder, Mr Nelson has lost his life. Then he explains about the disappearance of this new explosive which you have recovered from the seabed.'

Farrell stopped him from going on. 'It might be an idea if we found a better place to talk,' he said.

Muammar raised his eyebrows. 'The garden perhaps? Would that be sufficiently private?'

'No. Travers has men outside. I was followed here. Do you have somewhere with a radio?'

'Yes, I understand.' Muammar despatched his son to find one before escorting Farrell into a small room off the hall. 'While we wait you must please allow me to say one thing. It is by my hand all this has come to pass. In my haste to acquire cheap emeralds from Iran I have not only brought pain and dishonour to my family, but brought misfortune to other people. I cannot forget that I, myself, was responsible for introducing you and Mr Nelson to these men from Intech.'

Before Farrell could reply, Salim entered the room carrying a small portable radio. He placed it on the windowsill and grinned. 'Decadent western rock and roll, or a nice programme of Muslim prayers?'

'Anything.' Farrell fiddled with the radio himself until he found some music, leaving Muammar to dismiss his son and close the door.

'I do not believe there are listening devices in my home,' Muammar said.

'I don't know whether there are or not. I'm pretty damn sure there's a tap on my phone, though, and maybe one on yours as well.'

'I see. Was I sufficiently discreet when I telephoned you?'

'I think so.' Farrell hesitated. 'Look, I have to ask you this right away. Do you know for sure that Volchek has Almira? Did Travers explain?'

Muammar nodded. 'Mr Travers is also certain you have somewhere hidden these flasks which belong to Intech. If indeed that is the case, then I wish to make you an offer for them.'

'What do you mean?'

'To safeguard my daughter I am prepared to pay whatever is necessary. If you require one million American dollars then I shall find one million American dollars.'

Farrell unbuttoned his shirt to reveal the girdle. 'You don't have to pay anything to anyone,' he said. 'You don't really believe I'm here to sell you these, do you?'

145

'Please excuse me. I have insulted you.' Muammar seemed genuinely embarrassed. 'I was not certain you had them.'

'Apart from what Travers told you, what makes you believe Volchek has Almira?'

'I shall show you.' Reaching beneath a fold in his robe Muammar produced a sheet of paper and a photograph. 'One hour before I telephoned you these are delivered to my home in Muscat. They are given to my sister by a stranger.'

Like the photos in Farrell's pocket, this one also was a polaroid, a picture of Almira being held up against a car door by Hasan Rajavi. She was fully clothed and appeared to be unharmed.

Farrell put the photograph aside and studied the sheet of paper. It was an unsigned note, handwritten in Arabic with a small map covering the lower half of the page.

He gave the note back to Muammar. 'What does it say?'

'It is from the Russian Volchek, but written by Rajavi, I think. It is to state that the price for my daughter's safe return is sixteen flasks of this substance which he calls red mercury. Intech say I should obtain the flasks from you by whatever means I choose. When I have them they are to be delivered to a village high in the Hajar mountains.'

'How much do you know about red mercury?' Farrell asked.

'From Mr Travers I understand it is a new and most powerful form of high-explosive.'

'That's one hell of an understatement.' Farrell rebuttoned his shirt. 'This stuff isn't just high-explosive. Does the map show exactly where you're supposed to hand over the flasks?'

'Yes. My daughter is at this moment being taken there — to a very difficult and very remote place. It has been chosen, I believe, because Volchek is concerned that whoever delivers the flasks may be followed by the ISS. In his note he warns me to be careful. This Russian is a man who himself is very careful, do you not think so?'

'The bastard hasn't got much choice,' Farrell said. 'Being in Oman makes him a stranger in a strange land, and he knows Travers and the ISS are after him. There may be other people as well. Volchek's dealing with something half the world wants to get their hands on.'

'Yet you are willing to give this red mercury to me? Why should this be, I wonder? Although I make no judgement, either as a Muslim or as a father, I must ask you if it is simply because my daughter shares your bed.'

147

'It's more complicated than that.' Farrell met his eyes. 'But I'm not giving the flasks to you. I'm going to fix this myself. All you have to do is help.'

'Have you considered how very dangerous it will be? If Iran is so anxious to obtain red mercury, perhaps other countries in the Middle East are equally anxious. Then, of course, there is no guarantee that Volchek will permit you or my daughter to live, whether or not you give him what he wishes. Would it therefore not be better to let me handle matters?'

'How?' Farrell asked.

'By sending the flasks with a friend who, in your own words, is not a stranger in a strange land — not a European, but someone accustomed in the ways of my people, and at home in the high mountains and the desert. I am fortunate in having such a friend. He is Ali-Khaleefa, a Dhofari with whom I have already spoken.'

Farrell had met Ali-Khaleefa on several occasions. He was Muammar's stable manager, a tough, leathery old man who treated Almira as though he was her second father.

'Do you agree with my proposal?' Muammar enquired.

For the first time today Farrell found himself close to smiling. 'If you've already

148

spoken to Ali-Khaleefa you must've been pretty sure I had the flasks,' he said.

Muammar spread his hands. 'I had hoped. But you have not said if you will allow my friend to deliver them.'

'Only if he takes me with him. It's a two-man job.'

'That is your decision?'

'Yes.'

'Very well. Then we have many arrangements to make but little time in which to make them.' Muammar hesitated. 'Before we begin, may I please ask you something which is more personal?'

'Go ahead.'

'You have seen my daughter's arm, yet you do not mind that she is disfigured in such a way?'

'No,' Farrell said. 'I don't mind.'

'So for her you will trade the red mercury with the men from Intech — the same men who have killed your friend Tony Nelson?'

Concealed in Muammar's remark was a suggestion that Farrell was overlooking an opportunity for vengeance, and even a hint that he was being less than honest in declaring his reasons for wanting to go. But Muammar didn't understand, Farrell thought. How could he? Only Almira could understand why this had to be done this way,

149

and why, until she was safe again, everything else would have to wait.

* * *

Just as Muammar's sister had greeted Farrell on his arrival at the beach house, now it was Aunt Latifa who accompanied him to the car to say goodbye.

'Please you will be careful,' she whispered. 'My brother is relying on you.'

'I know.' Farrell approached the Mercedes with his eyes on the trees, looking for the men he was sure were there. But it was too dark, and when he tried to listen for footsteps or voices all he could hear was the distant sound of surf breaking on the beach.

'My brother has shut the front gate,' Aunt Latifa explained. 'In order for you to leave you must first stop to open it.'

'So they can see it's me?'

She nodded.

He reached into his pocket for the letter. 'Would you mail this for me?'

'It will be my pleasure. Allah be with you. And with Miss Almira.'

'Thank you.' He kissed her on the cheek and climbed into the car where Salim was crouching uncomfortably on the floor on the passenger side.

The young man muttered something in Arabic, then began swearing fluently in English.

'Have you got a problem?' Farrell asked.

'I got shit all over my clothes crawling over the flower bed and I need a cigarette.'

Deciding it was best to ignore him, Farrell drove to the gate and stepped out into the Mercedes' headlights.

The Nissan was where he expected it to be, parked on the roadside some distance away beneath a tree, facing towards Mutrah with the engine running. Although its lights came on almost as soon as Farrell had the Mercedes underway, the driver waited for some seconds before he pulled out from the kerb to take up his customary position a hundred yards behind.

'How much of a lead have you got?' Salim asked.

'Not enough.' Farrell accelerated slightly before settling down to the job in hand, driving conservatively, but adjusting his speed at intersections to provide an opportunity for other traffic to join the convoy.

The technique was unsuccessful. The driver of the Nissan was unwilling to fall back, and with few cars on the road, already the first potential drop-off point was drawing near.

It came up quickly — too quickly for Farrell to even consider jamming on the brakes. He saw a building slide past the window, the large brick-built factory with the alleyway that Muammar had described. A moment later it was gone, wasted and swallowed up in the darkness.

Farrell began trying harder, counting down the minutes to the second drop-off where he believed he might stand a better chance.

Salim had guessed things were not going well. 'Use the reeds along the coast road,' he said. 'Then you won't have to stop completely. If you try jumping while we're going through town, you'll probably smack into a wall or something.'

Farrell was surprised to hear that Salim cared. Over the course of the evening the young man had been surly and ill-mannered, apparently as indifferent to the wishes of his father as he was to the fate of Almira.

'Can you get up here behind the wheel in time?' Farrell asked.

'I can move a hell of a lot faster than you can. Anyone who's spent as long as you have screwing my sister has got to be a real slow bastard.'

The remark was too childish to warrant a reply, leaving Farrell only to consider the pleasure he would get from kicking Salim in the head at a later date.

He increased his speed, doubtful now that the plan would work at all unless his luck improved.

The first real chance came with the appearance of a large van in his mirror. It was a white van, already ahead of the Nissan, travelling fast and about to overtake the Mercedes until Farrell put his foot down.

For nearly seven minutes he kept it behind him, using it to block the Nissan's view while he made up his mind and waited for a gleam of moonlight on the ocean.

When he was sure, he nudged Salim with his foot. 'Get ready to take over,' he said. 'I'm going to slide into the passenger seat.'

Manoeuvring himself across the car was difficult enough. Doing it without losing speed while Salim slipped behind the wheel proved even harder. As a result, the second drop-off point was less than 200 yards ahead before Farrell was ready in position.

'Reeds.' Salim pointed to the shore line. 'Say when.'

'You're driving.' Farrell cracked open the passenger door. 'Whenever you see a soft spot.'

'OK. Here we go.' To alert the driver of the van, Salim stabbed at the brakes, waited for a second and then stood on them — this time making the Mercedes slither dangerously close to the verge.

Long before the reeds started whipping at his face Farrell knew he had jumped too early. He was conscious of the Mercedes accelerating away and heard the door slam shut behind him. Then he hit the sand, landing awkwardly on his injured shoulder.

He was still rolling when, with horn blowing and lights flashing, the van swept by.

The Nissan, though, was a good sixty yards behind it giving him time to bury his face before more headlights lit up the foreshore. But soon the Nissan too was gone and the road was once again in darkness.

Lying in a clump of tangled reeds with his mouth full of grit, Farrell was having difficulty in breathing. The sand was only partly to blame, he discovered. Most of the problem was bruising — the after-effect of rolling several yards with sixteen heavy steel tubes strapped around his waist.

But the subterfuge had worked and the flasks themselves were undamaged. Now, provided nothing prevented Ali-Khaleefa from coming to collect him, the first hurdle had been overcome.

He scrambled to his feet and walked down to the water's edge where he rinsed the sand out of his mouth, and gingerly swung his arm

154

to see if it still worked. Like yesterday, after cranking over the engine on the fishing boat, there was a slight stiffness in his shoulder, but nothing more serious apart from an extension of the bruising along his ribs.

Farrell wasn't worried about the bruising. Instead he was conscious of a hollowness somewhere inside his head where the doubts were beginning, an emptiness that was being made worse by the dull expanse of sea stretched out in front of him. It was draining away his confidence the longer he stared at it, robbing him of his sense of purpose and making him wonder if he was already too late, and if all this would yet turn out to be for nothing.

To regain his optimism he took Almira's ear-rings from his pocket and held them up in the moonlight. But he could detect no sparkle, and when he tried to recall the last time she had worn them, all he could see was the self-same photograph of her kneeling on the bed.

6

Once, at a coastal settlement on the peninsula in the middle of summer, Farrell had encountered Omani women laying out gutted fish on rocks made so hot by the sun that they made a perfect cooking surface. He could remember the smell and how the juices had bubbled and boiled on to the sand. There were other summer days he could remember — sweltering days when the sun had burned down with the intensity of a blow-torch. But he had never before experienced a midday temperature like this, nor had he ever imagined how hot the desert wind could become on its long journey through the mountain passes to the sea.

Beside him at the wheel of the Land Rover, Ali-Khaleefa seemed insensitive to the heat that was sucking Farrell's breath away. Since they'd turned off the road an hour ago the Omani had said little, keeping his attention on the deteriorating track while he negotiated his way around potholes and the sand-filled ruts that had reduced their speed to almost nothing.

Farrell wiped the grit off his face and tried

to forget he was sitting in a pool of sweat. Even after he'd moistened the grab handle it was still too hot to hold, and when he inadvertently touched the dashboard to steady himself, it felt as though his hand was on fire.

'I need some water,' he said. 'You'll have to stop for a minute.'

'First we must find shade.' Ali-Khaleefa pointed ahead to a rock-shelf. 'I shall see if I can drive there.' He dropped a gear, but predictably, as soon as the Land Rover left the track it lost all headway, sinking to its axles into another pocket of *sabkha*, the chalky layer of powder lying beneath the crust of sand and gravel.

Farrell got out and walked alone to the rock-shelf, leaving Ali-Khaleefa to reverse his way out and try again. The Omani made it on his second attempt, arriving with rooster-tails of sand spurting from all four wheels.

'If we carry on like this we're going to break something.' Farrell reached for the water bottle, and swallowed several mouthfuls from it. 'Are you sure you know where you're going?'

'I am sure.' The Omani grinned. 'Once it was believed the old trails through the Hajar would stay open only for the camels, but now, as you see, with four-wheel-drive it is

157

sometimes possible.'

'Sometimes?' Farrell said.

'This is not a difficult track — slower than the sand road I have shown you on the map, but I promise the ISS will not look for us along this way.'

Farrell didn't doubt it. Overnight, after Ali-Khaleefa had picked him up from the coast, they had driven west in the comparative safety of darkness, travelling inland to Samail before turning south and entering a huge scrub-filled wadi shortly before dawn. There Farrell had called a halt, reluctant to continue in daylight in case Travers had cast a net out over half the country. Now, though, after being persuaded to embark on what had turned out to be a near-vertical drive through a rocky valley on the northwestern flank of the wadi, he was convinced no one was ever going to find them. He was equally certain that if the afternoon became any hotter his eyes would melt.

'You wish to see where we are?' Ali-Khaleefa spread his map out on the bonnet.

'What about the village?' Farrell asked. 'Show me that first.'

'Here.' Ali-Khaleefa placed a finger on an area that appeared to consist mainly of ravines. 'But it is not a proper village — only what is left of one. Many centuries ago there is much trade in these parts with frankincense and the *laqat* incense gum for the Romans. Later the people of the village try to live by other means, but more than one hundred years before today, the water in the underground *falaj* becomes bad, and many people die. For this reason the village has no name.'

'Did someone poison the water?'

The Omani shook his head. 'It is from how you call it — minerals.'

'So it's a ghost town,' Farrell said.

'The Bedu sometimes camp there when they travel, but for a short while only.'

'And where the hell are we?'

'I think as close as this.' Ali-Khaleefa moved his finger about an inch on the map. 'Had we taken the sand road we would be already there. By this route we have perhaps one or two hours more.'

Farrell leaned back against the rock-shelf to think, wondering if it would be best to arrive unannounced, or whether he should plan his approach more carefully. So far he had planned nothing, keeping his mind on the problem of getting to the village without revealing its location to Travers or the ISS. But in this barren moonscape it was hard to believe his precautions had been necessary, and nearly as difficult to believe that he would soon need to be ready to exchange the red mercury for Almira.

Concerned about the temperature in the Land Rover, he went to check on the flasks. They were packed in a long canvas case, once again bound into a bundle to prevent them from rattling against the two rifles and the spare magazines of ammunition that Muammar had provided.

The flasks were hot, but not dangerously so, Farrell decided. If red mercury had a low tolerance to heat or shock it would have blown long ago. Again he found himself trying to picture what the explosion of 16,000 sticks of dynamite might be like. Not that there would be anyone to see it or hear it if anything happened up here, he thought, and no one left to tell Almira he had failed her for a second time.

Ali-Khaleefa came to see what he was doing. 'The flasks are OK?' he asked.

'Seem to be. I don't know what it takes to set this stuff off.'

The Omani grinned. 'We not try to find out, I think. Now please you must drink some more. For a European it is easy to dehydrate.'

Farrell tried to swallow some water from his bottle but gagged on the second mouthful. 'I can't,' he said.

'You are nervous perhaps?'

160

'Yeah.'

'I also.' Sitting down on a mudguard that would have been too hot for Farrell to touch, Ali-Khaleefa began to roll a cigarette. 'I had not expected to come here again with guns,' he said. 'Twenty-five years ago when I was too young to believe I would ever die, I have fought for the Popular Front for the Liberation of Oman. Then, because the mountains of the Jebel and the Hajar were as familiar to me as the lines upon my hands, I had no fear. But I am no longer young, and now among these hills and valleys I smell much danger.'

'But you've been coming up here for years,' Farrell said. 'Muammar told me.'

'It is not the same. Since the car accident in which her mother dies I have taught Miss Almira to ride her father's horses in the Hajar, how she is to watch for the wolves, the panthers and the hyena. I have shown her how to be careful of the wild animals, the insects and the poisonous plants until there is nothing more she can learn from me. But today I come again with a rifle — perhaps to save her from these men who want the red mercury, so it is important for me to remember how to again be brave. You understand these feelings?'

'Yes, I understand.' The explanation had

161

been unnecessary. Farrell knew exactly what Ali-Khaleefa was endeavouring to explain — just as he knew there was no one he would rather have with him. This was the man Muammar had described; someone who could move effortlessly through the mountains, someone whose eyes could see a dust trail twenty miles away and, at the next minute, pick out the delicate tracks of scorpions in the sand. Twice Farrell had been warned to be cautious when he relieved himself, and twice there had been snakes where Ali-Khaleefa said there would be snakes. A man who was truly at home in the Hajar, Farrell thought, and maybe that would provide the edge they needed.

The Omani drew heavily on his cigarette before he stubbed it out on a rock. 'These people who have taken Miss Almira are to be trusted?' he asked.

'They killed Tony Nelson.'

'I understand. But what will they gain by killing again?'

'They still have to get the flasks out of the country. Maybe they won't want to leave anything behind that could trip them up later.'

'And at the village, Volchek and his companion will be alone?'

Farrell showed him the photo of Almira

being held with a knife to her throat. 'This guy's probably with them.'

'Ah.' Ali-Khaleefa spat in derision. 'How can any man do this thing? Do you see how she tries to cover her arm from him?'

'Yes.' Farrell retrieved the photograph. 'I wish I knew who the hell he is.'

'The knife is not a *khanjar* so he is not an Omani. When I find this one I shall make him smooth like a woman between his legs. Then, if he does not beg forgiveness, I shall cut out his liver and feed it to him.'

'That's not on the agenda,' Farrell said. 'You and I had better get something straight. We're here to make an exchange, that's all.'

'How can you say this when these men have murdered your friend?'

'It's real easy: I can't afford to screw up.' Farrell paused. 'I need a guarantee from you — no surprises, and I call the shots.'

'You wish me to shake your hand like an Englishman?'

'No. I want your word as a Dhofari.'

'Then, of course, I will give it to you.' Ali-Khaleefa smiled. 'Now, shall we continue? Or will we wait until the sun has moved so it will be cooler?'

'Are you sure about the one or two hours to get there?'

'Perhaps less if the track is good.'

163

Farrell consulted his watch. 'If we leave now we'll be there around midday,' he said. 'I suppose that's OK.'

Ali-Khaleefa went to restart the Land Rover. He rolled another cigarette while Farrell got in. 'You are ready?' he asked.

'Yeah.' Farrell lowered himself on to a seat that felt more like a hot-plate.

'Soon the drive will be easier.' Ali-Khaleefa lit his cigarette before engaging the crawler gear and setting off up the valley again in the usual series of bone-jarring lurches.

Farrell hung on, occasionally wondering if they would tip over and marvelling at the ability of the transmission and suspension to absorb shock-loads that would have reduced any other vehicle to scrap.

The Land Rover seemed to be unbreakable. Despite the radiator boiling from time to time and the crunching noises coming from underneath whenever the chassis bounced off a rock or boulder, it continued responding to Ali-Khaleefa's commands, climbing higher and higher until at last they emerged from the head of the valley.

Here the terrain was kinder. For as far as Farrell could see, everything was baked to the same dull red colour; the soil, the rocks, the ridges and even the scree littering the bottom of each ravine. The Land Rover too was red, smothered inside and out in a thick film of dust.

Ali-Khaleefa stopped to inspect his map before squinting into the sun and getting out to look at their wheel marks. 'We leave a trail behind us,' he said.

'So what,' Farrell said. 'Nobody's going to see it. We might as well be on another bloody planet.'

'We follow this ridge.' Ali-Khaleefa pointed. 'In maybe one mile it joins with the sand road to the village. Then it will be like driving on the highway again.'

'Do you think they'll hear us or see us coming?'

'You can be sure of it. In the old days these villages have been built on high ground for people to defend themselves against invaders. Anyone who is there will see our dust. We cannot approach secretly. Is that not why Miss Almira has been brought here?'

'So we can't double-cross Volchek, you mean?' Farrell said.

'Yes. Mr Muammar has said the ISS could attempt to follow us. By keeping Miss Almira in such a place it will be easy for the Russian to see we travel alone.'

Farrell nodded. 'Have you got any good ideas?'

'In such circumstances it is best not to be

too clever, I think. We have nothing to gain and much to lose.'

'So we just drive straight up and hand over the red mercury?'

'No. I will remain behind one hundred yards in the Land Rover with a rifle while you take the flasks ahead on foot. If the Russian is the man I believe him to be, he will do the same with Miss Almira. Because we may be watched with binoculars it is necessary to conduct our business openly, but not without precautions. Do you, yourself, have a better way for us to do this?'

'No.' Although Farrell's shirt was wringing wet, and sweat was running like acid over his ribs where the girdle had rubbed his skin away, his mouth was so dry that his tongue was sticking to his gums.

'Then we shall do it?' The Omani looked at him.

'Yeah. We'll do it.'

In contrast to the slow, jolting climb up from the wadi, the short drive to the sand road was easy going, and once the Land Rover was on the new surface, even if it did fall short of the highway quality that Ali-Khaleefa had promised, it was good enough for them to pick up speed and create a welcome draught of air through the cab.

The countryside was changing now. To the

166

west, where the bare peaks of the Hajar range were glowing in the sunshine, a heat-haze was shimmering against a dusky, orange-coloured sky. The peculiar colours were adding to Farrell's sense of having gone back in time. He'd been in the mountains before, but not in mid-summer and never had he been this high. Yet they were still in the foothills, travelling on what appeared to be a gentle but unending slope to nowhere. To his right, the panorama of the eastern Hajar was similarly unreal, a tapestry of faded colour bordered by an ocean that was more blue than the sky. In different circumstances Farrell would have found the views spectacular. Instead it was as though he was hallucinating, moving through an imaginary landscape of artificial colour on his way to the edge of the world.

His first glimpse of their destination came less than a minute after Ali-Khaleefa told him to get prepared. At the top of the slope, flanked on three sides by steeper inclines of yellow and red-veined rock, the village was a collection of derelict, mud-brick buildings, some of them no more than heaps of rubble. Those that remained intact were shells, their windows staring out over an empty plateau like rows of sightless eyes.

Ali-Khaleefa brought the Land Rover to a halt. 'There are camels,' he said. 'And smoke.'

Farrell could see the smoke, a thin column rising from somewhere in the centre of the village. He could see the camels too, a group of them tethered in the shade of what had once been fortified walls or battlements.

He was reaching for the bag containing the flasks and the rifles when Ali-Khaleefa stopped him.

'Wait,' the Omani said quietly. 'At this range I do not trust my aim.' He nosed the Land Rover forward, keeping it in low gear while he searched the hills and buildings for any signs of life.

'What do you think?' Farrell was apprehensive.

'I do not know. There are no vehicles. Only camels and the smoke.'

'If Volchek's here, the bastard's probably watching us.' Farrell was looking for a glint of sunlight off binoculars, not yet willing to believe that the village could be occupied only by wandering Bedu tribesmen.

Three hundred yards from the camels, Ali-Khaleefa suddenly switched off the ignition and kicked open his door. 'Listen,' he said.

For a moment Farrell could detect nothing. Up here the air was so still and so silent that it seemed as though the whole world was asleep. But then he heard it. Funnelling out of one of the ravines was the distinctive throb of helicopter rotor blades.

'Jesus.' Grabbing the bag he pulled out one of the rifles and fitted a magazine.

Ali-Khaleefa's face was expressionless. 'We do not yet know who it is,' he said. 'Perhaps it is Volchek bringing Miss Almira.'

'Perhaps it isn't.' Farrell chambered a round, listening and looking, hearing the chopping noise grow louder as the still-invisible helicopter drew closer.

'It comes quickly,' Ali-Khaleefa grunted. 'We must find cover, I think.'

There was no cover. No rocks, no cliffs, no trees — only the crumbling walls and buildings of the village.

The Omani restarted the Land Rover, spinning its wheels as he headed for the protection of the nearest cluster of houses.

He was too late. Farrell heard the whine of a turbine. A second later, rising from a gully like a giant dragonfly, the helicopter soared above the plateau and began to bank. It was an Omani Air Force helicopter, painted in desert camouflage, flying fast and low now the pilot could see their wheel tracks.

Swerving to throw up a screen of dust Ali-Khaleefa swung the Land Rover one way and then the other. But the helicopter was already passing overhead, sweeping the dust

169

aside in the downdraught of its rotor.

'We're not going to make it,' Farrell yelled. 'Get back into the valley where they can't land. They must know we've got the flasks.' He struggled with his rifle, uncertain whether he should use it.

Before they could change direction, the helicopter was in front of them, hovering at an altitude of less than thirty feet. Its attitude was threatening as though the pilot was daring them to make a run for safety.

Out-manoeuvred, Ali-Khaleefa did the only thing he could do. He changed gear, shouted at Farrell to hold on, and accelerated furiously in a straight line toward the buildings.

It was a mistake.

Streaking out from pods on each side of the helicopter's fuselage, the rockets came in waves, blasting out craters in the ground all around them.

The Land Rover stood no chance. Travelling at nearly forty miles an hour, the right front wheel hit one of the holes so violently that Farrell heard the suspension crack. The impact threw him against the windshield and slowed the vehicle to a standstill.

Ali-Khaleefa hadn't given up. He tried again, navigating his way round two more craters before the wheel collapsed, and a second wave of rockets blew out all the windows.

Blinded by dust, Farrell disembarked still holding the rifle. The walls of the village were no further than 200 yards away, but he was never going to reach them. The helicopter had landed and men were spilling out of it — armed soldiers, two of them crouched low, approaching the wrecked Land Rover, their weapons at the ready.

Ali-Khaleefa shouted above the noise. When Farrell failed to respond, the Omani jumped out and gripped the rifle barrel.

'They will kill you,' he said. 'What purpose will it serve if you die here?'

Farrell couldn't answer him, unable to believe he could have journeyed this far only to have been hunted down within sight of the place he had come to find. Helplessly he looked in the direction of the village, wondering if Almira was there or if she had ever been there.

'Please, you let go of the gun,' Ali-Khaleefa said.

There was barely time for Farrell to drop it before the soldiers reached him. They were young men in full battledress, holding their machine pistols nervously in both hands while their eyes flickered first over him and then over Ali-Khaleefa.

One of them motioned with his gun, indicating that Ali-Khaleefa should stand beside Farrell. The other soldier went to the Land Rover.

Farrell was working out the seconds, trying to decide how long it would take him to reach the houses if he could somehow retrieve the flasks from the Land Rover and magically outrun the bullets that were bound to follow. He abandoned the idea, cursing whoever had betrayed the location of the village and put Almira's life in danger.

The soldier who had been rummaging around in the Land Rover had found what he was looking for. After checking the stencilling on the sides of the flasks against a piece of paper and relaying a message over his radio, he hurried back to the helicopter carrying the bundle under his arm.

His companion remained behind, gun levelled, speaking in Arabic to Ali-Khaleefa.

'What does he want?' Farrell asked.

'He has explained we are under military arrest and that both of us are to be taken immediately to the Muscat airbase.' The Omani hesitated. 'I have said that because you must stay here he will have to shoot you in the legs before you agree to leave. But I think without the flasks our cause is lost.'

Again Farrell scanned the ruins of the village. The noise of the helicopter was disturbing the camels, but if anyone was watching they were keeping well hidden. Except for the same wispy column of smoke curling upwards in the sunshine, nothing was moving.

'We must go with these men,' Ali-Khaleefa said. 'Later we shall return for Miss Almira. I swear to you we will do this.'

Farrell had no intention of going anywhere. Faced with only one option he was waiting for the right instant to kick out at the soldier and start his run.

He had no opportunity to do either.

The soldier's face became blank. Simultaneously his knees buckled, and as blood began leaking from his ears, he sank slowly to the ground. A second, unnecessary bullet tore half his jaw away.

Unlike Farrell who was about to set off after the flasks, Ali-Khaleefa had identified the source of danger. The Omani acted swiftly, hurling Farrell bodily into the nearest rocket crater.

'What the hell are you doing?' Farrell yelled.

'You will not succeed.' Ali-Khaleefa raised his head a few inches. 'See what is happening.'

173

Twenty yards from the helicopter the other soldier was sprinting for his life through a hail of bullets coming from the village.

He never made it, crashing into a heap with the bundle of flasks spilling from his hands.

But he had been close enough. While the pilot prepared to take off, other soldiers retrieved the flasks, dragging their companion's body into the helicopter and returning the fire with automatic weapons.

An increase in the speed of the helicopter's rotor was accompanied by the high-pitched whine of its accelerating turbine. The pilot had overreacted. For an instant the helicopter had seemed unstable, rising on one skid and bouncing. But suddenly it was airborne, gaining altitude rapidly before it went into a turn.

'Oh Jesus.' Farrell scrambled to his feet. 'They're going to attack the houses. Almira's there.' He began to run, then stopped.

From a launch-point somewhere deep inside the village a tiny, wire-guided missile was climbing skywards. It swept across the plateau, gathering speed as it travelled along its line of sight and homed in on its target.

Too late the pilot saw the danger. He was completing his turn when the missile hit the tail section and blew most of it away.

Leaving a spiral of dense black smoke

behind it the helicopter began to spin.

Farrell watched the nose dip, watched the rotor beating sideways against the sun. Then, as if in slow motion, he saw the whole fuselage crumple into the ground in a shower of sparks and flying debris.

He waited for the flames, for the flash and the whoosh of igniting fuel. But the fire flickering beneath the rocket pods was not yet spreading and the remainder of the debris was smouldering too far away to be a hazard.

Ali-Khaleefa was on his feet as well. 'So Volchek still can get the flasks,' he said. 'Look.'

From the shadows of the village wall a four-wheel-drive Mitsubishi Pajero had emerged. It accelerated, heading for what remained of the helicopter.

'He tries now, I think.' Ali-Khaleefa shielded his eyes.

Farrell's reply was drowned out by the thud of a rocket firing in its launch tube. The sound was followed by a fountain of sparks erupting from the wreckage and the crack of exploding ammunition.

'If anyone's going to salvage anything they'll have to hurry,' Farrell said. 'The whole bloody thing could go at any minute.'

For a while he thought he was wrong. No sooner had the Pajero left the village than the

175

flames began to die. They sputtered before disappearing altogether. And then, without a warning of any kind, across the empty reaches of the Hajar, the sky exploded.

Emanating from sixteen small steel flasks buried in the wreckage came a flash of incandescent light brighter than the sun. And from the light burst a fireball — a gigantic, swirling sphere of flame, riding on a shock wave travelling faster than the speed of sound.

Hammering at the very air itself, the blast from the detonation was worse than the flame front. To Farrell, conscious only of a roar so deafening that he seemed to feel it and hear it with every part of his body, the heat was bad enough. It seared his face and hands, but it was the blast that picked him up like a paper doll and slammed him back against the Land Rover.

Incapable of deciding whether it was over or not, he slumped, allowing himself to slide down the Land Rover's door until he could slide no further. Not until he was sure it was safe to do so did he open his eyes, and then only slowly, frightened of what he might see.

Except for a saucer-shaped depression nearly a hundred yards across, there was nothing to see. Scoured clean by the detonation, the plateau was unchanged.

There was no smoke, no fire, no burning debris, and of the wrecked helicopter and the bodies of its crew, not a trace remained. Even the dust had gone, driven away to hang in a motionless halo around a mountain village that had just borne witness to the violence of the world's newest high-explosive.

In shock and with his eyes full of grit, Farrell tried not to think about Almira while he looked for Ali-Khaleefa. The Omani was nearby, sitting on the ground nursing his leg. Rocking backward and forward with the pain, he endeavoured to speak when Farrell crawled over to see how serious it was. 'Is it broken?' Farrell knew it was a stupid question.

'I try to run, but after I am thrown in the air, my leg is snapped.'

'I'll get help. Don't move.'

'Wait.' Ali-Khaleefa seized Farrell's arm. 'We have visitors.'

The Pajero was approaching. Unharmed, it was skirting the depression, heading directly for them.

Farrell stood up to meet it, expecting to see Volchek. But it was Hasan Rajavi who was driving, and beside him, in place of Volchek, sat the man who had held the knife to Almira's throat.

'Do not make them kill you.' Ali-Khaleefa

struggled to his knees. 'Allow them to say what it is they want from you.'

There was no indication that Rajavi wanted anything. Leaving the Pajero's engine running he drew up alongside and spoke through his open window. 'You enjoy the bang, Englishman?' he asked.

'Where's Almira?' The knot in Farrell's stomach tightened. 'Where is she?'

'Of what value could the girl be to us now the red mercury is lost? You lead the helicopter here yet you expect we will keep our part of the bargain? When the ISS come for you, tell the man Travers this is for him.' Rajavi wound up his window, pausing just long enough to spit in Farrell's face.

Buried in the sand somewhere at Farrell's feet lay the rifle he'd dropped. And somewhere in the Land Rover was the other one. He didn't search for them. Nor did he watch Rajavi drive away. Instead, once he had made Ali-Khaleefa as comfortable as he could, he set off for the ruins of a village with no name on what he knew would be the longest walk he would ever have to make.

7

Many of the Bedu were nervous, backing away from Farrell as though they believed he had caused the explosion. He approached the group of men directly, too numb to observe the usual protocol, confronting three tribesmen who began to raise their rifles. 'I'm looking for someone,' he said. 'Do you understand English?'

His question was met with silence.

'A girl.' Farrell cupped his hands over his chest to simulate breasts. 'An Omani girl.'

A young man said something and pointed to a low building about eighty yards away where several goats were tethered alongside the rubble of a collapsed wall. The building was the source of the wispy smoke — smoke that was drifting upward to mingle now with the hanging halo of dust.

Farrell began walking again, keeping his mind blank, refusing to contemplate what he might find when he got there. When he reached the doorway he hesitated, uncertain of how a stranger might be received if the building was occupied.

It was occupied — by a dozen or more

veiled women who retreated to line up against the far wall of the room. All he could see of them were their eyes staring at him in distrust through the slits in their indigo-dyed *burqas*.

'It's OK.' Farrell reached into his pocket for one of the polaroid photos. But before he could display Almira's picture, a woman adorned in a heavy silver necklace moved forward. She bowed and made him put the photo away.

'What?' He wasn't sure what she meant. Drenched in sweat, straining to read the expression in her eyes, he waited for clarification. 'Please,' he said. 'I have to know what happened to her.'

Pulling him by his sleeve the woman led him from the room, taking him along a corridor deep in charcoal and dried goat dung. At a door at the end she bowed her head again and left him.

Although a heavy wooden beam across the doorway told Farrell he was in the right place, if he could have avoided opening the door he would have done so. His nerve gone, he fumbled as he tried to remove the beam from two holes in the stonework.

In the end it fell out, lodging itself against the partly opened door. And through the gap he saw what he had feared most.

The prison was tiny, illuminated by a high

rectangular window through which the sun was shining. A discarded missile launcher lay on the dirt floor in one corner of the room. In another corner, huddled in the only patch of shade, was the broken, shapeless figure of Almira.

Wrenching the door open he stepped inside, knowing she was dead, freezing when he heard her call his name and saw her rise unsteadily to her feet.

Before she could fall, Farrell had her in his arms.

She clung to him, trying to keep her face hidden while tears began streaming down her face.

Farrell could taste her tears. He let them trickle into his mouth and inside his shirt, holding her until he was controlled enough to prise her arms away from him so he could look at her.

She raised her head, attempting to smile but failing because of a series of deep cuts across her mouth. Both her lips were bruised and the cuts were bleeding.

He wiped the blood away with his finger. 'Rajavi?'

'No. The other man. I heard a helicopter, then there were gunshots and a terrible explosion. I thought the whole village had been blown up. Afterwards the man came and said they'd tried to disable the helicopter, but that everything had gone wrong.'

'Why did he smack you in the face?'

'He didn't. He tried to force his gun into my mouth. To kill me, I suppose.'

'Why didn't he?'

'Rajavi came back in time. They had a big argument about what to do because something called the RM was gone. I didn't know what they meant.'

'Red mercury,' Farrell said. 'That's what was in the flasks. It's a new kind of super high-explosive. Volchek was going to exchange you for it.'

'Volchek wasn't here. Just Rajavi and that other man.' She wiped her face. 'I didn't ever expect to see you again.'

'You don't know the half of it,' Farrell said. 'This is the second time in two days I've expected to find you dead.'

'Oh.' She put her arms round him again. 'Perhaps I am. Perhaps this is all a dream.'

'I don't think so.' Farrell didn't want to tell her how close to a nightmare it had been, and how far it was from being over. They had two hours, he thought, maybe less if the helicopter's radio silence had already alerted the Muscat airbase.

'Are you OK apart from your mouth?' he asked.

'Sort of. You have to tell me what's going on though. How did you get here?'

'We can't talk now. Ali-Khaleefa's lying out in the sun with a broken leg. As soon as I've got something fixed up for him we have to lose ourselves in case Travers sends a back-up.'

'Ali-Khaleefa?' Her eyes widened. 'Why did he come?'

'Long story.' Farrell looked at her. 'Rajavi didn't tell you about Tony Nelson, did he?'

'Tell me what?'

'Nelson's dead. Someone cut his throat.'

'No. Oh no.' She went white, suddenly letting go of him and turning her back.

'There isn't time for any of this,' Farrell said gently. 'I need to know if you can get the Bedu to help us.'

When she was slow to answer he twisted her round to face him. 'Listen to me,' he said. 'The explosion you heard was sixteen flasks of red mercury vaporizing a whole helicopter and its crew. If the ISS think we had something to do with it, or if Travers believes I've still got the flasks, we're going to be hunted down like rats. The longer we stay here the easier we'll be to find.'

Still she remained silent.

'You can speak to the Bedu,' Farrell said, 'I can't. So you have to get us out of this, and

183

you have to do it right now. Do you understand?'

'Yes.' Some of her colour returned.

'So what do we do?'

'If we give the Bedu something they'll help us. They might do it anyway.'

'OK.' Farrell set off back along the corridor towing her behind him.

On this occasion, either because the women had seen him before, or because Almira was with him, they appeared less timid. Avoiding eye contact they carried on skinning and gutting two goat carcasses which were laid out on a long stone table by the fire.

Almira searched out the woman with the silver necklace, speaking to her quietly while Farrell waited by the door. The relief was still with him, but with Ali-Khaleefa injured and with no transport of any kind, his confidence was seeping away again.

The Bedu woman brushed past him, head lowered as she hurried away.

'All done,' Almira said. 'As long as her husband agrees. Give me your watch.'

'Why?' He handed it to her.

'I've said my father is a very rich man who'll pay ten thousand American dollars if the Bedu can get Ali-Khaleefa to the Muscat hospital in two days. All I need to do is give them a letter.'

'What's the watch for?'

'That's for us — unless you brought money.' She glanced at him. 'Did you?'

'No. Tell them they can have what's left of the Land Rover. There are a couple of brand new Weatherby rifles lying around out there too if they can find them. Will that be enough?'

She nodded. 'The ISS won't send another helicopter, will they?'

'Probably. This isn't about Intech selling explosives to Iran anymore. We've got ourselves mixed up in some kind of international race to develop new weapon systems. Travers is just as likely to send in half an airborne division. He's after anyone who's ever heard of red mercury.'

'The woman says we should stay here until it's dark. It'll be safer for us to travel at night.'

'What about Ali-Khaleefa?'

'The men have gone to fetch him. He can pretend he's one of them if the ISS decide to search the village.'

'And where exactly are you and I travelling to?' Farrell asked.

She smiled, wincing from the cuts across her lips. 'I can get us to the coast. Remember me telling you there are things I'm good at?'

'Like walking around mountains in the dark?'

'Yes. When we reach the Gulf we'll contact my father to say we're all right, and then you can get us a boat.'

'To where? The Greek islands are a hell of a long way from the Gulf of Oman.'

'I don't mind where.' She stood on tiptoe to kiss him. 'We've been a bit busy to say hello, haven't we?'

Farrell didn't answer. He was watching a group of approaching Bedu tribesmen who had turned the corner by the wall. Four of them were carrying Ali-Khaleefa on a stretcher constructed from a woven *ghadaf* mat.

Almira went to meet them, embracing the injured Dhofari who, although embarrassed by the attention, was unable to disguise his relief at seeing her.

The Bedu woman with the necklace had returned as well. She stopped to talk with Almira again, leaving the men to carry Ali-Khaleefa into the room.

In the doorway the Omani made them put the stretcher down so he could reach out to grip Farrell's arm. 'You must not remain in the mountains,' he said.

'It's OK,' Farrell said. 'Don't worry about us. The Bedu are going to take you to hospital, and Almira's fixed it so we can stay here until it's dark.'

'I understand this. But what will you do

186

then?' Ali-Khaleefa tightened his grip. 'There will still be much danger for you and Miss Almira, I think.'

'No one will know where we are. We're going to head for the coast.'

'Ah. I see. Because you are skilled in the ways of the sea you will take Miss Almira away from Oman to a place where all this madness can be forgotten.'

'I'll look after her,' Farrell said. 'You have to tell her father for me. It's important.'

'Of course.' Ali-Khaleefa paused. 'You have my word.'

Almira came to interrupt. 'We need to go to the *falaj*,' she said, 'so we can find it in a hurry. If a helicopter comes and it's flying fast, the Bedu think we'll only have a few minutes' warning.'

'You will be careful,' Ali-Khaleefa said. 'You understand about the water?'

'Yes.' She bent down to kiss him on his cheek. 'The women say they have a herb to take away the pain. Promise me you won't spit it out.'

'Ah. So I have also to give you my word. Already it seems life is hard for a man who has only one good leg.' The Omani managed a smile before he released Farrell's arm and allowed the stretcher bearers to carry him away.

'Do we have to hide in a damn well or something?' Farrell asked.

'An underground tunnel. The woman told me where it is. We ought to go and look.'

The tunnel was not a tunnel. It was a hole in the ground surrounded by camel-thorn bushes on the eastern boundary of the village. Farrell knelt down to peer inside, but the sun was already low and the hole was inclined away from the light, making it difficult for him to see anything. The smell, though, was overpowering — the stench from the decaying bodies of animals that had either fallen to the bottom in their hunt for moisture, or those that had succumbed to the poisoned water before they had managed to clamber out again. It was not a hiding place Farrell would have chosen, and although he guessed the smell alone would be enough to put off any searchers, he wondered if Almira knew what she was letting herself in for.

But, as he had so often done before, forty minutes later when the faint chop of another rotor echoed up out of the ravines, he found he had misjudged her.

She ran ahead of him, pushing through the thorns at the entrance and sliding feet-first into the hole, dislodging clumps of soil and rubble in her haste.

'Easy,' Farrell warned. 'Not too far. What

about *jebel* hornets? You said they like nesting in these things.'

'We'd have heard them if there were any. It's what you can't hear you have to worry about — vipers and centipedes mostly.' She stopped sliding and turned on to her stomach.

In the dark Farrell couldn't see her properly, but he suspected she was mocking him. 'Have you been inside a *falaj* before?' he asked.

'Not like this. Usually they're really sweet and clean. Some of them go a hundred and fifty feet down in the ground. There's one under the desert that's supposed to be fifty miles long, but I don't know where it is.'

'Good,' Farrell said.

'There's a ledge here.' She suddenly disappeared. 'Feel with your feet and then move to your right.'

Unlike the soft, damp walls of the entrance, the ledge was formed from a shelf of bare rock just wide enough to allow them to sit side by side. By now, partly because of the disgusting smell, but mainly because of a lack of light which made it impossible to see what might be crawling over their legs, Farrell was having trouble with his imagination.

The chopping noise was louder, funnelling down from the surface into the tiny chamber

189

in which they were crouched. He could picture the helicopter flying low over the depression in the plateau, its crew searching for wreckage they would never find.

'How long do you think they'll stay?' Almira asked.

'Until they're convinced we're not in the village. It might depend on what the Bedu tell them if they're suspicious enough to land.'

'The Bedu won't give us away — not with Ali-Khaleefa there.'

'Yeah.' Farrell took her hand. 'Are you sure we can make it down to the wadi in the dark?'

'There's a moon. We can either follow the ravine, or take a short-cut past the waterfall. I don't know which is best.'

'You're supposed to be good at this,' Farrell said. 'You decide.'

'All right.' She shivered. 'Waiting here's worse than being shut up by myself in that little room.'

'Shush for a minute.' Farrell was listening to the helicopter. The beating noise was softer and a good deal closer than it had been a second ago.

'Put your arms round me,' she said. 'Please.'

Farrell held her, feeling her shivers turn to trembling.

'Hey.' He pulled her hair away from her

face. 'We're going to be OK. All we have to do is wait until they've gone away.'

'It's not that.' She hesitated. 'It's Tony Nelson. I can't stop thinking about him. Everything's gone so terribly wrong. If I'd never met you none of this would've happened, would it?'

'Sure it would. I'd have still gone to pick up the emeralds, and I'd still have taken the courier on board the *Stingray*. Without you I'd have drowned. You know that.'

She said nothing, keeping her head buried against his shoulder while Farrell tried not to wonder how long they might have to stay here, and listened for voices above the noise of the now stationary helicopter.

There were no voices, just the whine of a gas turbine and the rhythmic swish of an idling rotor. But whoever was looking for them was nearby, Farrell could tell. He could feel the presence of men searching through the camel-thorn for some sign of the Englishman and the Omani girl they had been sent to capture. He pushed the thought aside, telling himself that no matter how unpleasant this stinking, snake-infested hole happened to be, for the minute it was their only guarantee of safety.

He was glad Almira had given his watch away. Last night on the drive to the wadi,

Farrell had counted the hours. Now, in circumstances that could hardly be more different, a watch would again have been his enemy — a means to show how slowly time could pass when he was willing it to go quickly.

He had no idea how long it was before the village became quiet again. All he knew was that the helicopter had gone, the noise from it rising and falling in intensity as it flew back eastwards over the foothills in the direction from which it had first come.

In her rush to reach the surface, Almira began to scramble over him.

'Hang on.' Farrell blocked the way. 'They could have left someone behind.'

'I don't care. I can't stay in here any more.'

He made her wait, crawling up the slope on his stomach with her holding on to both his ankles.

Outside it was dusk. To the west over the ragged tops of the Hajar range where the sky was a deep orange colour, an aircraft vapour trail hung like a silver thread from one peak to another. Closer to the village there was dust in the air again, this time not from the explosion but left behind by the helicopter's down-draught.

After Farrell had wormed his way further into the thorn bushes and helped Almira from

192

the hole, she lay beside him gulping in fresh air.

'How do we know if the ISS left someone?' she asked.

'We don't.' He stood up and pulled her to her feet. 'Are you game to find out?'

She nodded. 'This is crazy. Things like this don't happen to people.'

'Try telling that to Tony Nelson.' He began walking, moving cautiously until they reached the village centre and the remains of the wall.

Ahead of them, apart from lights flickering in the windows of the building, everything was as it had been. The voices he could hear were the voices of the Bedu; the goats and camels were standing quietly, and, if Travers had laid a trap, Farrell was unable to detect it.

Keeping Almira behind him, he approached the building, wishing he could believe the Bedu would try to warn them of any danger. But there was no warning and perhaps, Farrell decided, no danger either.

'What do you think?' Almira whispered.

'I think it's OK. Stay here for a second.' He stepped into the doorway.

Inside the room the atmosphere was thick with the smoke from oil lamps, and filled with the smell of cooking. Men were either sprawled on the floor or squatting on mats,

193

talking, eating and drinking. They glanced up, but there was none of the wariness Farrell had encountered earlier, and even an odd nod of recognition here and there. Of the women there was no sign.

A tall weatherbeaten Bedu came to greet his visitor. Over his robe he wore a coffee-coloured *bisht* cloak open at the waist to reveal an ornate *khanjar* in a decorated silver sheath. '*Tafaddal*,' he said. '*Tafaddal, tafaddal.*'

Because Farrell was familiar with the expression, understanding that its repetition was a form of politeness, he was careful to shake hands and introduce himself before drawing Almira from the shadows.

She smiled and began speaking easily to the Bedu in Arabic. The conversation continued for nearly a minute, ending in more smiles.

'No ISS,' Farrell said.

'No. It was the Air Force. Apparently once they found the rocket launcher they hardly bothered to look for us.'

'Why the hell not?'

'Because we're dead. You see, after you and I were taken on board the first helicopter, two strangers who were here fired a missile at it. The Air Force commander was told we were killed along with the crew in what the Bedu

194

said was an explosion that was so large they thought a piece of the sun had fallen to earth. They say if they pretend to be simple nomads people always believe them.'

Farrell was impressed. He was relieved as well, wondering if their luck had begun to change.

'Try to look pleased.' Almira escorted him into the room. 'We're invited to dinner, and I have to thank you for the watch and the rifles. Our host says they're very fine rifles and that Ali-Khaleefa has promised him more ammunition for them.'

'Where is Ali-Khaleefa?'

'Over there. You go and talk to him while I write the note to my father.'

The Omani was sitting on the floor, clearly no longer in pain, his leg freshly splinted and propped up in front of him on a pile of bloodstained goat skins. 'Soon you will be on your way,' he said. 'But there is less need for you to hurry now, I think. Once the Air Force commander makes his report the ISS will look not for you but for Rajavi and his bastard friend.'

'As long as Travers buys the story,' Farrell said.

'I shall hope.' Ali-Khaleefa lowered his face. 'There is something I wish to ask you. One day when all this is forgotten, you will

195

write to me perhaps?'

'Count on it,' Farrell said.

'Then I shall say goodbye to you now. May Allah be with you.'

With some reluctance Farrell left him and went to join Almira who was kneeling on a mat at the stone table. Where the carcasses had been this afternoon a variety of food was spread out, including the stewed heads of the two goats.

After declining the offer of one and hearing the popping noise as the man next to him skilfully twisted the jaw away from the skull, Farrell decided to stick with a front leg and a large bowl of what he thought was camel's milk. He drank the sweet milk first, finding it quenched his thirst, but at the same time took the edge off his appetite.

Almira saw him put down the leg. 'Aren't you hungry?' she said.

'I'd rather get going. Have you done the letter?'

'Yes. I'll just go and see Ali-Khaleefa, then we'll leave.'

While she was gone Farrell thanked his host, expressing his gratitude for the hospitality by another exchange of handshakes. The tribesman remained courteous, but ill at ease in the presence of a westerner and evidently relieved that his guests were about to depart.

When Almira came back she handed the man her note, receiving in return a small carved sandalwood box.

Farrell waited until they were alone outside before he asked her what was in it.

'What I asked for. Morphine, a snake-bite kit and antibiotics.' She smiled briefly. 'Don't look so surprised. The Bedu are very sophisticated people.'

Farrell wasn't surprised. But as they walked from the village to stand together on the arid, moonlit plateau, he couldn't help wondering if the contents of the box meant their descent to sea level would be more interesting than he had first imagined.

★ ★ ★

In the light of early morning the waterfall was a cascade of white foam and glistening raindrops. Above it, set against the red-veined cliff over which the water ran, a rainbow hung in the mist, reaching from one side to the other of a narrow rock-pool.

'Is the water OK to drink?' Farrell asked.

'Yes.' Almira kicked off her shoes. 'We can swim as well.'

He was reluctant to stay out in the open for too long, but the idea was irresistible. They were both filthy, streaked in sweat from a night of continuous exertion, and provided there was some cover nearby where they could wait out the hours of daylight, Farrell thought the risk was minimal.

He undressed, stood for a second and then launched himself out over the pool in a shallow dive. The water was like ice, so cold it took his breath away. But the feeling was wonderful, a sense of freedom from having escaped the heat and the dust at last.

When he turned to see if Almira was going to follow him she was already poised to dive. She'd put on his dirty shirt, but otherwise was naked, her figure outlined against the sky as though she was a sprite in a painting or in a dream.

He watched her body arch out over the pool and slide into the water leaving barely a ripple on the surface.

She bobbed up beside him gasping.

Gently cleaning the dirt from her lips, Farrell checked the cuts. They had healed over, but the swelling and the bruising was worse.

'Stop it.' She pushed his hand away. 'You don't look any better than I do. What are those marks on your ribs?'

'I jumped out of your car with a bunch of steel flasks wrapped round me.'

'What happened to my car?'

'Nothing. Salim was driving.'

Her expression changed. 'I've got some catching up to do, haven't I? I didn't realize my brother was involved in any of this. How much did you tell him? How much does he know about the red mercury?'

'A fair bit. You and I need to have a talk about Salim.'

'I don't want to.' She began to swim away, kicking out when Farrell grabbed her.

'It's important,' he said.

'Let me go. You're going to tear your shirt if you don't.'

He started undoing the buttons, misunderstanding why she was wearing it until she began fighting him. Releasing her at once, he looked away, remaining in the pool until he was sure she was out of the water and had slipped on her blouse to cover her arm. The incident had spoiled the atmosphere and brought back the reality of their situation to Farrell.

At the edge of the pool he put on his clothes, wondering if it would be possible to find enough shade behind one of the larger rocks, or whether they should look for somewhere more secure.

'There aren't any caves around, are there?' he asked.

'We can't use caves.'

'Don't tell me — snakes and scorpions, right?' Farrell's overnight course on mountain travel had increased his respect for Omani wild life.

She shook her head. '*Muesebeckis* — giant ticks that live in the goat dung. There are bat ticks sometimes too. If you get bitten by one of those you break out all over in poisonous ulcers.'

'Great,' Farrell said. 'Is there anything up here that doesn't bite or sting?'

She smiled. 'You haven't seen a camel spider yet — big furry ones over four inches long. They have a beak and inject you with a fluid so they can eat you while you're asleep.'

'I'm not going to sleep.' He swatted at a mosquito. 'What about staying right here?'

'Suppose Travers doesn't believe we're dead? If he decides to keep looking for us, this is exactly the kind of place he'd expect us to be, isn't it?'

'Probably. Where else is there?'

'I'll show you.' She slipped her shoes back on. 'It'll only be scrub and stuff, though.'

The scrub consisted of sunbaked thorn-apples and a few gnarled acacia and *mughir* trees growing on one of the steppes about a mile away from the waterfall. But there was shade from a rock outcrop and shelter from a wind already hot enough to sting Farrell's face. Yesterday the blast from the explosion had burned his cheeks and forehead, and now he'd washed off the protective film of dust, his skin was tender and inflamed.

'Here.' Almira sat down in a sand-filled hollow and made herself comfortable. 'What did you mean about my brother?'

'I thought you didn't want to talk about him?'

'I do now. Tell me.'

'OK.' Farrell pulled the three crumpled photographs from his pocket.

'What are those?'

'Volchek left them at my apartment.' He gave her the worst one first and saw her cheeks flush. 'Is that the guy who tried to ram the pistol in your mouth?'

She nodded.

'These aren't so embarrassing.' He handed over the other two. 'Someone took them when we were up at Khabura.'

'I don't understand what they have to do with my brother.'

'Who told Travers I had the flasks and gave him the location of the village? I don't think it was your father or your aunt, do you?'

'That doesn't mean it was Salim.'

'Look at the photos again — at the cars behind the jetty in the background. There's a red one — maybe your brother made a mistake when he was taking snapshots of us.'

She studied the photographs again. 'Why would Salim have followed us to Khabura? Anyway I can't tell if it's a Porsche. You can't either.'

'Yeah, I know.'

She gave the photos back to him, then produced the little wooden box and took out a cigarette and a single match. Farrell saw that her hands were shaking. 'Some snake-bite kit,' he said.

'I wasn't telling lies. The other things are in here too.' She held up the match. 'Are you going to light my cigarette for me?'

He grinned. 'Still trying?'

'Be nice to me.' She helped him shield the match from the breeze. 'Ever since I was sixteen I've known how much my brother hates me, but I didn't think he wanted me dead. That's what might have happened, isn't it?'

'It's what Salim could have figured would happen if the ISS took the flasks from me before I reached the village. I'd have had nothing to exchange for you. You're only alive because once the red mercury blew up, Volchek and Rajavi couldn't use you any-more.'

She thought for a moment. 'I suppose my brother could've seen it as a way to get rid of me. It's not like him though — you know, thinking things through. Usually he's too busy to bother with anything much except sex and cocaine.'

'Like his sister,' Farrell said.

'I don't take drugs.' Her eyes flashed. 'You know I don't.'

'That's not what I said.'

She relaxed slightly. 'I don't understand what you mean.'

'It's going to be a hell of a long day, and your hair's still wet.'

'Wet hair?'

'I like the smell. And you know very well what I mean.'

'I'm too tired. So are you. We need to rest.'

Farrell watched her stub out her half-finished cigarette and replace it alongside a syringe and some capsules in the box. If her expression hadn't given her away, he would still have backed his intuition. She was being too deliberate, pretending she was indifferent to his proposition.

To show her subterfuge had failed he pushed her down into the soft, warm sand and kissed her very gently on the mouth.

'You don't have to be careful,' she whispered. 'The cuts don't hurt. You took all the hurt away a long time ago.'

★ ★ ★

The first night of their journey across the foothills and ravines had been hard going. Their second night of travel had been equally exhausting. Even in daylight Almira's short-cut would have been difficult, requiring them to negotiate a near-vertical channel in a rock face above the wadi — a descent that had not only sapped their strength, but brought them out at the bottom much later than Farrell had wanted.

But the worst was over, and now, in the first light of dawn, he could see that the bed of the great wadi stretching out before them was encouragingly flat.

Leaning against the trunk of a juniper tree Almira inspected her blistered feet. 'We should've kept one of the rifles,' she said. 'If I don't get some food soon I'll run out of energy altogether.'

Farrell doubted it. For much of the night she had led the way, helping him in the rock-channel where she'd been as sure-footed as a cat, not once complaining when he had to stop to grope for a hand-hold or search for a crevice that she would have found in half the time. He could tell how tired she was, but apart from her swollen mouth and blistered feet, she was still in good shape, if anything,

204

more determined and more stubborn than when they'd started.

'No waterfalls?' he said.

'Not down here. There's a waterhole somewhere, though. Just a tiny one. If we don't want to be tramping across the wadi in broad daylight we ought to look for it right away.'

Farrell wasn't sure precautions were necessary anymore. For the last thirty-six hours there had been nothing to indicate that anyone was searching for them — no spotter planes and no helicopters — the sky as empty and silent as the mountains themselves had been.

Above the juniper tree, on an early-morning hunt for breakfast, a dragonfly was hovering. It darted forward, missing whatever it had seen before flying off to somewhere else. Farrell watched it go, straining his eyes until it became a dot against the horizon.

'Is something the matter?' Almira asked.

'I don't know if anyone's after us or not. Maybe I got it wrong.'

'This time tomorrow we won't have to worry one way or the other. Instead of being surrounded by cliffs and rocks we'll be way out to sea.'

Farrell tried to imagine the sea.

'Where are you going to take us? So we can

live happily ever after, I mean?' She threw a handful of dried juniper berries at him.

'Depends how big a boat I can borrow.'

'You don't have to borrow anything. My father will buy us whatever we need — he was planning to buy a new boat for Tony anyway.'

Farrell shook his head, 'We can't risk contacting your father.'

'Because you don't trust my brother?'

'Because we're not taking any chances. If you want a happy ending, let me handle the boat.' He smiled at her. 'You might have to wait a bit for the Greek islands.'

'So much for promises.' She wrinkled her nose.

Daylight was creeping up the tree trunk. In another minute it would reach her waist, and a minute after that she'd be standing in sunshine. Farrell watched her shadow begin to form, again remembering the morning he'd first met her. A long time ago, he thought, before his fascination with her had turned his life upside down and before he'd come to understand why he never tired of looking at her.

'We'd better find that water,' he said.

She nodded, 'Find somewhere to sleep too.'

Leaving the shelter of the foothills they followed camel tracks through straggly

206

clumps of *gai'sh* bushes before emerging out on to the wadi proper where already the distant valleys were bathed in sunlight. Here the rocks were the colour of rich cream and the surface softer and more difficult to walk on.

Soon, when they began sinking ankle deep with each step, Farrell called a halt, intending to look for a route that would take them to firmer ground. What he saw instead were dust trails.

There were four vehicles, less than half a mile away, travelling on converging paths, dust billowing from their tyres as they came racing across the sand.

Caught in the open with nowhere to go and with his heart beating so hard he could feel it, for Farrell there was an awful inevitability to the end. He stood quite still, holding Almira's hand, knowing that his promises had indeed been for nothing and that the future in which he had once believed was over even before it had begun.

8

By cheating and taking very small steps Farrell could pretend the cell was nine and a half steps square. The degree to which he could cheat was limited by the channel running diagonally across the floor, an open concrete trench that served as a toilet, not only for him, but also for other occupants of the building.

This morning, because of the flood of urine and faeces, he stopped his pacing early and endeavoured to work out what time it was while he listened to the sound of men coughing and talking as the cell-block slowly came to life.

On the previous three days, breakfast had arrived before any sunlight had begun to filter through the bars on the window. Today was an exception.

Instead of a tray being poked through the slot in the wall there was the noise of a key scraping in the lock and the door opened.

Travers was outside, holding a handkerchief over his nose to combat the stench. 'Christ,' he said. 'I figured it would be bad, but not as bad as this.'

'What do you want?' Farrell remained where he was.

'Time for you and I to have a talk. There's a shower at the end of the corridor. You'll find a razor and some clean clothes on the washstand. Tell the guard when you're done.'

'Then what?' Farrell asked.

'Then we talk.' Travers turned to leave. 'Try to get your head sorted out before that, will you?'

Farrell's attempt to clear his head was less than successful. By the time he'd finished in the shower he'd decided that there was nothing much to sort out. In the absence of any clues as to what Travers was doing here he was no further ahead than he'd been since his capture, and not inclined to believe the American was the bearer of good news.

He shaved and dressed automatically, following the guard to a small air-conditioned room where Travers was waiting with his brief-case open on the table in front of him.

'Tough break.' Travers looked at him.

'For who?' Farrell sat down on the only other chair in the room.

'Who do you think?'

'Is Almira OK?'

'She's lucky she didn't end up the same way Nelson did.'

'No bloody thanks to you and the ISS,'

Farrell said. 'You damn near killed her. It wasn't luck. It was because Rajavi decided she didn't matter anymore.'

'So I understand. She told me about it.'

'Who told you I was taking the flasks to the village?'

'You're not here to ask questions. And I'm sure as hell not here to answer them.'

'Just one,' Farrell said. 'How did you know we weren't killed in the explosion?'

Travers smiled. 'I didn't. The ISS weren't looking for you the other morning. After the Air Force got a radio call to say their chopper was going down we guessed there'd been a foul up. I figured we might still have been able to grab Volchek and Rajavi on their way down from the village. We missed them, but ran into you and your girlfriend. Like I said, tough break.'

'Volchek wasn't at the village,' Farrell said. 'Only Rajavi and another guy.'

'Miss Muammar's explained all that. She's told us the whole thing from start to finish.'

'So you haven't found Rajavi and the guy he had with him. And you haven't found Volchek either.'

Travers shook his head. 'They'll be out of the country by now. But we'll run them down sooner or later — maybe when Intech try to resupply Iran.' He paused to cough. 'I have some questions for you.'

'I thought you'd got it all from Almira.'

'Are you acquainted with an Omani called Ali-Khaleefa?'

Farrell pretended to think. 'Yeah. I remember — the old guy at Khabura who rented the fishing boat to Nelson. What's he done?'

'You're wasting your breath,' Travers said. 'You're not as good at this as you think you are.'

'What else do you want to ask me?'

'Forget it. I can't be bothered. You're a pain in the arse, Farrell. Here, sign this.' Travers slid a sheet of paper across the table.

'What is it?'

'A release form. You don't want to stay locked up in this place forever, do you?'

Farrell felt his stomach muscles tighten. 'Why are you letting me go?'

'Why not? You're a nuisance. The Omanis don't want any trouble from the British Consulate, and you're no good to me — not now.'

Farrell signed the form unread, worried that things were going wrong somewhere.

'OK.' Travers retrieved the piece of paper and slipped it into his case. 'There'll be a car coming to collect you around ten.'

'Don't bother. I'll have Almira pick me up.'

'I don't think so.' Travers removed his glasses.

'Why?'

'She's been detained. The Omani Internal Security Service have got her.'

'What the hell for?'

'For her participation in a fatal attack on a Royal Oman Air Force helicopter. Undermining state security by consorting with foreign terrorists, and the unlawful importation of uncut emeralds believed to be stolen from the Government of Iran. Do you want me to go on?'

The distortion of the truth was worse than Farrell could have possibly imagined. He was bewildered, not yet able to absorb what he'd heard.

'Remember when I said you were out of your depth?' Travers' expression was impassive. 'You should've started swimming when I gave you the chance. The Omani authorities need someone to blame. Look at it from their point of view: Volchek or Rajavi would have been fine, but they haven't got Volchek or Rajavi.'

'For Christ's sake, if they wanted someone to take the can, why didn't you give them me?'

'I've told you; because you're a British national. You can make waves. She can't.'

Travers replaced his glasses before sliding another piece of paper across the table. 'I brought this for you. It confirms your No Objection Certificate has been cancelled. Which means you're going to be on a free plane ride to London before midday. Nice and quick. Nice and clean.'

Farrell controlled his voice. 'What about Almira?'

'What about her? She's not my problem. And she's not yours either; not anymore. Forget about her. Think how much you'll enjoy being back in the UK instead. Last I heard it was raining there and London was having a cold snap.'

'I have to see her,' Farrell said.

'Not a chance.' Travers stood up. 'You've seen enough of Miss Muammar. Shame about that arm of hers. Still, when you have someone who looks like her to play with in bed I suppose you don't notice her arm much.'

'Fix it so I can talk to her on the phone.' Farrell was desperate now.

'I don't owe you any favours.' Travers shut his brief-case. 'I'll do this for you, though; if I run into her again, I'll tell her you said goodbye.'

* * *

Seen through the window of the aircraft the coastline of Oman was a long curve of glittering beaches. Floating white between the Portuguese forts guarding the entrance to Muscat harbour, the Royal Palace was shimmering in the heat-haze, still beautiful and still faintly unreal — all that remained of another time, and for Farrell, a reminder of how and where everything had started.

In his pocket was all he had to show for what might have been; the shrapnel from his shoulder, three soiled photographs of Almira and the two silver pendants she had left behind in his apartment — the ear-rings he had carried with him to the mountains, but forgotten to give her. He held them up to the sunlight, understanding now, that just as the sparkle had always been an illusion, so the idea of a fresh start had been nothing more than a stupid dream.

9

The letter was limp, damp from the rain and from lying too long on Farrell's doormat. Because it was an airmail letter, and because the postmark was still recognizable, he took the envelope into the lounge and placed it unopened on the mantelpiece, wondering if he could bring himself to live for another month on someone else's money. Or would today be the day on which everything changed? Farrell didn't think so. After three months, three of Muammar's cheques and the letters from Aunt Latifa that he'd thrown away because he couldn't bear to keep them, he wasn't expecting anything to change.

He wasn't expecting the rain to stop either. In London at this time of year all the days were the same — predictable and depressing, a succession of grey skies, drizzle and temperatures that were already so low that his face hurt if he went out too early or came home too late.

This morning, after his walk to get a paper from the shop on the corner, it was his hands that were aching from the cold — a warning, Farrell decided. In a few days it would be

November, and this was a taste of what it was going to be like if he didn't get his act together before the onset of the really cold weather.

He went to the kitchen where he made himself two cups of black coffee and tried to forget about the envelope in the other room while he glanced through the paper.

The situations vacant section carried the usual crop of jobs. Most were unattractive or unsuitable and, as usual, the few overseas appointments were for places that offered little in the way of climate and even less in terms of finding somewhere interesting to lose himself. Not that there were ever any worthwhile jobs, Farrell thought. In twelve weeks of looking he had found only two which sounded promising and they'd both been taken before he'd even telephoned.

Carrying a cup of coffee with him he went to stand at the window. It was the only window with anything like a view — the main reason he'd rented the Kensington flat — but with the coming of the rain, the view had become increasingly dismal. Worse than either the wet or the cold was the lack of colour outside. He was aware of it now, a dullness that seemed to be sucking his life away; a sense of being trapped, of being unable to move forwards.

Twice in the last week, in an effort to blank out the weather, he had drunk himself insensible, using brandy as a substitute for sunshine. The exercise had been only temporarily successful — a short-term hit instead of the longer lasting and more effective technique of making himself recall the blue of the Gulf in early morning or how the shadows had drifted across the sunlit ravines of the Jebel Akhdar in late evening.

Today Farrell knew the letter would be an excuse to remember everything else — the whole thing — pretending that by doing so he might yet drive some of his despondency away. Remembering hadn't worked so far, but things hadn't been this bad before, nor had he been inclined before to even consider what he was considering now.

So was this to be the turning point? The day on which he'd finally recognize that only by abandoning his hopes could he start to create any sort of future for himself?

The letter would help him decide. The damn letter that could have come at any time except today when he was least prepared for it.

He retrieved the envelope from the mantelpiece, endeavouring not to predict what he would do if there was no fresh news or if the situation had taken a turn for the worse.

217

Inside the envelope was a cheque for $5,000 drawn on Muammar's New York bank and a note from Aunt Latifa to say that, although Almira had been moved to a less secure jail, the family had still not been allowed to see her. The envelope also contained two snapshots. One of them had been taken inside the courtyard at the Muscat villa. It showed Almira's two Salukis sitting in the rear seat of her brother's car with Aunt Latifa waving a disapproving finger at them through the window. The second photo was of an elegant Arab horse standing by the rails outside Muammar's stables. But it was what was scrawled in ball-point across the top of the picture that caught Farrell's attention — a verse from somewhere — YET MAN IS BORN INTO TROUBLE AS SPARKS FLY UPWARDS FROM A FIRE — a saying or quotation that he guessed could only have been sent by one person. He turned the photo over to find the signature of Ali-Khaleefa on the back of it.

The cheque and the note from Aunt Latifa had rekindled the sense of loss. But the photos made it worse. Again, by treating him as though he was part of their lives, the Muammar household were doing exactly what Farrell most wanted them not to do. Instead of blame there was unsolicited financial support. Instead of reproach there were photos of the dogs and a horse. And in place of bitterness there was Ali-Khaleefa's message to persuade Farrell that misfortune was somehow preordained.

Unconsciously, the most vivid of his memories began to return; of the villa, the beach house and the stables; of days so hot that Farrell would once have gladly exchanged them for the chill of London in late October, and of a girl with cut lips standing beside him in the deep warm sand of the wadi while she tried to smile her goodbye. It was the last time he had seen her, a frozen moment of time that haunted Farrell still.

As he had done so often before, he attempted to erase the picture, willing himself to forget so it would never reappear, so he would never again have to confront it, or remember how she had looked on that morning.

But just as the dreams came to him at night, the other memories were coming now — few enough, but still too many for him to believe that he could build a future in which she would play no part.

If thinking things through would have lifted his spirits Farrell might have been prepared to go on, but with the photos and the cheque in front of him, he knew he could not. He could no more go on like this than he could go on waiting for the right job to come along or for the sun to shine. Waiting was not an option. Nor was remembering. Instead it was time to break out of the trap — to discover what would happen if he went full circle.

From the drawer beneath his bed he recovered the three crumpled polaroid photos of Almira, placing them on the kitchen table beside the photos that had come in the mail. For a while he studied them. Then he tore them up, ripping them into smaller and smaller pieces. He was equally severe with Aunt Latifa's note and the cheque, reducing them methodically to tiny scraps of paper until all evidence of the past had been destroyed and he was in a better frame of mind.

Despite being uncertain of how long he could maintain his optimism, for the present he thought he was on top of things again — sufficiently encouraged to take the next step and phone for a taxi.

Only when he went to the bedroom to change his shirt did he catch sight of himself in the mirror. Imprinted on his shoulder was the puckered scar from the shrapnel — his own personal memento, unerasable and, if he'd needed one, enough of a reminder to make him doubt the wisdom of what he was about to do.

★ ★ ★

Catching the train had not been a good idea. A rental car would have enabled him to change his mind halfway, and by having to concentrate on driving in the wet, there would have been less opportunity for him to re-examine his motives for the trip. As it was, by the time he stepped out on to the platform at Bristol, the spontaneity of his decision had gone, and with it had gone his sense of purpose.

Farrell turned up the collar of his coat and joined the queue of people standing outside the station at the taxi rank. They were commuters, carrying umbrellas, or sheltering from the rain beneath brief-cases or sodden newspapers. Except for a little girl holding her mother's hand, no one smiled. Absorbed in themselves they were drab, featureless figures in what to Farrell seemed to be a uniformly drab and featureless afternoon.

He was annoyed with himself for making the observation. The UK was not the Middle East any more than Bristol was Muscat or Mutrah, and the quicker he understood that, the sooner he'd overcome the feeling of being somewhere he didn't belong.

It was past five o'clock before he managed to get a taxi and nearly six when he stopped the driver at the end of a narrow, unlit lane in Cleeve.

'This is fine.' Farrell gave him a handful of notes. 'Do me a favour will you? Stay here for five minutes in case I come back.'

'Number eighteen'll be way down there.' The driver pointed. 'You're going to get wet.'

'Yeah.' Farrell stepped out into the rain. 'Thanks for the ride.'

The majority of the houses in the lane were expensive period cottages, either carefully preserved or recently renovated. He walked past them, searching for a number on a gate post or a front door.

Smaller than the others and flanked by a low brick wall, the cottage he was seeking had a garden so overgrown that he had to squeeze between the car in the driveway and a hedge in order to reach the porch.

He knocked on the door twice, hearing footsteps a moment before the outside light came on and the door swung open.

'Oh God.' Mary Farrell stood framed in the light from the hallway.

'Hi.' Now he was here, he had no real idea of what to say. 'I should've phoned. If this is a bad time I can come back.'

'When you happen to be passing through next?'

'I'm not passing through,' Farrell said. 'I've been in England for a while.'

'I know. I didn't think that meant I should expect a visit.'

Farrell stopped groping for words. She was unchanged except for her hair being longer. Her face and her figure were as he remembered, her eyes still unfathomable and the set of her mouth the same as it had always been.

'Look,' he said. 'If this is awkward I can just as easily leave.'

'That's it, is it? After seven years my husband appears on my doorstep, says hello and disappears again. Don't you want to come in?'

Farrell was confused now. At the end of the lane the taxi would be waiting. All he had to do was walk away — return to London, to his empty flat, and forget he'd ever been here. He was about to check on the taxi's headlights when she spoke again.

'You don't have to go,' she said. 'Not unless you want to.'

'I could use a cup of coffee. I'm pretty wet.'

'Well, you'd better stop standing out there then, hadn't you?' She stepped aside to let him in.

Farrell wasn't just wet; he was soaked. He was also so cold that he couldn't control his shivering.

'God in Heaven.' She stared at him. 'You look dreadful.'

'Thanks.' He took off his coat and gave it to her. 'If you don't want puddles on your floor, chuck that outside.'

'I'll find you something dry to put on while you go and have a hot shower to warm up.' She hesitated. 'You don't have to rush off anywhere, do you?'

Farrell smiled. 'I'm too bloody cold to rush anywhere.'

'Your blood's thinned out. You've been away too long. When I first came back to live it took me three years to get used to the climate. Sometimes at the end of the winter I wish I never had come back.'

He avoided comment, wondering if her remark had been unintentional or whether he was supposed to have read something into it. With Mary you could never tell, he thought. Her manner too was unchanged. Already she seemed to have overcome her surprise, apparently accepting the arrival of her estranged husband as though nothing had ever gone wrong between them.

In the shower he spent nearly half an hour letting the hot water scour away a different

224

set of recollections — not those of a slender, satin-skinned girl in Oman, but of his first summer living with Mary in Kuwait and of how often Tony Nelson had told him she was unhappy. Then, because of the money and because running night freight across the Persian Gulf had been the most exciting thing Farrell had ever done, almost up until the day Mary left, he had managed to pretend his marriage was working.

He should've listened to Nelson, Farrell thought. Except for the fatal decision to dive for the red mercury, Nelson had got everything right, and if he was still alive today he'd still be offering the same damned advice — never pass up an opportunity; always remember where you are; and never go back to anywhere you've been before — catch-phrases that were as meaningless now as they had been then — except perhaps for one — the warning about never going back.

★ ★ ★

The flames were hypnotic, long ribbons of colour, drawing Farrell deeper into the fire the longer he looked at them.

'Don't.' He prevented Mary from putting on another log. 'It's fine like it is. I haven't sat in front of an open fire for years.'

She tucked her legs beneath her on the chair, making herself more comfortable while she waited.

Farrell knew she was waiting — expecting him to begin talking now that the meal was over and he'd drunk enough brandy to make it easier.

'Do you feel better?' she asked.

He nodded. 'You didn't have to wrap me up in a bathrobe and cook me dinner.'

'I know. I know why you're here too. You came to tell me about Tony, didn't you?'

'I already did in my letter.'

'Hardly.' She smiled slightly. 'Tony's parents had the body flown home. I went over to Ireland and stayed with them for a while. I found out more from them than from your letter. You never were any good at writing letters.'

Farrell's eyes were on the flames again. 'I worked with Nelson for nine years,' he said. 'And you'd known him longer that that.'

'You're making it hard for yourself.' She sipped at her drink. 'You didn't come all the way down here on a horrible day like this just to say hello. I'm not supposed to believe this is a social visit, am I?'

'Nelson should still be alive,' Farrell said quietly. 'Everything got screwed up — everything.'

226

'Why explain to me?'

'I don't know who else would want to listen.' He paused. 'Or anyone else I'd want to tell. It's not just about Tony.'

'Oh. Shall I get more brandy?'

'No. I'm OK, thanks.' Farrell dragged his mind back to Oman, to Mutrah, to the day he had berthed the *Stingray* under the gaze of a girl standing on a rock. But when he tried to remember why he had allowed her to accompany him on the pick-up, the words refused to come. He could no more describe his reasons for taking her than he could describe Almira herself. Gradually, though, as the images became clearer, they were easier to translate, and soon he was speaking more freely, staring alternately at the fire and into the unblinking eyes of his wife.

It took him over an hour to provide her with an account of the events leading up to his deportation from Oman — a long hour during which she remained sitting in the same position, neither interrupting nor showing any sign of emotion. Farrell too was careful to stay detached, keeping his voice level whenever he mentioned Almira. Only twice did he have to backtrack in order to clarify something, and only twice did he stop speaking for a moment because he was uncertain of how to go on.

Now he'd finished he refilled his glass, searching for any feeling of relief. But there was none — no sense of having accomplished what he'd set out to do. Nor was there any discernible reaction from his wife.

'Well?' he asked.

'I don't know what to say.'

'How about what a good job it is that you decided to come back to England?'

'Is that what you think?'

Farrell shrugged. 'It wouldn't be a bad guess, would it? I've just proved you were right. Here you are with a nice teaching job and a comfortable home while I've been hiding from helicopter gunships up in some stinking mountain village at the end of the world.'

'That doesn't mean I was right and you were wrong to stay in the Middle East. Trying to save that girl's life wasn't wrong.'

'I didn't save her life. She was lucky.'

'Did you sleep with her?'

He nodded.

'How old was she?'

'Twenty-four, I think. I'm not sure.'

'Were you in love with her?'

This time he didn't reply. All the questions had been in the past tense — how old was she? Were you in love with her? — confirmation of what Farrell had been trying to make himself believe, that Oman was buried along with Almira in an irrecoverable past.

'John.' Mary Farrell was endeavouring to regain his attention. 'I'm sorry. I didn't mean to pry.'

'It's OK.'

'So what are you going to do now you're back home?'

'Find a job overseas somewhere. I don't feel at home in England — not just because of the weather. I don't know what the hell it is.'

'It's you,' she said. 'You haven't changed.'

'Nor have you. You look great.' Despite being lightheaded from the brandy, Farrell sensed he had outstayed his welcome. 'Thanks for dinner, and for listening too.' He stood up.

'Where are you going?'

'There'll be a motel around. Point me at your phone so I can call a taxi.'

'Don't be silly. It's past eleven and you can hardly stand up. Anyway your clothes won't be dry yet. There's a perfectly good bed in the spare room. Stay here.'

Farrell shook his head.

'John, this house is more yours than it is mine. I bought it with the money you gave me — after you and Tony sold all those wretched machine-guns to the Arab Emirates

— remember? I won't let you go out again in the rain tonight.' She jumped up from her chair to prevent him from falling over. 'Look at you. You're not fit to go anywhere.'

'OK.' Farrell steadied himself by taking hold of the mantelpiece. 'How did you hear I was in England?'

'You don't want to know how.'

'Yes I do.'

'I wasn't going to say.' She looked away. 'It was that American — the man you mentioned — Richard Travers. He phoned me from London about a week ago to ask if I knew where you were.'

'Shit.' Farrell tightened his grip on the mantelpiece. 'What did you tell him?'

'That you were living in Oman. But he said you weren't anymore — that you were in England. He left me his phone number.'

'What did he want?'

'I don't know. Well, not really. Something about having a job for you.' She hesitated. 'You're not going to phone him, are you? I don't think that would be a terribly good idea.'

'No.' Farrell didn't think it would be either.

'I'll make us some coffee. Or will coffee stop you sleeping?'

'All I need is a bed.' Farrell held on to her arm. 'Where do I find it?'

'I'll show you. Watch where you're going and don't trip over the rug.' She led him to a small bedroom and switched on the light. 'I'll wake you before I leave in the morning.'

'OK.' He glanced at her. 'Do you know what Nelson told me once?'

'Do I have to guess?'

'He said I was the most stupid bastard he'd ever met — because I let you go.'

She smiled at him. 'You didn't let me go, John: you made me go. But that was a long time ago before we both grew up, wasn't it? Now stop thinking about all the bad times and get some sleep.'

Once she'd gone, Farrell sat down on the bed with some misgiving. If he could stop thinking altogether he thought he might stand a chance of an untroubled night. But, as he suspected, the minute his head hit the pillow, he knew the brandy wasn't going to work.

To guard against dreams, for a while he deliberately kept his mind unfocused, willing himself to remain awake. Only when a faint trace of fragrance drifted across his face did he become aware of already being in the middle of a dream he had experienced before, a semi-factual fantasy in which Almira joined him in a bedroom at her father's beach house on a sleepy afternoon. For reasons he had not yet been able to understand she seemed reluctant to make love, refusing to kiss him when he held her down until she relented in a burst of passion that always caught him by surprise.

Tonight, although the fragrance was stronger, the dream was more confused, and instead of having to wait for her response, she returned his kiss immediately. In this version there was also another difference, one that was muddling and distorting his image of her.

If Mary Farrell had known her perfume would be the same as the perfume in her husband's dream, she would certainly not have been unwise enough to call in to say goodnight on her way to bed. And perhaps if Farrell had been unaware of her presence she could have crept away undiscovered. By now though he was half awake.

'I thought I'd check to make sure you were all right,' she said.

Farrell was far from being all right. She was too close to him. Too available.

'Poor John,' she whispered. 'You're such a mess, aren't you?'

Opening his eyes was a mistake, so was his attempt to pretend this was not taking place at all. She was bending over him, a smile playing on her lips while she slipped off her housecoat. Beneath it she was naked, standing motionless as though expecting him

232

to take the initiative.

'For Christ's sake,' Farrell mumbled. 'You don't want to do this.'

'Why shouldn't I?' She prevented him from sitting up. 'Almira's gone. You can't have her anymore. You have to forget her.'

When she kissed him Farrell became wide awake. For some seconds he tried to avoid touching her, to lie still, ignoring her perfume and relying on the brandy to keep him still. But as her hands slid beneath the sheets to lie warm upon his stomach, he knew the alcohol would fail him as surely as he was being betrayed by his own weakness — by the fanciful belief that this was a way to blank out the past.

When she pulled the bed clothes away Farrell shut his eyes again. She was breathing quickly, lying beside him now while she brushed her lips across his chest. Soon her tongue was flickering over his skin like a flame from the fire and soon, after she had curled up, he felt her reach out shamelessly for what she wanted.

But with both her hands and her mouth busy she became too eager. He stopped her by pulling gently on her hair, making her uncurl so he could kiss her breasts. She too had closed her eyes, panting while she parted her thighs, offering herself to him, demanding that he touch her and explore her with his fingers.

For Farrell, adrift in a dream in which he was no longer able to distinguish Almira from Mary, all the memories were one. By prolonging the present he could recreate the past. They were the same, a blur of what he had once sought and lost fused with what he was seeking now.

She would not allow him to tease her. Quickly she guided him inside her, moving her whole body in unison with his until her urgency drove everything from Farrell's mind except the need for his own release. It began at once, before he was ready, a driving spear of pleasure to coincide with her orgasm, her trembling and her cries.

Even after it was over and he was holding her in his arms, the pleasure remained for several minutes, delaying the return of reality long enough for the brandy to again take over. He let it, welcoming the dizziness so there would be no need to wonder what the hell was happening.

For Mary Farrell the act of making love had been prompted by impulse rather than desire. She was surprised at herself, unsure now it was done why she had behaved in such a way. Not out of sympathy or sentiment, she realized, but for a less worthy reason altogether — a need to compete, to demonstrate to herself that, if she chose to, she could reclaim the man she had married. Or because of guilt? Did she owe him this? Had she simply wanted to convince him that, no matter how beautiful or how irresistible the Omani girl had been in bed, there were other women who could offer him more?

She found the notion as distasteful as it was disquieting — particularly if she compared this experience with other occasions in recent years when she had taken a lover. But there was no comparison. For longer than she could remember, nothing had approached the sensuous intensity of tonight. Which meant she had until morning, she thought. After that, if the disquiet had not gone away, she would either have to put a stop to things immediately or be very careful with herself indeed.

★　★　★

Above seventy miles an hour the rental car was unsafe. A combination of poor wheel balance and a misaligned suspension made it judder so much that Farrell was not prepared to push his luck on the motorway.

He reduced speed, cutting it back further before he reached the off-ramp when he saw the line of cars and trucks ahead of him. Three days ago his first trip by train had taken him nothing like as long as the drive had this afternoon. Then it hadn't mattered so much because there had been no warning of what he was walking in to. Today, though, because he could predict what her reaction would be, he was not expecting any surprises.

The drive from Bristol to Cleeve was more pleasant. As well as the road being dry, the sun was shining and, under more favourable circumstances, he would have enjoyed the countryside. Instead Farrell barely noticed. Anxious to get his visit over with, he began to increase his speed again, only reducing it when the judder returned. He made himself drive more slowly, following a truck all the way into Cleeve and arriving outside the cottage shortly after 4.30.

Mary's car was parked in the driveway. The bonnet was warm to touch, but he guessed she'd been home for some time — long enough to play back the message he'd left on her machine this morning.

She met him at the door.

'Hi,' Farrell said.

'You haven't just driven down from London, have you?'

'What do you expect if you don't answer my calls?'

'You know why I haven't answered them.' She hesitated. 'I'm not going to talk on the doorstep. You'd better come in.'

Farrell followed her into the kitchen and watched while she filled the coffee percolator. 'I figured maybe we didn't get things sorted out properly,' he said.

'Yes we did.' She sat down on a bar stool and crossed her legs. 'You shouldn't have come. You said you wouldn't.'

'Yeah, well.' He couldn't help noticing her clothes, a dark, knee-length skirt, black stockings and high heels — the only damn schoolteacher who could ever look like she did.

'For God's sake, stop it.' She had seen his eyes straying. 'So I went to bed with you — once in seven years. That doesn't mean anything. I felt sorry for you.'

'Do you sleep with everyone you feel sorry for?' Before he'd finished speaking, Farrell wished he'd kept his mouth shut.

'I told you Tuesday morning.' Her cheeks were flushed. 'We spent two hours talking. It was a mistake. I make mistakes. So does everyone else, but I'm not going to make another one over you. If I start thinking about us again, everything will go wrong, and I won't let that happen. I don't need you, John; I haven't done for a long time. You can't just walk back into my life and turn everything on its head. Go away to wherever you're going and leave me alone.'

'I didn't turn anything on its head — you did.'

'Well, I'm sorry. It wasn't supposed to be like that.' She fumbled with the percolator. 'You don't need me. You never did.'

'What the hell's that supposed to mean?'

'I lived with you for nearly two years. You're the same now as you were when we were together in Kuwait — still searching for some perfect, non-existent place or some crazy job you'll never find.' She paused. 'Maybe it was different then, I don't know. At least I had you to myself. But now you'll always be wondering about that girl in Oman, won't you?'

'No.' If Farrell had believed in his own lie he could have made it sound more convincing. But her expression told him there was no point in trying.

'It's funny, I almost believed I could make you forget her.' She handed him a cup of coffee. 'Was she really that pretty?'

'She got thrown out of a car when she was fifteen. Her left arm's three-quarters scar tissue. I'm not here to talk about her.'

'Why are you here then?'

'To make you understand something. You

238

see, maybe you made a mistake the other night and maybe I'm screwed up because of what happened in Oman, but no matter what you believe, one of these days I'm going to find the right place and the right crazy job.'

'Haven't I heard that before somewhere?' She managed a smile. 'So what if you do?'

'So between now and then you'd better not write me off.'

'I don't think starting over again would be a very good idea.'

Farrell finished his coffee. Learning that his drive to Bristol had been a wasted effort was only confirmation of what he had suspected. That he would fail to change her mind had been predictable, a long shot he should never have considered in the first place.

'Look, John, I'm sorry.' She got up from her stool and came to stand beside him. 'I don't know what else I can say.'

'You don't have to say anything. I'll get out of your hair.'

She waited for him to put on his coat before accompanying him to the front door.

'Take care of yourself,' he said.

She nodded. 'I hope things work out for you.'

For a second Farrell thought he might kiss her goodbye, but she had already stepped back, putting herself beyond his reach so that when he turned to leave even the lingering smell of her perfume had deserted him.

* * *

According to the newspaper the frosts of the past few days were likely to continue for some time. For early November they were not uncommon, the paper said, although the temperatures had been lower than expected.

Farrell was becoming resigned to the cold. Since his return from Bristol twelve days ago each night had been cooler than the one before, and each morning, when he came here to stand at the window of his flat, there was a little less warmth from the sun.

Worrying about how much colder it might get was as fruitless as searching for a job, he thought. The damned weather would do whatever it wanted to do, and if there were any suitable jobs he'd have found one by now.

This morning he was inclined to blame Mary for his low spirits. She had been on his mind since he'd woken up — a sign that unless he did something about it the day was not going to be a good one.

Having decided to ignore the cold he was preparing to go out when the clack of the letter box told him the mail had arrived.

Yesterday he had received a note from the

New York bank asking if he would please acknowledge the safe receipt of Muammar's October cheque. Today, as if fate was conspiring to keep the pressure on, a letter from Oman lay on the doormat.

Because this was the wrong end of the month for Aunt Latifa's communication, Farrell opened it at once. Instead of a letter the envelope contained a brief article clipped from an Arab-language newspaper. Printed in English along the bottom margin in ball-point pen were the words IT IS TO SAY CHARGES AGAINST ALMIRA ARE STILL NOT LAID.

Taking the clipping into the kitchen with him Farrell sat down at the table. Two weeks ago he would have been able to persuade himself that no news was good news. He might even have been able to believe he could carry on waiting for something positive to occur. But that was before Mary, before she'd told him what he'd already known, and before he'd realized the futility of believing in anything at all.

To make certain that he was not about to make another mistake, for nearly five minutes he sat quietly where he was. Then he started punching buttons on the phone.

He heard her number ringing and heard her say Mary Farrell when she answered.

'It's me,' he said. 'Don't hang up.'

'I wasn't going to.'

'Look,' Farrell said. 'If you still have it, I need that number for Travers — the one he gave you.'

'Oh.'

'Did you throw it away?'

'No. It's here somewhere. I scribbled it on the cover of the phone book.' She read out the number to him.

'Thanks.' Because she sounded so distant, Farrell wondered if he should expand the conversation or whether it would be better to cut his losses.

In the end, like everything else he'd wondered about in the last three months, it didn't matter. Before he could say goodbye, she said it for him.

10

For a Grosvenor Street building displaying the logo of American Travel, the foyer was something of a let-down. Apart from a receptionist's desk and a solitary pot plant, the furnishings consisted of nothing more than a nondescript plastic table.

The woman behind the desk glanced up from her magazine. She was about thirty, quite attractive and had long, dark hair tied back with a red ribbon. Farrell thought the ribbon looked out of place.

'Good morning.' She smiled at him. 'Can I help you?'

He returned her smile. 'My name's Farrell. Is this where I find Richard Travers?'

'Yes it is. If you'd like to go on up I'll tell him you're here. It's the first office you come to — you can't miss it.'

'Thanks.' He began walking away, but stopped when she called after him.

'Would you like coffee?' she asked. 'Or would you prefer tea?'

'Coffee's fine, thank you. Black no sugar.' Farrell continued to the stairs, taking them two at a time until he reached the landing where he found Travers waiting for him.

The American appeared weary, standing in the doorway of his office while he polished his glasses with the end of his tie. 'You found your way then?' he said.

Farrell nodded. 'I hope this isn't going to be a waste of time.'

'So do I. Come on in and we'll see.'

As well as being windowless, the office was nearly as austere as the foyer had been. There was a desk, a phone, two chairs and an electric heater. Standing on the desk, half-buried in documents, maps and sheets of paper was a slide projector.

'Help yourself.' Travers waved at one of the chairs. 'How's your wife?'

'Fine. How's yours?'

Travers put his glasses back on and peered over the top of them. 'We're not going to get far if you still have a chip on your shoulder. Either you're interested in hearing what I have to say, or you're not.'

'I wouldn't have come unless I was interested. What are we going to talk about?'

'I told you on the phone. You might be able to help me and maybe I can help you.'

'OK.' Farrell draped his coat over the back of a chair before he sat down. 'How long have you been working for American Travel?'

Travers smiled slightly. 'I can't figure out

244

why we bother to write it on the door. Everyone knows what goes on here.'

'Why should somebody from the US National Security Council want to discuss anything with me? Except for banging our heads together in Oman you and I don't have a lot in common, do we?'

'Let's just say that Britain, the US and some other countries have got a problem you might be able to help us solve. Oman isn't involved — not anymore.'

'Who are the other countries?' Farrell said.

'What do you care? Have you suddenly become politically aligned or something?'

'No. I just want to know where I stand, that's all.'

'You don't stand anywhere. This conversation is off the record. Once in a while we approach people privately to see if they're willing to undertake certain projects we don't want to do ourselves. You're one of those people.'

'Why am I?'

'Because no foreign government will believe someone like you has found themselves an agenda that coincides with the strategic objectives of the West. You've never worked for anyone but yourself; you don't care about anyone except yourself, and you have a suspect career history.'

'Suppose I tell you to stick your job?'

'Why don't you wait until you hear what it is?'

'Let's get something straight first,' Farrell said. 'You've decided I can give you a hand on some unofficial, international deal?'

'Right. One of these projects where it's worth trying an easy solution before we try anything else.'

'You mean safe,' Farrell said. 'The least damaging if it goes wrong.'

'Sure. You're what we call a low risk flyer. If you foul up we don't lose a hell of a lot. If you're successful we get a cheap win.'

Farrell leaned back in his chair. So far there was no suggestion of the American being anything but honest. Nor did he seem to be in a hurry to explain. Part of the pitch? Farrell wondered. Or because Travers knew better than to play his hand too early?

'Have a look at some pictures.' Travers began clearing paper away from the slide projector. 'Someone's borrowed the damn screen so you'll have to see them on the wall.'

The coffee arrived while Travers was shuffling through a box of slides. The woman from reception searched for a place to put her tray, gave up and left the office still carrying it. She returned holding a cup in each hand.

'Here.' Farrell found some space on the desk.

'Oh, thank you. I'm sorry things are so cramped.' She hurried away, closing the door quietly behind her.

'Every time I come over from the States it's the same,' Travers complained. 'If we can't do it properly I don't know why we run a UK office.'

'If the US and the UK are working together on this, why aren't British Intelligence handling it? Why am I talking to you?'

'British Intelligence don't know much about John Farrell; I do. I also happen to know more about red mercury than anyone in the UK does. Anyway, the fewer people involved the better.' Travers switched on the projector. 'Cut the room lights, will you?'

Farrell turned off the lights and went back to his chair.

'OK,' Travers said. 'Here we go. Recognize this?'

Projected on the wall was a high resolution picture of the Hajar mountain plateau. Because of the extraordinary definition, for a moment Farrell failed to realize that it was an aerial photograph.

'We flew in a team to check out the crater,' Travers explained. 'Three scientists, a geologist, a couple of explosives experts and a photographer. The poor bastards spent a whole day up there. They said it was the hottest damn place they'd ever been.'

'What were they looking for?' Farrell was attempting to pick out some sign of the village or the derelict wall.

'They were asked to estimate the level of explosive energy. You saw what sixteen little flasks of red mercury can do, but you have no idea what that means in terms of destructive capability, overpressure, burst intensity, flash temperature and the rest of it.'

'I've got more idea than you think,' Farrell said. 'What did these experts decide?'

'That the crater had resulted from the detonation of an unknown type of high-explosive having the same energy as five tons of conventional TNT.'

Farrell was not surprised. 'Didn't you tell them it was red mercury?' he asked.

'Not until they'd released their report. Even after I did tell them, to start with they wouldn't believe sixteen flasks could do anything like that. I had to get information from Russia before anyone would listen seriously. Once the scientists calculated the mass energy equivalent they just about haemorrhaged.'

'Is mass energy equivalent how you compare different explosives?' Farrell said.

'One way. The sums go like this. According to the Russian research people, each flask holds three hundred grams of red mercury gel. Sixteen flasks gives you just under five kilogrammes, or around ten pounds of the stuff altogether. When the Pentagon heard the numbers they flipped. They didn't want to believe ten pounds of red mercury gel could do the same damage as a truck load of TNT. You must admit it's pretty hard to imagine.'

For Farrell it wasn't hard at all. Since he had witnessed the fireball three months ago he had forgotten nothing. The explosion was as clear as if it had happened yesterday — the flash, the heat and being slammed back against the Land Rover so hard that he thought his head had come off. 'So what happened?' he asked.

'Our first idea was to try and stop MINATOM from producing any more gel. You can guess how successful that was. The Russians claimed they weren't violating any international treaty and said they'd manufacture as much damn gel as they felt like. Since then we've concentrated on where the stuff is going. This next slide will show you exactly where.'

The new picture was of lower quality, a black and white satellite photograph taken from very high altitude. Although the detail was fuzzy, the missile launchers were unmistakable even to Farrell's untrained eyes. The launchers looked like toys or models perched on the surface of a barren, artificial world.

'IRBMs,' Travers said. 'Intermediate range ballistic missiles — North Korean RODONG-TWOs. They're pretty damn good.'

'How big are they?'

'About forty-five feet long with a half-ton warhead on them. If you try hard you can just see the warheads. They're protruding from the beds of the mobile transporters.'

Farrell was curious now. 'Why have you been taking satellite photographs of North Korea?' he asked.

'We haven't. What do you think of this one?'

The next slide was a good deal clearer. Farrell guessed it had either been computer enhanced or perhaps taken from a satellite in a lower orbit. It showed four RODONG launchers travelling in convoy along a coastal road that ended abruptly at the foot of what appeared to be a mountain range. As well as the definition being much better, the slide was also in colour.

'OK,' Farrell said. 'If these aren't pictures of North Korea and they're not pictures of Oman, where were they taken?'

'Iran. The first shot was of the north-west region — not far from the Iraqi border. The one you're looking at now covers an area of the coast along the Persian Gulf. Forget Iran for a minute. What do you know about co-operative weapon development projects between countries?'

'Not much,' Farrell said.

'They're fairly common. While the major powers are scrambling to sign nuclear test ban treaties and non-proliferation agreements so they can keep the lid on things, the governments of non-aligned countries have started joining forces to share the cost of developing new aircraft, warships and submarines. For the purpose of this discussion we're concerned with a joint weapons development programme between North Korea and Iran. It's been running since the late eighties. The Koreans' part of the deal is for them to develop the booster and guidance systems for a new generation of long-range missiles while Iran concentrates on the development of nuclear warheads. The Koreans have done real well with their RODONG ONE and TWO, and with their new missile, the TAEPODONG, but Iran hasn't exactly come up with the goods they promised. They've come up with something else instead.'

Farrell had already guessed. 'Red mercury

warheads,' he said.

'Right. In a lot of ways non-nuclear explosives are a better choice for both Iran and North Korea. If the bastards ever get around to using them, they can't be accused of launching a nuclear attack on anyone. That means other countries will have to think hard before they decide on nuclear retaliation.'

'You're not talking about half-ton red mercury warheads, are you?' Farrell asked.

'Shit no. Even if Iran could get enough gel from the Russians, which they can't, they don't need half a ton for a warhead. A hundred pounds will do it.' Travers paused. 'What you saw in Oman was the explosion of less than ten pounds of gel. Multiply the energy of that bang by ten times and you can understand why the Koreans and Iranians are so pleased with themselves.'

Farrell was endeavouring to visualize the explosion from a hundred pounds of the gel. 'Do you know how much they have?' he said.

'No. But that's not the reason we're worried. Think about the weight difference. Instead of having to launch a thousand pounds of conventional high-explosive, all Iran has to do is put a suitcaseful of red mercury into the sharp end of a RODONG missile. They get a hell of a lot more destructive energy for a fraction of the weight.

I don't have to spell out the advantage of that, do I?'

'Range,' Farrell said slowly. 'Lighter warheads give their missiles greater range.'

'Which allows Iran to position their launchers wherever they want and target places they could never hope to reach before.' Travers adjusted his glasses. 'Tel Aviv and Haifa, for example.'

'Why would Iran target Israel?'

'Ask the next Revolutionary Guard you meet. Iran is a rogue Islamic state. They're still trying to sabotage the Middle East peace process. They're unstable, paranoid and they won't stop financing the PLO, Hizballah or the Hamas terrorists. It doesn't matter how much pressure the US or Britain puts on them, they're as committed to their goddamn Islamic *jihad* to fight Israeli occupation as they've ever been. You can't influence the Iranians and you can't trust them either. That's bad enough, but once they've secured a reliable supply of red mercury they'll be able to destabilize the whole damn region. Now do you realize why someone needs to do something?'

Farrell nodded. 'What's this got to do with me?'

Travers pointed to the picture on the wall. 'The guts of it are right there. See the road?'

Although the road along the Iranian coastline was clearly visible in the foreground, there were no landmarks Farrell recognized and the terrain inland was equally unfamiliar to him. 'Where does it go?' he asked.

'Not far — to a huge underground manufacturing facility the Iranians blasted out of the rock about ten years ago. They call it their Khvormuj Mugharet complex. It was originally designed to be a facility for producing chemical and biological weapons. Right now the new warheads are being assembled here.' Travers stopped Farrell from interrupting. 'Let me finish. Until recently we had no proof that either warheads or missiles were being stored in this part of the country. But in the last month, at least half-a-dozen operational launchers have been moved down from the north. They're not just being refitted with red mercury warheads, they're based permanently on the coast.'

'You haven't answered my question,' Farrell said. 'Why tell me?'

'Turn on the light and I'll explain.'

Farrell was becoming concerned. He was being supplied with what could be classified information as though he was already committed — an indication, he thought, of how few options he might be given when the crunch came.

While he attended to the lights Travers unfolded a map and draped it over the projector. It was a large-scale map of Iran on which someone had written a number of notes.

'OK.' Travers used a pencil point to trace the route of the road. 'The underground complex is south of Bushehr on the coast here.' He drew a circle. 'Now then, if you're an Iranian and you've just driven your mobile RODONG launcher out from its nice underground bunker ready to fire a missile at Israel, what military advantage do you see in being way down here on the Gulf instead of being up in the north-west of the country where you'd be much closer to your target?'

Farrell spent some seconds inspecting the map before he answered. 'A flight path that follows the border between Iraq and Saudi Arabia,' he said. 'Is that what you mean?'

'Yes. If you launch an extended range RODONG TWO from the Gulf coast it doesn't have to overfly Baghdad or Damascus. There's less risk of provoking Iraq and Syria because you're not lobbing missiles across their major cities or their airspace. All you have to worry about is Jordan, and no one cares what they think. If Jordan gets nervous they can't do anything about it. Your missile takes the least politically provocative route.'

By now Farrell had anticipated what was coming next. 'You don't have to go on,' he said. 'I've got the idea. Iran's converted their underground complex into a military base where they're assembling red mercury warheads, and you don't like it.'

Travers peered over his glasses. 'Which is where you come in.'

'I'm supposed to stop Iran destabilizing the whole of the Middle East?'

'Trust me. You can guess who's selling the gel to Iran, can't you?'

'Intech,' Farrell said.

'Two shipments so far, both originating from their Moscow office. We've been able to trace each one. Volchek accompanies the flasks to Tehran by air. From there they go by road — travelling at night under armed military escort. Intech have Hasan Rajavi riding shot-gun to make sure there isn't another foul-up, but the guy in charge is a brigadier-general from the covert action division of the Iranian Revolutionary Guards. We've had him under surveillance since he left Oman.'

Something stirred inside Farrell's head. 'What's his name?'

'Bozorgian. Massoud Bozorgian. Why?'

'And he was in Oman?'

'He arrived there the day after you met Volchek and Rajavi at Nelson's office — probably because Volchek asked the Iranians for some help.' Opening a drawer, Travers withdrew a photograph and slid it across the desk. 'That's him.'

Farrell recognized the man immediately. In the mountains it had been Bozorgian in the passenger seat of the Pajero. And, in the photo of Almira kneeling on the bed in Farrell's Mutrah apartment, Bozorgian had been the man with the knife.

'Ugly bastard, isn't he?' Travers remarked.

'He was up in the Hajar with Rajavi. I think he killed Nelson.'

'Do you know that for certain?'

Farrell shook his head.

'Let's move on then. Now I've given you a run-down on the background I'll spell out the project for you. It's real simple. We believe the next Intech shipment of gel is due in to Tehran some time in the next six weeks. That means it'll be travelling south before Christmas.' Travers paused. 'Before it reaches the Khvormuj complex we intend to have someone plant a detonating device alongside the flasks. Once the shipment is deep underground, the device will be triggered by a timer.'

'And I'm this someone?' Farrell said.

'You're out of your mind. Find a better way.'

'If there was a better way I wouldn't be talking to you. Apart from the last fifty or sixty miles down from Bushehr we're not sure of the route. We don't know if the trucks stop during the day either. Even if they do, getting to them in broad daylight isn't worth considering. About all we will know is the date the flasks arrive in Tehran and roughly when they'll be trucked out.'

'Who's going to tell you that?' Farrell asked.

'We have some friendly dissidents in Tehran and we're in touch with a group called the People's Mujahedin.'

'Get them to do it. Why can't they wire up one of the trucks before it leaves?'

'They're not the kind of people who have access to military warehouses. And blowing up a vehicle won't necessarily do the job. We have to trigger the gel itself. I'm told red mercury has a high tolerance to shock. What do you think of the idea so far?'

In any other circumstances Farrell would have rejected the proposal out of hand, but in this instance he knew his choices were limited. Showing no interest he slid his chair back from the desk. 'You don't want me for this,' he said. 'You've got the wrong person.'

'Listen. We'll put you into a comfortable

hotel in Kuwait City with all expenses paid. You used to work out of Kuwait so you know your way around there — just like you know your way around the top end of the Gulf. You'll be provided with a boat of your choice and any equipment you need — and I mean any equipment. After you've got yourself set up you can sit around and wait for a phone call. When you get it you'll have twelve or fourteen hours to cross the Gulf and take up your position on the Iranian coast.'

'No thanks,' Farrell said.

Travers stabbed at the map with his finger. 'The road runs close to the water for nearly ten miles. It'll be dark when the trucks come through, so all you have to do is pick the right place and arrange for some kind of diversion to hold them up for a few minutes.'

'You're making it sound like a trip up the Thames,' Farrell grunted. 'For Christ's sake why not just send in a cruise missile?'

'That'd be harder than trying to do the job by surface bombing. Don't kid yourself about the Iranians, Farrell. They're not stupid. We have intelligence on the complex from the German engineers who supplied the excavating equipment that was used to build the place. The main chambers are under at least a hundred and fifty feet of solid rock, and the entrance is at the end of a narrow valley

259

between two mountains. The valley isn't straight and the road winds around a couple of massive rock outcrops before it reaches the first outer chamber. Then there are doors — one metre thick, steel doors. Have you got the picture?'

'Yes.'

'You've missed the point anyway,' Travers said. 'No one's going to risk an international incident on this sort of scale. You can forget military intervention. If Israel or the West are implicated — no matter how slightly — there'll be so much shit flying around we'll never dig ourselves out. This way, if things go wrong we're squeaky clean. If the Iranians grab you, we don't care.'

'Unless I tell them the truth.'

'Tell whoever you like whatever you want. Officially you don't exist. It's not our fault if you've been following Intech around on some misguided personal vendetta because of what happened to Tony Nelson. You're expendable, Farrell. That's what makes you so attractive to us.'

'Maybe it's time I heard what's going to make this attractive to me.'

'How does two hundred thousand US dollars sound?'

Surprised by the offer, Farrell was slow to reply.

'Well?' Travers asked.

'I don't want your money or your job — not on those terms.'

'Don't be smart with me. If you're open to negotiation, say so. What do you have in mind?'

Farrell was remembering Nelson — how the Irishman had intuitively understood when he should push, when not to push and when to walk away.

'I'm waiting,' Travers said.

'Step one, I get on a plane to Muscat. Step two, Almira Muammar goes back with me from Muscat to Kuwait — no strings, no complications. If she's not part of the deal, you and I have nothing more to say to each other.'

'What makes you believe I can get her released?' Travers fiddled with his pencil.

'Who was it that persuaded the ISS to lock her up? You always figured you might need me, didn't you? You've had her on ice all this time.'

'It hasn't occurred to you that you might be wrong?'

'No.' To avoid antagonizing Travers unnecessarily, Farrell decided to compromise. 'Do you want to hear the rest?'

Travers nodded.

'Step three, as long as I'm guaranteed a

hundred per cent control in Kuwait, I'll see what I can do for you in Iran. If I pull it off I'll take your two hundred thousand dollars. If I screw up you can keep it.'

'I see. Why should I trust you, I wonder, when you and your girlfriend could choose to forego the money and vanish?'

'Look at it the other way round,' Farrell said. 'Suppose I do a good job and then find out you never intended to pay me.'

'Which makes the exercise difficult, doesn't it?' The American stood up from his desk. 'You were right. I'm afraid there's nothing more we have to say to each other.'

This time Farrell was not only surprised, he was caught offguard. With no reply prepared, and without a fall-back position from which he could renegotiate, he felt the initiative begin to slip away from him.

'Look,' he said. 'Whoever else you get to do the job you'll still have to trust them, and they won't know the coast as well as I do. In the last seven years I've spent more nights out in the Gulf than you've spent home in bed.'

'Perhaps, but that doesn't overcome the problem of Miss Muammar, does it? I'm not your enemy. Farrell, but I'm not your friend either. I'll discuss the girl's future, but only after you've completed the project. My offer of two hundred thousand dollars stands, of course.'

'So if I fail, Almira stays in some God-awful Omani jail.'

Travers shrugged. 'I get paid to do my job the best way I know how. I'm sorry we can't do business. Now, if you have nothing more to say, perhaps you'll excuse me. I need to send some faxes.'

Aware that he'd been outmanoeuvred but too disillusioned to reopen the conversation, Farrell gave up. He collected his coat and headed for the door.

'Leave your phone number with the receptionist,' Travers said.

'Why?'

'You never know. I'm not as lucky as you are. You're only accountable to yourself. I'm not.'

If the remark had been made by anyone else Farrell would have paid it little attention. In this case he thought he knew better. 'I figured I might take off somewhere for the weekend,' he said. 'Maybe I should wait to see if the weather clears up.'

'Good idea. You should know one way or the other in a couple of days.' Travers picked up his phone. 'Thanks for coming.'

★ ★ ★

After a weekend of fruitless speculation and having spent much of Sunday night wondering how badly he had managed to misinterpret the situation, by breakfast-time on Monday Farrell was no longer expecting his phone to ring.

When it did, it made him jump.

He picked up the receiver and said hello.

'Meet me in Kensington Gardens.' Travers sounded in a hurry. 'Can you do that?'

'Have you changed your mind?'

'By the Peter Pan statue in an hour. Don't be late.' The line went dead.

Farrell put down the phone, not yet sure whether the call was good news, but preferring to believe that it was.

By the time he left the flat his confidence was higher and he hardly noticed the chill on his walk to the south bank of the Serpentine where he started looking for Travers in the mist.

The American was standing beside the statue, insulated from the cold by a thick overcoat, gloves and a sheepskin hat. He remained where he was, waiting for Farrell to join him.

'Morning,' Farrell said. 'Did you get thrown out of your office?'

'I thought you might be too pissed off to come to the office. It's best we talk out here

264

anyway.' Travers produced an envelope. 'I brought this for you.'

'What is it?'

'Your airline ticket to Muscat, and a couple of tickets from Muscat to Kuwait — one for you, one for your pretty friend.'

Farrell decided to be cautious, reluctant to believe that his fortunes could have improved quite so dramatically over the course of a weekend. 'Couldn't you find anyone else?' he said.

'There isn't time now. Intech's next shipment of gel to Tehran is due in just over two weeks. I recommended against using you but we haven't got much choice. You're it whether I like the idea or not.'

'Look,' Farrell said. 'I want the whole story, not half of it. If you've got fresh information I want to hear it. How do you know when Intech's shipping the flasks?'

'It's none of your business, but I can tell you where the information came from. You see, the Russians might be unreceptive to requests from the West asking them to close down their Yekaterinburg lab and their research centres at Dubna and Krasnoyarsk, but providing they get paid for the gel they're prepared to listen to what Washington and London have to say. The Russians aren't going to cry into their vodka if there's a big bang in the Gulf.' Travers turned up his collar. 'An unstable Middle East is no more help to the new administration in Moscow than it is to us.'

'Does that mean the Russians know what you're planning to do in Iran?'

'You didn't listen to me properly last week. We're not planning anything, Farrell. You're the one with the plan.'

'What's the deal with Almira?'

'Once I know you're on the plane tomorrow she'll be released. You'll have one night to say hello in Muscat, then I want you standing by in Kuwait. Do you have a problem with the arrangements?'

Farrell shook his head.

'You haven't asked about the money.'

'Should I have done?' Farrell pocketed the envelope.

'No. Two hundred grand if you pull it off — but only if you do. There's only one catch. I'm not having you and your friend disappearing before you've done what you're being paid for. You'll both surrender your passports on arrival in Kuwait.'

'To you?'

'I'm going home, Farrell, to spend a nice Christmas with my family in Virginia. Someone else will be handling things in Kuwait.'

'Who?'

'Don't worry about who. They'll provide funds, equipment and anything else you need. You'll find hotel reservations, contact phone numbers and cash in the envelope along with your tickets.'

It was all so simple, Farrell thought, and faintly unreal. A phone call from Moscow to some faceless State Department bureaucrat in Washington had been followed by another call from Washington to London — and suddenly, the lives of two ordinary people had been brought together again. He felt ill at ease, wanting to anticipate what it would be like to see Almira again, but finding himself unable to do so.

'I have some advice,' Travers said. 'I'll walk you to your car.'

'I didn't bring a car.'

'Walk anyway.' Travers stamped his feet. 'If I get any damn colder I'm going to freeze to the ground.'

Along the banks of the Serpentine more people were gathering, some on morning constitutionals, tourists with cameras and even a few hardy joggers. Farrell watched them all, conscious of having somehow become divorced from whatever it was that made the scene so normal. A day from now he'd be gone, gone from London and from

England, and in place of the uncomfortable memories of Mary there would be Almira. But only after another night run, he thought — an unwanted trip that could see his future snatched away as easily as it had been before.

'You might not need me to tell you this,' Travers said. 'I realize you won't be in Muscat long, but if I were you I'd be careful what I said.'

'To whom?' Farrell kept walking.

'Remember asking me how I discovered where you were supposed to hand over those flasks — at that deserted village in the mountains?'

'I remember. How did you?'

'Same way I found out that you and Nelson had dredged up the flasks. While you were driving back from the peninsula with them in your trunk that evening, the US Embassy in Muscat got a phone call from someone who said they had information to sell. They asked for me by name.'

'Salim,' Farrell said.

'I'd already met him when I called to see his father, so the little bastard knew who I was and what I was doing in Oman. He said he'd supplied Nelson with scuba divers and that they'd just phoned him from Khabura. He offered to tell me what they had to say for a thousand dollars.'

'Which you gave him.'

'Not right away. I arranged to meet him in Mutrah around seven o'clock. He took me to the car-park outside Nelson's office and said you'd be showing up there later with the box. That's why I was waiting for you.'

'Salim wasn't ever up at Khabura then?' Farrell stopped walking.

'Did you think he was?'

'Someone photographed me and Almira by the jetty.'

'That would've been Volchek protecting his investment. Don't forget he'd already forked out a thirty-grand down payment for you to recover the box. He'd have sent Bozorgian to keep an eye on you. Does it matter?'

'I guess not,' Farrell was thinking. 'Was Salim working for you all along?'

'I wouldn't call it working. He'd sell anything to anyone. I paid him for information — like a photocopy of the map Volchek delivered to Muammar — the one showing the location of the village. I don't think young Salim cared what happened to his sister.'

'He cared,' Farrell said. 'He had it all figured out. Salim was hoping like hell that you'd run me down before I could exchange the flasks for Almira.'

Travers raised his eyebrows. 'Well then, you don't need any advice about keeping your mouth shut in Oman, do you?'

'No.'

'One last thing,' Travers said. 'This project isn't about you getting even for Nelson. I don't want to hear about any nasty accidents to Rajavi and Bozorgian. Providing they're underground when the complex blows they'll get what they deserve anyway. But if you fall over, I might need them again. Do you understand?'

'What about Volchek?'

'Leave him to us. Do you have any more questions?'

Farrell was past asking questions. By now it was not the discussion that seemed unreal. It was everything — the pale green of the Serpentine, the sound from traffic along Bayswater Road, and the misty morning air — all combining to exaggerate his sense of separateness. A week ago, standing outside Bristol station in the rain, he'd experienced the feeling of not belonging anywhere. This morning the feeling had returned, but overlaid with the knowledge that he was being manipulated.

'Right. I'll be off then.' Travers removed a glove. 'Best of luck.'

'Thanks.' After Farrell had shaken hands and said goodbye, for some minutes he stood alone beside the lake watching a boy launch a model boat. It was a radio-controlled launch with a whip aerial and a fragile plastic hull.

Because of the concrete edges of the lake, and because of poor visibility in the mist, it seemed doubtful that the boat would return in one piece. But the Serpentine was not the Persian Gulf, Farrell told himself. And now his luck had finally changed; if there was mist where he was going, it would be more of an advantage than a hazard.

11

The man at the immigration desk was unhappy. After flicking through Farrell's passport he went back to the first page and began again.

'What is the purpose of your visit to Oman?' he asked.

'Stopover,' Farrell said.

The man consulted a list of names on a clipboard before he returned the passport. 'Enjoy your stay,' he said.

Farrell headed for the arrival area, scanning the crowd for Almira as soon as he was through the door.

There was no sign of her. Instead, Ghassan Muammar came to meet him. Grasping Farrell's hand, he shook it earnestly. 'I have not the words to express my pleasure at seeing you again,' he said. 'After all that has gone before I have hardly dared hope that we would renew our acquaintance so soon.'

'Is Almira home?'

'Since last night. Because she is nervous at the prospect of greeting you, she has asked if I would come to the airport. You understand perhaps?'

Farrell nodded. 'Is she OK?'

'She is well, although my sister tells me there have been some tears. Now, please, where is your luggage?'

'This is it.' Farrell lifted his cabin bag. 'I'm travelling light.'

'Then we shall leave at once. My car is close by.'

Outside the terminal building Farrell stopped to let the heat wash over him. For early December, the afternoon was not particularly warm, but after the biting cold of London, the air was almost sensuous. Already his skin was moist and his eyes were hurting from the light.

He accompanied Muammar to the Range Rover, wondering if Almira had been released early because Travers had always been certain his offer would be accepted.

'Please. You will sit in the front.' Muammar held the door open. 'We have much to discuss.'

Farrell waited until the car was underway before asking more questions. 'How did you hear?' he said.

'I am telephoned by a man from the Internal Security Service. First I am told Almira is of no further interest to the authorities, and then that you will arrive from London on flight 379 today.'

'Did you collect her?' Farrell said.

'It was not necessary. I am informed she will be brought by car. Yesterday at five o'clock she is delivered safely to my home.' Muammar frowned. 'For weeks I have worked to undo this injustice to my daughter. I have spent many thousands of rial and sought advice from many people, yet in my heart I had not believed I would be successful. For this reason I am certain it is to you I owe my gratitude. Forgive me, therefore, if I ask how you have brought this about.'

'It's better if I don't explain. Better for you and for me.'

'You have done some business with the ISS?'

Farrell shook his head. 'It's not exactly over yet. I have to leave again tomorrow, and I need to take Almira with me. I don't think it's a good idea for her to stay in Oman.'

'I see.' Muammar slowed for some traffic lights. 'It seems that yet again I must rely on you to do for my daughter what in the past I myself have failed to do.'

For the first time since Travers had disappeared into the mist of Kensington Gardens, Farrell found himself beginning to tense up. All of yesterday, for most of last night and for the entire duration of his flight

274

from Heathrow he had avoided rehearsing anything — holding his images of Almira at bay until he could be certain it was safe to remember her smile, the glow of her skin and the touch of her lips. Now, suddenly, his imagination was in overload. After over three months of either trying to forget her or trying to remember her, Farrell was no longer struggling to separate Almira from Mary but guard against his rising sense of expectation. He was brought back to earth by Muammar speaking to him again.

'I trust you are not tired from your journey?' Muammar enquired.

'No, I'm fine. Why?'

'By way of a celebration, my sister is preparing a dinner for you. Ali-Khaleefa will join us, and my son will also be present. I hope this will be satisfactory?'

'It sounds great.' Farrell grinned. 'I could use a celebration. Is Ali-Khaleefa OK?'

'He has a steel pin in his leg, but otherwise he is moderately well.'

'Can he walk all right?'

'Certainly.' Muammar swung off the main road and started on the climb up to the Qurm Heights. 'He is very much looking forward to seeing you.'

Farrell was staring out of the window, conscious of viewing everything as if for the

275

first time. The palm trees, the Islamic architecture of the houses and the bright, clean streets seemed fresh and new. And, already replacing the repressive dullness of England was a feeling of freedom generated by sunshine, open space and glimpses of the coast.

Both Salukis were loose in the courtyard, barking excitedly when Farrell got out of the Range Rover to open the gates. Preferring to walk the short distance to the villa, he fussed the dogs and waved Muammar through. On the north side of the courtyard Salim's Porsche was parked in the shade of a palm and alongside it, where Almira's Mercedes stood with its doors open, the housemaid was watering a flower bed.

Aunt Latifa hurried to welcome him. She was dressed in a tunic with long flowing sleeves, gathered in at the waist over brightly coloured silk trousers. She was also wearing her best ear-rings and an extremely large brooch.

In case she was uncertain of how to say hello, Farrell kissed her on both cheeks and gave her a hug.

Unable to conceal her delight, she took his hands and began towing him towards the porch.

'Where's Almira?' Farrell asked.

'The silly girl remains in her room. She is not yet sure of herself.'

The opportunity for Farrell to enquire further was cut short by Salim who came to shake hands. Unlike his father and his aunt, he was wearing western clothes and seemed to be on his way somewhere.

'How was London?' he asked.

'Cold,' Farrell said. 'You ought to try it sometime.'

'My father thinks it was you who arranged for Almira to come home. What the hell did you do?'

'Not a lot,' Farrell said. 'She shouldn't have been locked up to begin with, should she?'

Salim shrugged. 'She hasn't talked about it. You'll have to excuse me. I've got a date waiting. I'll see you at dinner tonight.'

Aunt Latifa was as anxious to get Farrell indoors as Salim had been to disappear. She led him in to the hall where her brother was standing by the door of his study.

'Mr Farrell,' he said. 'I am sorry for the discourtesy of my daughter. Unless you first wish to refresh yourself, perhaps if you were to knock on her door she will understand that she cannot stay in her room all day.'

'Look,' Farrell said. 'She is all right, isn't she?'

'She must tell you so herself,' Aunt Latifa

said. 'Go and see.'

Feeling increasingly uncomfortable Farrell went to the stairs, stopping at the foot of them to collect his thoughts before proceeding.

Upstairs it was cooler, and a breeze coming through the open windows was ruffling the curtains along the corridor. There was no other movement, no sound, and the door to Almira's room was closed.

Instead of knocking first he pushed it open, entering the bedroom unannounced.

She was standing by her dressing-table, dropping an unfastened bracelet as she swung round to face him.

Farrell had always known it would be like this. She was beautiful, more beautiful than anyone he'd ever seen — proof that every tiny thing he'd remembered was right — the ultimate justification for his obsession with her and for all the heartache and anxiety.

She refused to meet his eyes, retreating until her back was against the dressing-table and she could go no further.

'Hey,' Farrell said gently. 'It's only me.'

She remained silent, her head lowered.

He went to her and placed his hands on her waist. 'Everything's OK,' he said. 'There's nothing to be scared of anymore.'

One by one tears started rolling down her

cheeks. 'Why have you come?' she whispered.

'Why do you think?' As surprised by her question as he was by her nervousness, he wondered how to reassure her.

'Did you mean any of those things you said to me? Do you even remember saying them? Were any of them true?'

'For Christ's sake,' Farrell said. 'Look at me.'

She shook her head.

'Of course they were true. All of them. Everything we said to each other. Why else would I be here?'

Tentatively she raised her face. 'A hundred and twenty-four days.' She spoke so quietly he could barely hear her. 'Have you any idea what it was like? Waking up each morning and going to sleep each night without knowing where you were, what you were doing, and if I'd ever see you again. How do I know you're telling me the truth?'

This time it was Farrell who didn't answer. Keeping both hands on her waist he pulled her towards him while he looked into her eyes. Although she was still crying, he thought she seemed less apprehensive.

When he kissed her she at first held back, but suddenly opened her mouth and wrapped her arms around him, refusing to let go even when she ran out of breath. Because the

279

closeness of her was already making his pulse race he was able to slow things down only by twisting away.

'Don't let go of me.' She tried to kiss him again, pressing her whole body against his.

'Take it easy.' With great difficulty Farrell made the effort to disengage himself from her embrace. 'Your father and Aunt Latifa are waiting for us. Don't you think we ought to go downstairs?'

'No.' She was panting. 'Not until I know everything. So far all you've done is make me cry and mess up my hair. I'm not going anywhere until you've talked to me.'

'There's going to be all the time in the world for us to talk. All you need to know right now is that you and I are going away together.'

'Where to?'

'Kuwait. We leave tomorrow.'

She wiped away her tears. 'Suppose I don't want to go to Kuwait with you.'

'Then you shouldn't have kissed me like that.' Carefully Farrell moved her sideways so the sunlight from the window fell across her face. 'Stand there a minute,' he said.

'Why?'

'Just do it.' He stepped back in order to see if he was right — to check that his impression was no different to his memory of her leaning against the juniper tree at daybreak on their last morning together in the wadi.

She was the same — arresting and still impossibly desirable. Today she was wearing a white blouse and the short yellow skirt he could remember from the summer — clothes that somehow increased her sensuality either because she had chosen them for that very reason or because she knew he liked them.

She spoilt the effect by stooping to pick up her bracelet. 'Why am I standing by the window?' she asked.

'So I can be sure it's you.'

'I can make it easier for you.'

'Downstairs,' Farrell said firmly. 'Now.'

Muammar was still in the hall, clearly relieved to see that his daughter had agreed to leave her room. 'Mr Farrell,' he said. 'May I speak with you alone?'

'Don't you dare.' Almira was indignant. 'I've only just said hello.'

'The fault is yours,' Muammar said, 'You will be patient while I discuss certain matters which are not of your concern. Please do not disgrace yourself further in front of our guest.'

'It's OK. This won't take long.' Trying not to show his amusement, Farrell squeezed her hand before accompanying Muammar to the study.

'This is most difficult for me.' The Omani closed the door. 'Although I appreciate you are unwilling to divulge your present circumstances, it is nevertheless my hope that you will be able to answer two questions which I have.'

'What are they?'

'From Ali-Khaleefa I have learned of the great explosion at the mountain village. Because of this, for many weeks now, I have wondered how it could be the ISS knew where to send their helicopters. I therefore wish you to tell me if it was my son who was responsible.'

Farrell thought before he replied. 'Yes,' he said. 'Salim was being paid by Richard Travers.'

'Then it is as I feared. By spoiling my children I have taken away from them their sense of what is right and what is wrong in this complicated world of ours.'

'No you haven't. Almira's fine. You shouldn't feel that way about her.'

'Perhaps. But for some months before she met you she was not only bored with herself but also, I believe, with her life in Oman. Her behaviour was of great concern to me. It is you I must thank for showing my daughter that where she finds excitement she will find danger.'

282

'She's known that for a while,' Farrell said. 'What else did you want to ask me?'

'I would like to understand why Almira was unharmed when you failed to deliver the red mercury to the men from Intech at the village.'

'I don't know why. Probably because they couldn't see any point in killing her. Maybe she was just lucky.'

Muammar nodded. 'Yes indeed. I respect your frankness. Now then, I insist you permit me to show my gratitude in a practical manner.'

Farrell stopped him. 'I don't want anything — just a favour.'

'And what is this favour?'

'There's a job I have to do. I realize Ali-Khaleefa has a pin in his leg, but I could really use his help.'

'Ah.' Muammar placed his fingertips together. 'You ask me for the only thing I cannot guarantee to provide. I must tell you that for some months Ali-Khaleefa suffers from a sickness — not because of the injury to his leg, but for another reason. When he is delivered to the hospital by the Bedu the doctors there take many x-rays of my friend. By this means they discover he has a cancer in his bones.'

'Can they fix it?

'It has spread from his prostate. I have learned that in some cases radiation treatment can be used and that surgery can sometimes be successful. But the doctors say once a man has this cancer in his bones, little can be done.' Muammar paused. 'It is a great sadness to me.'

'I'm sorry,' Farrell said. 'I'd never have asked if I'd known. I'll find someone else.'

'First you will let me speak with Ali-Khaleefa. I shall mention the matter to him this evening. Now, how else may I repay your kindness?'

'There isn't anything to repay.'

'No, no.' Muammar shook his head. 'Perhaps if my son had endangered only the life of his sister we would not be talking of this. But things are not so simple. By also putting you at risk when you were in the mountains he has dishonoured the name of my family in your eyes.'

'You've forgotten how well I know you,' Farrell said. 'And Aunt Latifa and Almira. All Salim needs is someone to straighten him out. He only did a couple of jobs for Travers.'

'Have you considered that at the same time he could have been working for Volchek? Mr Farrell, I know my son better than you imagine. Allow me to explain something. According to the men from Intech who called to see me in July there were supposed to be many emeralds circulating on the market in Oman — you may remember.'

'I remember,' Farrell said. 'What's that got to do with Salim?'

'Three weeks ago I am offered twenty kilos of uncut emeralds which are said to have come from MINATOM in Russia. These are the same emeralds you collected from the Iranian freighter — stones which, I can assure you, have not previously been for sale anywhere. What does this tell you?'

'That Intech just used the emeralds as an excuse to contact you — because someone had already told them what happened on board the *Stingray*.'

'Yes. Which is why I suspect Volchek and Rajavi may have initially visited my home when I was out. Perhaps instead of first discussing their business with me, they spoke with my son who later sold information to them concerning your accident at sea.'

'What if he did?'

'If my suspicions are correct and my son continued to have an association with Volchek or Rajavi, Salim might also have told them the flasks of red mercury could be found at Mr Nelson's office. My son, therefore, may in part be responsible for the terrible murder of your friend.'

It was plausible enough, Farrell thought. But even if Salim had been supplying information to whoever paid him, worrying about it now was pointless. It was over, finished and buried in the past.

'I apologize for burdening you with the problems of my family.' Going to the desk, Muammar picked up an ebony casket. 'I wish you to have this.'

Farrell took it from him and opened the lid. Inside, supported on a bed of red velvet, lay Muammar's sheathed *KHAN-JAR*. Because it was unheard of for an Omani to offer his knife to a European as a gift, Farrell knew that any refusal to accept it would be regarded as the greatest of insults.

'Thank you,' he said. 'I realize what this means to you.'

'You are my friend, Mr Farrell, a friend to whom I am entrusting my daughter. I have no doubt you will take good care of the *KHANJAR*.'

The statement had been made politely, but the request could not have been plainer.

'I'll look after it,' Farrell said. 'And I promise you'll never have to worry about your daughter.'

* * *

If Aunt Latifa had served one more course Farrell would have been inclined to write off the evening altogether. As it was, by the time coffee arrived he thought even Almira might consider it too late for them to go out. She was seated on the opposite side of the table, close enough for him to touch her ankle with his foot, but otherwise still out of reach.

'Mr Farrell.' Ali-Khaleefa spoke discreetly. 'I have waited to talk with you, but I fear the evening is passing.'

'I know. Shall I ask if it's OK for us to go outside? Or would that be rude?'

'I will do it.' The Omani stood up and went to speak to Muammar.

As if Almira had read Farrell's thoughts, she too left the table, thanking Aunt Latifa on her way from the room, but without glancing in his direction.

'You have had sufficient?' Aunt Latifa addressed the question first to her European guest and then to her brother.

'I haven't eaten this well for months,' Farrell said. 'You shouldn't have gone to so much trouble.'

'It is my pleasure. There is more coffee.'

Ali-Khaleefa came to the rescue. 'Forgive me if I go to the garden so I may smoke,' he said. 'Perhaps Mr Farrell would share my company there.'

Outside in the warm night air, despite his frustration at again being separated from Almira, Farrell was conscious of feeling more at ease than he had done for months.

'I wish to give you my answer.' Ali-Khaleefa began rolling a cigarette. 'I understand you have asked if I will help you in some small way. If it is true, although I do not yet know what I may do, I wish to offer my services.' He paused to light the cigarette. 'It is necessary for me to say, however, that I am not the same man who travelled with you to the village with no name.'

'It's not the same kind of job. We're not going to be driving up any mountains.'

'Ah. Then perhaps one good leg will be enough.' Ali-Khaleefa's face split into a grin. 'When will you tell me how I should prepare myself?'

'Later. The main thing is for you to be on a plane to Kuwait by tomorrow night. I'll be going on ahead with Almira so one of us can meet you at the airport. You can tell Mr Muammar if you have to, but no one else.'

'You will explain to me in Kuwait?'

Farrell nodded. 'Are you sure it's OK?'

'I am sure.'

Almira had come to the French windows. She too had been smoking, but threw her cigarette away before smiling happily at

288

Ali-Khaleefa and speaking to Farrell. 'If you'd rather spend the evening talking in the garden I'll go to the beach house by myself.'

'You're not going anywhere by yourself,' he said.

She dangled her car keys. 'Take me then.'

The slip of her tongue made it impossible for him to keep a straight face.

For a second she looked at him then began to giggle, only partly managing to recover her composure when Salim arrived to ask her something.

She handed the keys to Farrell. 'I'll meet you in the courtyard.'

Ali-Khaleefa walked with Farrell to the Mercedes where the Omani solemnly shook hands. 'You received the photograph which I have sent to you?' he asked.

'Yes, I did.'

'There is much truth in the saying.' Ali-Khaleefa smiled. 'When I join you in Kuwait we shall see, I think.'

Almira came running from the villa, holding a bottle of champagne in one hand and an envelope in the other. After kissing Ali-Khaleefa goodbye she climbed into the car, waiting impatiently for Farrell to get behind the wheel.

'What did Salim want?' he asked.

'Nothing.'

'Tell me.' Farrell swung the Mercedes out on to the road and put his foot down.

'He gave me these — four tabs of LSD.' She tossed the envelope out through the window. 'And he said he could sell us some really good cocaine.'

'Nice of him.'

'Aunt Latifa was nicer. The champagne's from her.'

'I don't think I need any,' Farrell said.

'It's for breakfast silly. I want to know about Kuwait now.'

'Afterwards. We don't need to talk about it until tomorrow.'

'After what?'

By ignoring her question, and by maintaining the pretence of being alone in the car, for most of the journey he was able to keep his mind on the driving. But no sooner had he turned the Mercedes into the driveway of the beach house than the weeks of waiting began to crowd in on him.

Leaving him to lock the car she skipped on ahead, vanishing into the house before Farrell reached the front door. Inside, enough lights had been switched on to lead him on a false trail. Three of her bracelets were scattered across the table in the kitchen, and, near the entrance to the conservatory, her shoes lay on the floor.

He found her in the lounge where she was standing barefoot in the centre of the room, her arms held loosely by her side.

'Have you really missed me?' Her voice was husky.

Farrell couldn't reply. The expression on her face was the expression he had never quite been able to forget, and if he'd ever wondered why his dreams of her had been so vivid, now he knew the reason.

Lips parted she was half smiling, her breasts rising and falling beneath the fabric of her blouse while she stared at him wide-eyed in anticipation.

'For Christ's sake, come here,' Farrell said.

'No.' Slowly unbuttoning her blouse she pulled it back to tie it behind her waist. Then, equally slowly, she undid her belt and allowed her skirt to slip to the floor.

Until now Farrell had been relying on his memory, never certain that the fascination she'd held for him could be as real as he wanted it to be. But it was. Her figure was as perfect as the colour and the texture of her skin. Above her brassiere, her breasts melted into the curve of her shoulders and her throat, and below her waist where tight black lace bikini briefs concealed nothing, so tantalizing was the swell between her thighs that he could not bear to take his eyes away.

When he went to kiss her, for several minutes she held his wrists, using her mouth and her tongue to heighten his desire until she fell victim to her own ardour. She helped him unfasten her brassiere and to remove her bikini, drawing in her breath whenever his hands strayed over her breasts or between her legs. Soon she began murmuring softly to him, first in Arabic, changing to English only after Farrell had picked her up in his arms and carried her to the bedroom.

He lay her naked on the bed, knowing she was watching his every movement as he struggled to remove his own clothes. He was still kneeling over her when she abandoned herself, grasping him with both hands and sitting up to kiss him with such ferocity that she bruised his lips.

Lowering her head onto the pillow again, he brushed a palm across her nipples. They were swollen, two tiny pink buds that she was eager to give him. He touched each one gently, lingering over them before drawing his other palm down between her breasts, spreading out his fingertips across the taut muscles of her stomach, but this time lingering too long.

'Please Farrell,' she whispered. 'Please don't stop. Please.'

There was no more chance of him stopping

than there was of her wanting him to. Overwhelmed in a perfumed world where the pleasure of caressing her was driving all reason from his mind, he tried to curb his need to be inside her.

But she refused to wait, gripping his wrists again to force his hands between her open thighs as though distrusting him to meet her own needs.

Now, whenever he touched her, instead of her skin being warm and moist, she was burning hot and wet with perspiration, squirming to make him hurry. Only when he began to enter her did she release his wrists in order to allow him to penetrate her fully.

Once she had accepted him, for a second or two she lay content with her eyes closed. But it was Farrell now who could not wait. She was like silk, contracting to arouse every nerve and every fibre of him until his remaining control was lost in the heady rush to possess her.

Murmuring his name once more she splayed her legs, urging him on, kissing, holding and finally raking her nails across his back as she joined him on her climb towards a climax so violent that it racked her entire body and left Farrell's heart slamming like a hammer against his ribs.

It was more than a minute before she had

recovered sufficiently to notice a tear in the sleeve of her blouse. On this occasion, instead of being embarrassed as she would have been in the past, she lay where she was, letting Farrell draw a sheet across her arm. She was breathless, still heaving from her exertions, but able to reach up to touch his cheek.

'A hundred and twenty-four days,' he said quietly. 'Is it really a hundred and twenty-four days since that morning at the waterfall?'

She nodded.

'We'd better make sure we never wait that long again — not unless we want to kill ourselves.'

'We don't have to wait.' She snuggled up to him. 'From now on we can make love every day.'

★ ★ ★

Except for a small boy playing ball with his father, the beach was deserted. Out in the Gulf a tanker was heading south leaving a smudge of wake behind it on a sea that seemed to be more blue than it had been yesterday.

On their walk here from the beach house, Farrell had again been aware of the colour and clarity of everything. Along the shore where the waves were breaking, the foam from them was a carpet of brilliant white bubbles, and in the sunlight the sand itself was glittering.

'You had too much champagne.' Almira threw a seashell at him. 'You've gone all quiet.'

'I don't feel like talking.'

'Is that another way of saying you're going to put off explaining things to me?'

'No.' He turned to look at her, uncertain of how to start. Earlier this morning while they were still in bed she had provided a stumbling account of her experiences over the last few months. Although parts of it had been harrowing, rather as Farrell had expected, the financial intervention of her father had made her imprisonment less distressing than it would otherwise have been. After describing her first week as being so bad that she had twice contemplated suicide, she had gone on to explain how things had suddenly improved when she'd been moved to an open compound, allowing her a greater degree of freedom and where she could at least hold her own among the other inmates. She had finished by telling him how she had spent each night trying to recall every minute she had spent with him, but that towards the end she'd found herself fantasizing about places they had never been to.

For Farrell, listening to her had been difficult. Reliving her ordeal with her had been even harder. As a result, not until they'd come here to the beach had he been able to properly rationalize his feelings. Now, with her sitting beside him in the sun, he was reluctant to spoil the moment by reopening a past that was best forgotten.

She picked up a handful of sand, letting the grains trickle through her fingers. 'It's your turn,' she said.

'OK.' Farrell began by skimming over his deportation from Oman before giving her a summary of his months alone in England. Avoiding any mention of his trips to Bristol, he told her about the cheques from her father, the card from Ali-Khaleefa and the letters from Aunt Latifa and how his search for a job had been no more successful than his attempts to accept his separation from her. Then, before she started asking questions, he described his two meetings with Travers, omitting some of the detail to guard against her becoming alarmed.

'You're not serious?' she said.

'Why do you think we're sitting here? If I'd turned Travers down you'd still be locked up and I'd still be freezing to death in England.'

'We're together now. Nothing else matters. If you think I'll let you do this, you're crazy.'

'Two hundred thousand dollars,' Farrell said. 'It's our start — for you and me.'

'My father will give us twice that much if I ask him. Don't you see?' She took his hands. 'There's no reason for you to do anything. We can disappear — just like we were going to do before.'

'I don't want your father's money. All I want is for you and me to have the kind of life where we're not always scratching around for money. You don't know how that feels — I do.'

'Tell me the truth,' she said.

'I am telling you the truth. We'll disappear afterwards — after it's done and we've got our passports back so we can live where we like without always having to look over our shoulders.'

'It's because of Tony Nelson.' She dropped his hands. 'Isn't it?'

'Look,' Farrell said. 'It'll be OK. I've told Travers I'll try, that's all. I promise I won't be taking any risks. You can ask Ali-Khaleefa to make sure I don't.'

'What do you mean?'

'He's going to Kuwait with us. I've already asked him.'

'Oh. I still don't like the idea of you carrying explosives across to Iran.' She paused for a second. 'I don't know whether to believe you. You could've made all this up so

297

I'll try to change your mind about going.'

Farrell had detected the thaw before she had finished speaking. 'You don't have to do it now,' he said. 'Wait until we're up in Kuwait.'

'Beginning tonight — after we've checked into our hotel room? Is that when I'm supposed to start being extra nice to you?'

The suggestion was provocative enough for Farrell to change the subject. 'You're not to say anything about Kuwait or Iran to Salim — not a word. It's best if you don't tell your father either.'

'Were you right about my brother?'

'The divers phoned him from Khabura while we were taking the box back to Nelson's office. Your brother sold Travers the information, and it was Salim who damn near got us both killed in the mountains. He might even have been working for Intech as well — I'm not sure.'

'Does my father know?'

Farrell nodded. 'Your brother had better hope I never come across him on a dark night somewhere.'

She picked up more sand, attempting to squeeze it into a ball. 'So who took those photos at Khabura?'

'Probably someone called Massoud Bozorgian — the bastard who stuck his gun in your

298

mouth. Travers says he's a brigadier general in the Iranian Revolutionary Guards. I think it was Bozorgian who killed Nelson.'

'Is he taking the flasks of red mercury to the missile base in Iran?'

'It's not just a missile base; it's where the Iranians are assembling their new warheads.'

'But will Bozorgian or Rajavi be on the convoy?'

'Maybe. Stop asking questions.' He jumped to his feet. 'Come on. Let's see if the water's warm enough for us to swim.'

She shook her head.

'Why not?'

'Because I don't want to.' She began to smile and then burst out laughing. 'There, that's what you've been waiting for me to say, isn't it?'

This was the moment, Farrell decided, right now — before her mood changed again and while the sunlight was still in her hair. Reaching into his pocket he took out the ear-rings and gave them to her. 'These are yours,' he said. 'I've been carrying them around the world with me.'

'Oh. Thank you.' She was embarrassed.

'Aren't you pleased?'

'Of course I am. I haven't anything to give you, though.'

'That's not what you said last night.'

She smiled again, standing up now to face him so he could help her put the ear-rings on.

There was no need for Farrell to check. Already they were catching the light, and already, where the silver pendants lay against her skin, he could see the diamonds sparkling.

12

Farrell already knew this was the one. With the taste of spray on his lips, and the full-throated roar of the diesels filling the cockpit with noise he spun the wheel, pushing the hull in to a long turn.

There was no pounding, no skipping, just a slight delay when he opened the throttles wide to commence the run back to the marina. He felt exhilarated, pleased to be back at sea in a boat that had the performance to match its specifications. It was a two-year-old Bluefin called the *Seawraith*, forty-eight feet long, fitted with twin Cummins diesels — the kind of boat that Farrell knew Nelson would have jumped at if he'd ever had the chance.

Ahead of them now, the chunky irregular skyline of Kuwait City was gleaming in the sun on a haze-free morning. At this time of year, when there were no dust storms and the north-west *shimal* wind had died away, visibility was often good, but today, except for some smog over the downtown area, the air was as clear as Farrell had ever seen it.

He cut back his speed, relieved to have

301

found what he wanted after wasting so much time evaluating boats that should have had more than enough power, but which for one reason or another had turned out to be disappointing.

Behind him in the cockpit, where Almira was continuing to ignore the agent from the charter company, Ali-Khaleefa seemed to have overcome his trepidation at venturing off-shore into, what for him was the foreign environment of the Gulf.

He came forward to study the instrument panel. 'The boat is good, I think,' he said. 'We shall use this one, yes?'

Farrell grinned at him. 'I thought you'd like it.'

'For a short while you will permit me to steer perhaps?'

Farrell gave him the wheel, glad that he'd asked. Although the Omani's face was more deeply lined and he occasionally seemed to be in pain, throughout the three days he'd been in Kuwait, as well as working tirelessly to locate boatyards, he had become more outgoing and more confident at sea.

Leaving him to refine his helmsmanship, Farrell went to open negotiations with the agent — a smooth-talking Arab who had spent much of the trip trying not to look at Almira.

'OK,' Farrell said. 'I'll need exclusive, unrestricted use from tomorrow onwards for the next three weeks. If you want to charge an extra premium for insurance because you don't know who I am, that's fine. And if the owners are worried about engine hours, I don't mind paying for anything over the first hundred.'

'You will provide your own crew?' The agent wrote something in his notebook.

'Yes. I'll arrange for a maintenance check and for fresh water and for all the fuel as well.'

'The boat is owned by a Kuwaiti company which imports desalination equipment for distribution in the Middle East. Until I have spoken on the phone with the president I cannot be sure of the cost for a three-week charter.'

'You don't have to be sure,' Farrell said. 'As long as you treat this as a straight deal, the cost doesn't matter much. If you'd like to draw up an agreement I'll have my representative call by your office with a cheque before nine o'clock tonight. How does that sound?'

The agent could not have been more pleased. 'I am glad to do this business with you,' he said.

'Good.' Farrell shook his hand. 'Don't be

surprised if the boat spends most of its time at the marina. We won't be going out very often.'

'Of course.' The agent swivelled his eyes back to Almira. 'I am certain you and your wife will have a most pleasant time.'

'We will.' Hoping Almira would keep her thoughts to herself, Farrell went to relieve Ali-Khaleefa leaving her to entertain the agent for the remainder of the return journey to the marina.

Although they made good time, it was gone four o'clock before the *Seawraith* had been tied up at its berth again and they were driving back through town on their way to drop Ali-Khaleefa at his hotel. Almira was at the wheel of the rental ute, a near-new Nissan double-cab equipped with a glass-fibre canopy and tinted windows.

'I can't remember where to go.' She swerved in front of a bus.

Farrell issued directions while she tried to avoid the worst of the traffic along the harbour front.

'What was all that about your representative signing the agreement?' she asked.

'You know what it's about.' Opening the glove compartment, he took out the fax that had been waiting for them on their arrival at the hotel. Despite the lack of a signature, each time he looked at it he could almost see Travers sitting at a desk somewhere. Farrell read the message out loud to her. 'Essential suitable vessel is selected not later than November twenty-sixth for hire, charter or purchase by your representative. Call your contact number to confirm compliance with these instructions prior to the above date.'

'Oh. So are you going to phone?'

'Soon as we get back.' Farrell pointed to a side street. 'Down there and round by the fountain.'

Ali-Khaleefa stopped her at the next corner. 'From here I can walk,' he said. 'You will collect me at nine o'clock tomorrow, yes?'

'Right.' Farrell twisted round in his seat. 'You know you can always get a room in our hotel if you'd rather,' he said. 'I can't see it matters if Travers finds out you're in Kuwait with us.'

Ali-Khaleefa shook his head. 'By myself I can drink much whiskey and enjoy a pretty girl without you knowing. A gentleman I have met assures me that these things are possible in Kuwait if you are careful how you ask.' He climbed out of the ute grinning at Almira. 'You will not tell your father this?'

She laughed. 'I will if you're not ready in the morning.' She reentered the stream of cars and buses, driving confidently through the downtown congestion until they reached the underground carpark of the Concord Plaza.

As soon as they were alone in the elevator she pretended to flirt with Farrell, but once inside their suite she disappeared into the shower leaving him to make his phone call to the contact number.

The woman who answered spoke impeccable English and sounded as though she had been expecting to hear from him. 'I'm so pleased you called,' she said. 'We have new information. Would it be all right if I brought it round to your hotel?'

'Sure.'

'I'll see you later this evening, then. Goodbye.'

Farrell was left wondering who she was, what information she had and why she hadn't enquired about the charter. He was trying to decide how best to approach the subject of more money when Almira emerged from the bathroom. She was drying her hair and wearing nothing but one of his shirts.

'Well?' She sat down close to him on the bed. 'What have you found out?'

'A woman's bringing some stuff round. Things could be starting to move.'

'Am I supposed to be happy about that?'

Farrell knew what was coming next. 'Don't start,' he said. 'I've told you twenty times. You're not going with us and that's the end of it. Go and put some clothes on.'

'Don't you want to take me to bed?'

Tempting though the idea was, he discounted it. Since their arrival at the hotel they had spent nearly as much time in bed as they had done looking at boats, and even if they weren't expecting a visitor, he'd already decided this evening was an opportunity for them to catch their breath.

She lit a cigarette. 'Guess what I missed most? Besides you, I mean.'

'Those.'

She nodded. 'Cigarettes are hard currency in jail. You can buy anything you want with them. Before I was moved I had to trade four whole packets a day for protection — you know, so I wasn't raped by other women.' She paused. 'I suppose I missed lots of other things too — like Aunt Latifa, my father and my dogs.'

'It's over with,' Farrell said quietly.

'I know. If we went to live on a Greek island somewhere, Aunt Latifa could send my dogs, couldn't she?'

'All I ever said was that we could spend a few days having a look around.'

'That was four months ago. Everything's

different now. If I'm not allowed to go with you on the *Seawraith*, you have to find me an island — unless I can persuade you to take me on the boat and to Greece as well. Look at me a minute.'

He was quick enough to prevent her from slipping off the shirt, but too slow to escape.

Pushing him down on the bed she sat on his legs and began unbuckling his belt. 'We could catch a plane tomorrow,' she said. 'Wouldn't that be wonderful?'

'Ali-Khaleefa might feel a bit let down, don't you think?'

'I washed my hair specially for you, but you haven't even noticed.' She allowed herself to go limp and fell on top of him. 'My father had a talk with me before we left.'

'About you behaving yourself?'

'He wanted me to know that he'll pay the hospital bills if Ali-Khaleefa gets really sick.'

'It won't be that quick. Is that all you talked about?'

She shook her head. 'I know he's given you his *KHANJAR* because he thinks you're an honourable man, and he told me he's making Salim go in the army.'

Farrell tried to imagine Salim in the army. 'Why didn't you say before?'

'We haven't talked properly before. We've either been rushing around or you've been too busy taking off my clothes — well, up to now you have.'

'Are you going to get off me?' he enquired.

'No.' She pinned him down by his shoulders. 'Not unless you answer a question. I want to know if you went to see your wife when you were in England.'

'Yes.'

'Was she pleased to see you? What happened? Did you make love to her?'

'No.' He replied without thinking, more unsettled by his lie than by her questions.

'I don't believe you.' She rolled off on to the bed. 'Still, it doesn't make any difference whether I do or not.'

'Meaning what?'

'The first day I was in jail the wardens made up a joke about my arm. They said only a Jew or a blind man would ever want to touch me, and then only if I was in a dark room.'

'They're wrong. How often have I told you?'

'If you'd spent half your life listening to Aunt Latifa and my father saying how sorry they are for you, you'd understand. Every time you look at me I wonder what you see and whether you're comparing me with your wife and other women.'

'Why the hell would I compare you with

anyone? I don't need to.'

'But your wife was really pretty. Tony told me she was. He said you were crazy about her.'

Farrell tried without success to make her face him. 'Listen,' he said. 'Do you remember how you used to make fun of Nelson's three wise sayings?'

'About never passing up an opportunity, remembering where you are and never going back to anywhere you've been before? I don't think they're very wise.'

'They are if you make your living shipping guns across the Gulf of Oman.'

'What's that got to do with your wife?'

'Nothing. I'm talking about us. The same rules work for you and me. We're not going to miss this opportunity; we both know where we are with each other, and neither of us is going back to anywhere or anyone. You're stuck with me and I'm stuck with you, arm and all.'

'But you're still leaving me behind when you take the *Seawraith* to Iran, aren't you?'

'Yes. And you're still putting on some clothes before our visitor arrives.'

'Only if you help me.' She seemed to suddenly regain her confidence, wrinkling her nose at him before getting off the bed.

Farrell watched her walk to the bedroom,

distracted by the shirt and by her smile as she turned to close the door behind her.

It took him less than a minute to decide to join her, but his intentions were frustrated by a telephone call to say that a lady was waiting to see him in the lobby.

He asked the man on the desk to send her up, then, after leaving the door to the suite ajar, he went to stand outside on the balcony. From the eleventh floor the noise from the traffic was barely audible, but he could smell the exhaust fumes, and the pollution hanging over the downtown area was worse than it had been this morning. Through the smog, here and there he could pick out some of the 200 mosques that were dotted around. They were everywhere, their domes standing out from the modern architecture in a city having more places to worship than it had trees.

He began counting the domes, but was interrupted by a knock on the door.

'It's open,' Farrell said.

The woman who came into the room was the receptionist from the London office of American Travel. She was carrying a briefcase and had a long cardboard tube under her arm.

Farrell took the tube from her. 'I didn't know it would be you,' he said.

'I should've explained on the phone. I'm

311

Rebecca Harris. Hello again.'

'You're my local representative?'

'American Travel, Kuwait, at your service.' She gave him a business card. 'We're arranging your hotel accommodation, the boat charter and, of course, we're supplying the explosives.' She smiled. 'With American Travel, you never travel alone. Isn't that nice?'

'Do you do this sort of thing all the time?' Farrell put the tube on the table.

'Only if we have someone operating in the Middle East. Mostly I'm stuck in England. Is Miss Muammar here?'

'She's in the other room, why?'

'I'm supposed to collect your passports before I start your briefing, but it doesn't matter. Perhaps you could give me the details of the boat first.'

'It's a forty-eight foot Bluefin fitted with three hundred horse-power diesels and long-range tanks. I've told the agent you'll be calling round to his office with a cheque.' Farrell handed her the brochure from the charter company. 'The boat's called the *Seawraith*.'

'What a lovely name. I do hope we get good advance intelligence — you know, so you don't have to rush. It's an awfully long way for you to go, isn't it?'

'As long as the weather holds, distance

doesn't matter,' Farrell said. 'Time's the problem. What are the chances of me getting over there the night before? It's going to be tough deciding how to play things if I've only got a few hours to have a look around.'

'I'm not sure how much notice you can expect. I can check for you, though. We think the flasks are arriving in Tehran two or three days from now. That means you'll have to be ready on the night of the twenty-ninth or the thirtieth. Is that all right?'

'I can leave Kuwait by the morning if I have to, but you haven't got the detonator for me yet.'

'It's a special high-energy percussion unit called a Maverick. It's being flown in from Britain tomorrow. Richard Travers says you can expect a hundred per cent result as long as it's placed within one foot of any flask of red mercury.'

'Assuming I can stop the damn convoy to begin with,' Farrell said. 'For all I know I'll be working out in the open with no cover.'

'I can show you what the area's like. I've brought new satellite photos, the best maps we have of the Khvormuj region and charts of Iran's western seaboard along the Gulf.' She emptied the contents of the cardboard tube on to the table, smoothing out the maps and charts before arranging them in order.

Farrell was inspecting a map when Almira chose to make her entrance. She was wearing a collar of braided gold around her throat and was dressed in jeans and a white silk jacket. Her expression was a warning of approaching trouble.

'This is Rebecca Harris from American Travel,' Farrell said.

'Really.' Almira ignored her. 'I thought you said she worked for the American National Security Council.'

'I do.' Rebecca studied Almira with interest. 'After hearing so much about you from Mr Travers it's nice to be able to say hello.'

'Well, now you have, and now you've delivered whatever it is you've come to deliver, you can write down a message for your Mr Travers. Tell him that if he'd come here instead of sending you, I'd have clawed his eyes out for taking away four months of my life, and that if I could stop his project, I would. I don't know how you've got the nerve to even speak to me. Look at you, all made up with mascara and lipstick, pretending to be so smart because you have this terribly important job. But you're not smart at all. You see, Ms Rebecca Harris, when this is over and you've been put back in your little box, your life is going to be as boring as it's always been — but mine isn't because I've got something you'll never have.'

The lady from American Travel appeared to be unconcerned. 'I'm sorry about what happened to you,' she said. 'But you're wrong: I don't have to pretend my job's important — I know it is. If Iran ever launches red mercury warheads against Israel, half the Middle East will go up in flames. I might be able to do something to help stop that.'

'You'd better carry on telling Farrell how lucky he is to be working for you then, hadn't you?' Almira collected the car keys from an ashtray on the table. 'Of course, you might only think he's working for you. Why don't you ask him if there's another reason why he's going to Iran?'

Farrell stopped her from saying any more. 'Have you finished?' he said.

'Yes.' She stood on tiptoe and kissed him hard on the mouth. 'I'm going out. Don't forget to hand over my passport. I wouldn't want Ms Harris to be worrying about anything while you're saving the Middle East from burning to the ground.'

When she'd gone Farrell slumped down in to a chair. 'I'm sorry,' he said. 'She's had a pretty rough time.'

'Yes, she has. When I was being briefed in

London Mr Travers told me how extraordinarily attractive she was, but I had no idea. She is quite stunning, isn't she? What did she mean about another reason for you accepting the project?'

'Rajavi and Bozorgian.' Farrell paused. 'I've got a bit of unfinished business with Mr Anatoli bloody Volchek too.'

'We're arranging for Volchek to be delayed in Tehran for a few days. If things turn out well, we'll be leaking disinformation to the Iranians to implicate Intech in the explosion. It's a way for us to choke off the red mercury supply route from Moscow. You know, you really shouldn't be worrying about these people from Intech when you have so much else on your mind.'

'I'm not worrying,' Farrell said. 'Is it OK if we go over my list of equipment now? I can get the stuff myself but not without more cash.'

'I'm not sure I understand.'

'Infra-red imaging scanner, long range acoustic detectors, halogen lights, night-vision binoculars, a Zodiac inflatable and I'll need a separate supply of detonators and some Semtex high-explosive. I might take a grenade launcher and some other bits and pieces as well.'

She raised her eyebrows. 'Is that all?'

'You don't want the *Seawraith* ending up

like the *Stingray*, do you?'

'Oh, I see. Of course not. Perhaps I do spend too much time in my little box. You make it sound so matter of fact.'

Farrell knew he had been playing down the risks — not for her benefit, but for his own — a way to persuade himself that equipment could compensate for a plan that was still full of holes.

He started examining the satellite photos, only half listening to what she was saying while he endeavoured to picture what the road or the cliffs would look like in the dark and wondering if Travers already had someone working on a fall-back solution.

By 10.30 he had made some progress towards refining his plan and with the help of the maps and charts his options had been gradually narrowed down to the point where he was ready to call it a day.

He accompanied Rebecca down to the lobby, said goodbye to her, then returned to the suite where he lay down on the bed to consider what advantage the tide and moon might offer if the 29th was to be the night.

Although he was still awake when he heard Almira let herself in, he kept his eyes shut until she came into the room and sat down beside him.

'Where have you been?' he asked.

'To see Ali-Khaleefa. We drove to the Sief palace and out to the harbour. He's really happy about going with you. He didn't say so, but I know he is.'

'That was some performance you put on for Rebecca Harris.'

'Mm.' She unfastened her gold collar. 'Are you too sleepy for me to apologize?'

Farrell thought he might be but the longer he looked at her the less certain he became, and when she leaned over to touch her lips against his, he found he was hardly sleepy at all.

★ ★ ★

Two weeks before, in London, Farrell had spent an entire weekend expecting the phone to ring. Then, when the call from Travers had finally come, it had signalled an end to the waiting. But the call this evening had left him flat. There was no relief, no excitement, only a vague sense of uneasiness.

He replaced the receiver, aware of the expression on Almira's face.

'When?' she asked.

'A hundred and sixty flasks left Tehran Wednesday evening. There's just one truck. It stops in Esfahan on Thursday and in Shiraz on Friday.'

'And travels down through Bushehr to the complex on Friday night. Is that what you've been told?'

He nodded. 'Rajavi and Bozorgian were identified coming out of some building called the Karim Khan 40 in Tehran. According to Rebecca, it's the headquarters of Iran's Vevak Intelligence and Security Ministry. You might not like Rebecca much, but she's doing a pretty damn good job.'

'No she's not. She's doing what she gets paid for. What about the escort?'

'Three guards from the QUDS Branch of the Revolutionary Guards — that's the outfit the Iranians call their Jerusalem Force. Nelson did business with them once.'

He picked up the Maverick percussion detonator and began zeroing the two digital timers on the side.

'Stop it.' Almira knocked the case out of his hands. 'Ever since that woman brought it over here you've been playing with those buttons. If you're not doing that you're on the *Seawraith* stripping down the guns you bought. Can't you see how on edge you are?'

'I'm fine.' He left her and went out on to the balcony. Where the sun had set, a thin band of cloud was still catching the light, but across the rest of the city the sky had turned a deep violet colour. He watched the cloud disappear into nothing, his mind already on tomorrow when he would be watching the sun go down on the other side of the Gulf.

She came to stand beside him, but seemed unwilling to reopen their conversation.

'At least there'll be time to set something up.' He kept his eyes on the sky. 'Having an extra night over there will make a hell of a difference.'

'Is that a clever way to say you're leaving in the morning?'

'Yes.'

'Suppose I'm not here when you get back?'

'Then you miss out on two hundred thousand dollars and a trip to Greece.'

'Farrell.' She stepped in front of him. 'Don't go.'

'It'll be OK. I'll be back with Ali-Khaleefa by Saturday evening. You're worrying about nothing. If it looks too hard or too dangerous, I won't try.'

'Yes you will. I know how you think. This is more important to you than I am. You can't forget Tony anymore than you can forget your pretty wife in England. You don't even want to forget them, do you?'

Because he knew that, if anything, she was more on edge than he was, he moved her out of the way and returned to the room intending to make his call to Ali-Khaleefa.

But she followed him inside and ripped the plug out of its socket.

'Now what?' Farrell said.

'If you're about to organize your crew, don't bother. I'll go and see Ali-Khaleefa. I don't want to spend the whole evening watching you fiddling with the timers on that stupid detonator thing.' She snatched up the car keys. 'Perhaps Ali-Khaleefa can explain why you don't care about me.'

'After he's done that, tell him to be ready at seven sharp in the morning. I need to be out of Kuwait Bay before nine.' Farrell grinned at her. 'If I gave your father back his *KHANJAR*, do you think he'd take you back as well?'

'If that's what you want.' She left the room, slamming the door behind her.

Farrell was not surprised. The tension had been building up between them all day and it was probably best for her to get out of the hotel for a few hours, he thought. And if anyone could calm her down, it would be Ali-Khaleefa.

Removing the Maverick from its box, he switched on the illuminated display and began to experiment again. Although the case was nearly nine inches long, the programming buttons were tiny and set too closely together for him to set the timers reliably if

321

he hurried. Which meant he had better not be in a hurry. Or if he was, he'd have to be damn careful not to make a mistake.

He tried twice more using his little finger, then his fingernail, finally abandoning the exercise when he realized he was doing precisely what Almira had predicted he would be doing.

Annoyed with himself and unwilling to remain alone in the hotel when his time could be spent more usefully checking things on the *Seawraith*, shortly before 8.30 he put the Maverick back in its box and went downstairs to summon a taxi.

It was dark when he arrived at the marina. On board a new yacht that was berthed at the end of pontoon fourteen, two Americans were having an argument and one of the larger launches had an engine ticking over, but otherwise the whole area was quiet.

He was halfway out on pontoon twenty-three when he saw a light flickering at a cabin window. Because the moon was throwing shadows from masts and spars onto the boats, it was difficult to know if the light was coming from the *Seawraith*, but Farrell was sure it was.

Keeping in the shadows he moved further along the pontoon until his suspicions were confirmed.

On her knees, crouched over a fuel tank holding a flashlight in one hand, Almira was using a wrench in a clumsy attempt to unscrew one of the filler caps.

For a second Farrell was too astonished to understand. Only when she had managed to remove the cap and began pouring something from a can into the tank did he realize what was happening.

Hoping to stop her in time, he shouted as he jumped on to the deck and swung himself inside the cockpit.

She scrambled to her feet, so frightened she couldn't speak.

'What the bloody hell do you think you're doing?' He wrenched the can out of her hand. It contained treacle — sweet, sticky syrup that he could smell and feel tacky against his fingers. There were other cans, three of them by her feet, unused, but with their lids off ready.

'You followed me.' She stuttered out the words.

Discovering that she'd resort to sabotage to stop him going had come as a shock. But it was the extent of her guilt that he found disturbing. She was biting her lip, clearly convinced he'd tailed her here from the hotel. He switched on the cabin lights in order to see her better.

'I knew Salim would tell you.' Her eyes clouded over. 'That's why you followed me, isn't it?'

Before he could ask for an explanation she made it worse. 'You've known all along.' She covered her face with her hands. 'You've been pretending ever since we left Muscat — because you knew the longer we were together — the more often we went to bed, the more you'd be able to hurt me.'

Farrell was bewildered, sensing he was on the verge of uncovering something too awful to contemplate. 'Why?' he asked.

She dropped her hands, but her legs seemed to buckle from under her and she slid down awkwardly against the bulkhead. 'Because I had to stop you from ever getting to Iran. I didn't know how to, so I gave a hundred dollars to a man in a chandler's shop. He said treacle would wreck the fuel injectors after two or three hours running. I thought if the engines failed while you were at sea you'd never be able to get back here in time to make repairs. It was the only way I could be sure nothing would happen to you.'

Farrell remained silent.

'You have to believe me,' she whispered. 'Whatever Salim told you about the game, I swear it was over before I ever made love with you.'

'Game?'

'I never really played it. You didn't give me a chance. As soon as I realized I was falling in love with you I gave my brother a cheque to pay off my part of the bet and I told Rajavi I wouldn't give him anymore information. You can't think I was trying to sabotage the *Seawraith* because I'm still working for Intech — not after all those things I've said to you.'

Farrell clenched his teeth. 'Maybe Salim didn't give me the whole story on the game.'

'He wouldn't — not if he thought he could still spoil things for me — between you and me, I mean.'

'When did this game of yours start?'

'The day after Volchek and Rajavi called to see my father about the emeralds. I overheard what they said, so I went to see Rajavi and told him the box had been thrown overboard from the *Stingray* — you know, because I thought it'd be exciting to help search for it. But I made the mistake of telling my brother what I'd done. That's when he came up with the idea of the game.'

She had been speaking so quietly he could hardly hear her. Now her voice tailed away to nothing.

'Go on,' Farrell said.

'Salim said it would be like playing chess, but using real people. I was supposed to get information from you that I could pass on to Rajavi while Salim helped Travers. My brother and I bet each other twelve thousand American dollars. If Intech had got back their red mercury, I would've won. If Travers had found it first, Salim would have won.' She stopped, red-faced and humiliated. 'Spoilt rich kids looking for kicks. That's what you think, isn't it?'

A minute ago he had been too numb to think, but now rage had taken over. Barely aware of what he was doing, he hurled the can of treacle at her. It missed her by less than an inch, spraying its contents across her face and down the front of her blouse.

'What in God's name were you thinking of?' he yelled. 'Tony Nelson died because of your fucking game.'

She curled up into a ball, pressing herself back between the bulkhead and the fuel tank surround. 'Farrell, please. Please, you have to listen to me. I'd stopped helping Rajavi days before that happened. Bozorgian already knew you and Tony had the flasks. You told me Bozorgian saw us at Khabura. I swear by the holy Koran and on the grave of my mother that I never did anything to hurt Tony or hurt you. All I ever did was talk to Rajavi about the box.'

Her words were without effect. In England,

night after night, Farrell had sought to dispel images of her that had been made erotic by her innocence. Now, instead of innocence, all he could see in her eyes was the reflection of his own disillusionment.

'You didn't give information to Intech,' he said. 'You sold it to them, didn't you?'

'No. I told Rajavi what he wanted to know for nothing — because I wanted to win the game. But that was before you changed everything for me — on that afternoon when you asked me to dinner. Before then I couldn't believe you'd want to go out with someone like me.'

'You offered me five thousand dollars to take you to Khabura.'

'Because I wasn't certain you were serious. It was an excuse for me to see you again.'

The picture forming in Farrell's mind was nearly complete. One by one, pieces of the jigsaw were falling into place — her reaction at the news of Nelson's murder; the reason why her life had been spared at the mountain village, and why, nine days ago at the villa when, instead of being eager to greet him, she had stayed in her bedroom expecting him to confront her with the truth.

'How the hell do I know if you're lying or not?' he said.

She began crying, trying ineffectually to

wipe away the mess of treacle from her face.

Farrell ignored her tears. 'You're no better than your shithead brother,' he said. 'You're just a whore. Did you pose for that photograph with Bozorgian in my apartment?'

'How can you talk to me like that? You can't — not when I haven't done anything wrong — not when I've been waiting my whole life to feel the way I feel about you. Farrell, I've been in love with you since that first night you kissed me. That's why I've always been too scared to tell you about the game.'

'Pity you couldn't win it. Unless, of course, you're still trying. Or is Intech paying you to stuff up the *Seawraith*?'

She stood up. 'If you think that, you might as well go ahead and kill me. Blame me for Tony Nelson if that's what you want.'

The despair in her face told him he had gone too far. His doubts were making him accuse her of betraying him when there was no evidence that she ever had. Whatever she'd done, however foolish she had been, Farrell knew he had to stop this — before the wounds became too deep — before he lost her completely. Now his rage had eased he wanted to forgive her, to admit he was being unreasonable, to hold her in his arms but somehow he couldn't find a way to do it.

She met his eyes. 'Salim never told you about the game at all, did he?'

'No.'

'Then you haven't been waiting to hurt me?'

'Don't be bloody silly.'

She looked away. 'So what happens about us?'

'Nothing. We go back to the hotel. It's less than nine hours before I leave and I need to get some sleep.'

'After saying such dreadful things to me aren't you frightened I might phone someone the minute you're gone?'

'Not now. You've just bought yourself a return ticket to Iran.'

'Oh.' She was too distressed to be relieved. 'Does that mean you don't trust me?'

'It means I think you're too strung out to be stuck in the hotel by yourself for three days.'

'But do you believe me?'

'I don't know.' He gathered up the cans of treacle. 'I guess I can always ask Rajavi when I see him.'

'Farrell, stop it, please. Whatever else you think, you must know I've always been in love with you — you must know that.'

To persuade himself, he left the cabin and

went to stand outside on the foredeck alone. The moon was higher now, casting a swathe of yellow light over the water to form an illuminated pathway. It was quite distinct, beginning at his feet and extending out across the Gulf in the clear night air. But when he strained his eyes towards the horizon, he found the end of the path was just too far away for him to see.

13

Everything was quiet. Riding at anchor on a glass-like sea the *Seawraith* was motionless, and now the midday tide had turned, the breeze had died leaving the air breathless and oppressive. On the shoreline 500 yards away where tiny waves had been breaking, all that remained were ripples, and even the flamingos had stopped feeding in the shallows of the lagoon.

After the ten-hour trip across the Gulf yesterday, and an exhausting night spent scaling the cliffs above the road, Farrell found the silence unnerving. Enforced idleness wasn't helping either. Although he hadn't expected the wait for tonight to be easy, the combination of silence and inactivity was making the time drag. He was also weary of examining his motives for coming. Even if the plan worked, what would he have accomplished? he wondered. Was he here for the reason Almira thought he was here? Or was it for the money — for their future together — for some half-imagined life he had promised her? He didn't know anymore.

Having spent the past thirty-six hours

331

endeavouring to put aside his distrust, to convince himself beyond question that she had told him the truth, by daybreak this morning he had reached only one conclusion: that it didn't matter what he thought. The attraction was still there, and because of it, because whenever she was with him his fascination with her was no less than it had been a day, or a week, or a month ago, he had discovered he could make himself believe whatever he wanted to believe.

He was considering whether or not he should let her sleep on when the smell of cigarette smoke told him Ali-Khaleefa was up and about.

Squinting in the sunlight the Omani came forward to join Farrell at the bow. 'You have been keeping watch?' he asked.

'Sort of. I'm not sure what for, though. Are you OK after last night?'

'A little stiff, but now we know where we will create the rockfalls, tonight will not be so hard, I think.'

'But more dangerous,' Farrell said. 'Whatever you do, don't give Almira the idea she can go with us again. She's going to damn well stay here even if I have to tie her up.'

Ali-Khaleefa drew on his cigarette. 'She has told me of her indiscretion and that now you may doubt her affection for you. So she fears you may not go through with what you have planned. She is frightened you may risk your life by first questioning Rajavi about her before killing him and the man Bozorgian to avenge the death of your friend.'

'Does she think the nice guards from the Iranian Jerusalem Force are going to stand around while I have a chat with Rajavi?'

'With Miss Almira it is often not possible to know what is inside her head. You must understand that for seven years she has waited for the happiness she says you have brought to her. Therefore I am sure she thinks only of herself and of you.' Ali-Khaleefa paused. 'I can tell you she knows you will never again take her into your bed if you are uncertain of her faithfulness.'

'Yeah, well, maybe she should've told me about the bet she made with her brother before things got out of hand.'

'But you cannot think she tries to sabotage the boat because still she has some contact with the men from Intech?'

'No. I just wish like hell I knew when she stopped. Her father only got half of the story. He knows Salim sold information to Travers and the Omani Security Service, but he never guessed his daughter was trying to win a game by doing business with Rajavi.'

'It is best he does not learn of such a thing.'

Ali-Khaleefa stopped talking abruptly and held up a hand. 'There are vehicles. Can you not hear them?'

Farrell was looking rather than listening, wondering if he should have anchored the *Seawraith* further off-shore where its presence would be less suspicious. Twice this morning trucks had lumbered by on the coast road, on both occasions heading away from the complex. But this sound was louder, and it was coming from the north.

There were five trucks in all, Iranian Army Mercedes painted in desert camouflage, travelling in an untidy convoy with the drivers eating the dust from the truck in front. They were in the middle of the road, moving slowly along the far side of the lagoon, disturbing some of the birds which took off to circle before returning to land among the reeds.

None of the drivers waved, evidently no more interested in the *Seawraith* than they were in the flamingos or the pelicans.

Ali-Khaleefa dropped his cigarette overboard. 'Tonight when the driver and the guards must stop to clear away the rocks we shall blast from the cliff, you are certain the truck will contain the red mercury?'

'Who knows?' Farrell said. 'I guess there's chance we could stop the wrong one. Are you getting jumpy?'

Ali-Khaleefa shook his head. 'Last night for over nine hours while we search for the two places to do our blasting, there is no traffic on the road, so I think we will be lucky. To be sure of this luck, at sunset yesterday and again this morning at daybreak when I kneel towards Mecca, I have prayed for good fortune in what we do. This cannot guarantee success for us, but by the grace of Allah and with our automatic rifles, we will together avoid the mistakes we have made before.'

Farrell thought so too. 'I'd better get Almira,' he said. 'She's been asleep long enough.'

It was unnecessary for him to fetch her. Awoken by the noise of the trucks she was already climbing the companionway, staring apprehensively towards the coast.

'What's happening?' she asked.

'Nothing,' Farrell said. 'Bit of local traffic. You missed it.'

'Oh.' Without thinking, she began to smile at him, but stopped herself in time. 'Is it all right if I swim? My hair's full of grit and dust from climbing those cliffs.'

'This isn't a cruise; you've got work to do. I'm giving you a crash course on how to handle the *Seawraith*. Having you along means that Ali-Khaleefa and I won't have to go so far in the Zodiac tonight. You can be our mobile base.'

'To make me feel useful? Have you been thinking of how to keep me on board?'

'Jesus.' Farrell was in no mood for this. 'You and I better have a talk.' He led her away. 'Listen,' he said. 'We're not playing another one of your bloody games. If you don't want to help, just say so.'

She flushed. 'I didn't mean it to sound like that. You're still angry with me, aren't you?'

'Not particularly.'

'Yes you are. You haven't touched me since we left the hotel yesterday morning. You've hardly even spoken to me.'

'What would you like me to say?'

'I need to know everything's all right with us.'

'Everything's fine,' Farrell said.

'How am I supposed to tell you I'm sorry if you won't let me?'

'This isn't exactly the right time, is it?'

'I don't care.'

He'd always known she was sorry, but when she leaned forwards and parted her lips to kiss him, he began to understand what she had really been trying to say. Although the taste of her and the fragrance of her skin were as seductive as ever, it was the soft, submissive way she offered her mouth that told him she was not only seeking forgiveness, but endeavouring to prove he could no more distrust her than he could resist her. Her kiss reinforced what Farrell already knew — that nothing had changed. The spell she cast was unbroken and would remain unbroken, because to doubt the existence of the spell would be even worse than doubting her.

For several minutes he held her to him, conscious of the sun warm on his back, running his fingers through the tangles in her hair while he watched a solitary flamingo take off from the lagoon.

Not for another twenty-four hours would he have cause to wonder why he kept his eyes on the flamingo for so long and to remember another time when, months ago in the Hajar mountains, he had watched a dragonfly disappear against the blueness of the sky.

★ ★ ★

A brilliant flash of light was followed by the crack of the blast reverberating out across the Gulf. A moment later, from the moonlit clifftop where they had been dislodged, more than a dozen rocks began their descent.

Gathering debris with them they created a fifty-foot-long avalanche that hit the base of the cliff in a cloud of dust. One of the rocks kept going. It was the size of a television set, rolling end over end across the road before it tipped over the edge to land in the water not far from where Ali-Khaleefa was standing.

'You use too much of the Semtex, I think.' Using the boulders of the sea-wall as steps, the Omani climbed up on to the roadside to inspect their handiwork.

Farrell accompanied him, switching on a halogen light to check on the depth of the rubble. Much of it was clay or fractured chips, and, because the rocks themselves were mostly of a size that could be driven over, the end result was better than he'd hoped for.

'We shall clear a way through, yes?' Ali-Khaleefa spat out a mouthful of dust.

'No. This isn't going to hold them up. It's worked out pretty well — just enough of a warning so they won't be suspicious when they come across the real roadblock.' Farrell inspected his watch. 'Let's find out if we can do it again.'

'So now we go one mile further on to do the same?'

'Except for trying to knock a few bigger rocks down.' Farrell directed his light seawards to alert Almira. 'I suppose we might as well get on with it.'

Ali-Khaleefa pushed the Zodiac in to deeper water, holding it steady for Farrell to

338

get in before he clambered over the side himself. 'You wish me to start the outboard engine?' he asked.

'It's not worth the trouble.' Farrell began using one of the oars as a paddle. 'Get ready to yell at Almira if she comes in too close.'

In the moonlight he could already pick out the white hull of the *Seawraith* coming to collect them, but Almira was being careful to follow instructions, keeping well clear of the reef and the rock out-crops that had been evident at low tide this afternoon.

Reducing the speed of the engines to an idle, she let the boat drift forwards until the Zodiac was alongside and she was able to catch the rope Farrell threw to her. For the first time since leaving Kuwait her eyes were bright, and when she held out a hand to help him on board, there was a real smile on her lips.

'That was an awfully loud bang,' she said. 'Aren't you worried about the noise?'

He shook his head. 'We're over fifteen miles from the complex and Travers says it's buried at the end of a valley. I don't think anyone will hear anything.'

'Are we going to the river-mouth right away?' She glanced at him. 'I can take us there.'

'Do you figure you can find it in the dark

without running aground?'

'It's not dark — not with the moon. I'll be able to see the headland and the bridge. Anyway, I know how to use the compass and the depth finder. It's only the radar I can't work. I couldn't make any sense of the picture.'

'All you'll get from the coast is reflection off the cliffs and a lot of clutter.' He eased open the throttles for her. 'The radar might tell you if there are any boats sneaking up on you from behind, though.'

'There won't be pirates here, will there?' Her expression changed. 'You're not serious?'

'Wouldn't hurt to keep an eye on those.' Farrell pointed out to sea where two pinpoints of light were travelling east across the main shipping lane. 'But don't spend all your time looking over your shoulder while we're away.' He left her at the wheel while he went to change into his wet suit and collect the detonating unit.

Although his uneasiness of the last few days had gone, once down below in the cabin, to reassure himself, he removed the Maverick from its box and switched on the display for one last time.

The row of zeros on the screen had the wrong effect. Soon, in their place, there would be numbers — real numbers — hours, minutes and, if he chose to programme them in, even seconds. After that, and if he ever got around to pulling out the arming pin, when the display next registered its neat, identical row of zeros, the Maverick was going to vaporize a mountain.

But for what? Farrell wondered. To repay a debt to Nelson that no one could repay? Or for some other ill-defined reason that allowed him to justify the cost of what he was about to do?

He tried to visualize the explosion. By themselves, 160 flasks in the truck would generate a shock wave ten times more severe than the one at the village had been. But confined underground, surrounded by thousands of gallons of rocket fuel and God knows how many warheads of red mercury, the violence of the blast would be unimaginable. Then there were the people at the complex to consider — scientists, technicians, military personnel and all the support staff. How many of them would perish? Could he balance their lives against the millions of Israelis who would die if Iranian warheads were ever to rain down on Haifa and Tel Aviv — an equally unimaginable scenario that only someone like Travers could contemplate because no ordinary person could begin to comprehend what disaster on such a scale might be like.

And so there were no answers, Farrell thought. There never had been and there never could be. In a world where power was measured in megatons of blast energy, and where anyone could justify anything, the questions were as meaningless as the concepts of right and wrong.

He stopped trying to rationalize his feelings, ignoring the display on the Maverick while he put on his wet suit and gathered together the few other items of equipment that he'd decided to take with him.

Before he could leave the cabin a change in the note of the exhausts told him Almira had throttled back the engines. He hurried to the cockpit to find her concentrating hard on her navigation. She was holding the *Seawraith* a constant distance from the shore, keeping her speed well down as she endeavoured to pick out the headland in the distance.

Farrell went to check on her course. 'Are you OK?' he asked.

'Mm. Ali-Khaleefa says you're leaving me a rifle. Is that because you're worried about something?'

'Insurance. Do you know how to use an M16?' He slipped a clip into one of the rifles and gave it to her.

'Do I have to prove I can?'

'Go ahead.' Farrell took the wheel from her. 'As many rounds as you want — straight out to sea.'

'You don't believe me, do you?' Steadying herself against the side of the cockpit she pulled back the slide and flipped off the safety. 'Are you ready?'

His reply was drowned out by her burst of fire. She held the trigger down for nearly three seconds, controlling the muzzle well without flinching from either the recoil or the noise.

Ali-Khaleefa was grinning. 'Now you see,' he said. 'I have told you how for many years while she is growing up I have taught her this.'

Farrell was not altogether surprised. Months ago in the poisoned *falaj* and later, during their descent to the wadi, he had learned not to be surprised by anything she could do.

'OK,' he said. 'We're only about ten minutes away from the headland and the river, so this is where you get your last instructions. Promise me you'll do exactly what I'm going to tell you.'

'All right.' She put down the rifle, keeping her eyes on his face. 'I promise.'

'As soon as Ali-Khaleefa and I leave in the Zodiac you're to take the *Seawraith* at least a mile off-shore. If you think there's a chance of anyone seeing you from the road, head on out for another half a mile. Once you've decided where you want to be, you drop the anchor and you stay there.' Farrell paused. 'No cigarettes, no lights and no noise — and I mean that. You'll hear us blasting the rocks for the roadblock, but once we've finished things are going to get real quiet.'

'For how long?'

'If our friends left Shiraz at dusk we can expect the truck through around two o'clock in the morning — it depends on how good the road is. You'll see the headlights before we will, and you'll be able to see where the truck stops as well.'

'How will I know if it's the right one?'

'You won't,' Farrell said. 'Nor will we until I have a look. But there wasn't any traffic last night so I don't think there'll be any false alarms.'

'Do I come and pick you up right after it's gone?'

'Yeah — nice and slowly. You'll only need to get excited if we start flashing one of the lights straight at you. If that happens you might want to speed up a bit, but keep your eyes open and for Christ's sake don't hit the bottom.'

'Do I use the gun?' She sounded hesitant.

'If there's trouble, I mean.'

'Up to you. Same thing if another boat gets curious. We're not taking the grenade launcher so you'll have plenty of fire-power. Do you know how to load it?'

'Ali-Khaleefa's showed me. I don't understand why you're leaving it behind. What about all the other equipment we've brought with us — the things you told Rebecca Harris you had to have?'

'I didn't know what we'd need until we got here.' Farrell could see the headland clearly now, a dark forbidding mass of rock on the far side of the river estuary where the road became sandwiched between the cliffs and the shoreline. He could see the long steel bridge too — perhaps too clearly. Last night, when he'd selected the river-mouth as the best location, because the moon had still been rising, the bridge had seemed less exposed and nothing like as obvious.

He cut the engines and began passing packets of Semtex to Ali-Khaleefa for storage in the front of the inflatable. Almira waited until he picked up the other M16 before she came to say her goodbye. 'I still don't want you to go,' she said.

'Never pass up an opportunity — remember?'

'Why are you wearing a wet suit?'

'Because it's black. I have to get across the road to the truck and back again without anyone seeing me.'

'What if someone does?'

'I head for the Zodiac while Ali-Khaleefa covers me with the rifle. We'll be on our way for you to collect us before anyone knows what's happened.'

'And then we leave?'

'Sure.' He paused. 'This is where you get to wish me good luck.'

Reaching out, she drew her fingertips across his lips. 'Farrell, if you don't come back in one piece, I'll kill you. You know that, don't you?'

'Yeah, I know that.' He smiled at her, then, quickly, before she could make him promise to be careful, he went to join Ali-Khaleefa in the Zodiac and to prepare himself for the trip to the river, the bridge and for his long overdue appointment with Rajavi and Bozorgian.

★ ★ ★

Farrell's nerves were fraying. For nearly five hours they had been waiting, but still there were no lights and still the night was silent.

Leaving the shelter of the boulders on the beach, for the third time in the last ten minutes, he climbed up on to the road to look and to listen.

Now the moon had sunk lower over the Gulf, the shadows from the litter of rocks were long dark streaks giving the road surface the appearance of wash-board, and, at the base of the cliff where the rubble had piled up, a million particles of reflective grit were glinting in moonlight that was far too bright.

Farrell walked fifty yards north, turned round to face the bridge and tried to imagine he was a truck driver. Ahead of him the road-block looked more contrived that it had done an hour ago, but the overall effect was unaltered by the shadows, and the impression remained one of a natural hazard that could be overridden without difficulty once some of the rocks had been manhandled out of the way or pushed aside by the truck itself.

He retraced his steps and sat down at the edge of the road, gazing out to sea, half hoping he might be able to catch a glimpse of the *Seawraith*, and half hoping he wouldn't. There was no sign of it. Nor was there any sign of the truck.

Ali-Khaleefa sauntered over to offer an opinion. He was carrying his M16 over his shoulder and had an unlit cigarette hanging from his lips. 'There has been a mistake, I think,' he said. 'It seems the woman from

American Travel is not correct with her date.'

'I don't know.' The knot in Farrell's stomach had been replaced by a feeling of frustration. 'I'm going to set the timer anyway. Maybe that'll make something happen.' He picked up the Maverick and used the end of a twig to punch in a delay of fifty minutes and no seconds.

Ali-Khaleefa inspected the row of numbers on the screen. 'You are sure such a time is not too short?'

'Depends when the flasks are unloaded. I don't want anyone at the complex discovering our surprise package ahead of time.'

'But the device must also not go off before the truck is underground.'

'Sure. The whole thing's a gamble. Do you think I ought to add another ten minutes?'

Ali-Khaleefa shrugged. 'If the explosion fails to destroy the warheads because the blast takes place in the open, the Americans and the British will try again one day. For me it is enough that Rajavi and his bastard friend will die. It is a pity only that the man Volchek will not die with them.'

'Volchek's luck won't run out until tomorrow. He's going to be stuck in Tehran overnight and there'll be a rope round his neck before we're back in Kuwait. Rebecca Harris is fixing things so the Iranians reach the wrong conclusion about Intech.'

'Then the Russian will wish he had accompanied the flasks to the Khvormuj Mugharet.' Ali-Khaleefa grinned. 'For any man it is better that the end is quick. The Iranians will not be kind to him.'

'Assuming we haven't made this whole bloody trip for nothing.' Farrell checked his watch, worried that he had either miscalculated the transit time from Shiraz or that for some reason the truck had never even left Tehran. In a few hours it would be dawn, and long before sunrise he knew they would have no choice but to abandon the exercise. Only Almira would be pleased, he thought. Two hundred thousand dollars poorer, but pleased. He wondered what she was doing and if she was becoming concerned.

'It is possible the Iranians are being cautious,' Ali-Khaleefa said. 'Perhaps from the offices of American Travel there has been a phone call made to someone in Tehran.'

'I don't think so. Travers runs a pretty tight operation. He wouldn't have given Rebecca Harris the job unless he was absolutely certain about her. If this turns out to be a wild-goose chase it won't be her fault.'

'You will tell me, please, what in English it means to chase the wild geese.'

There was no chance for Farrell to explain.

Ali-Khaleefa's expression became one of intense concentration. He was staring out to sea where there was a distant flicker of light. It was extremely faint, but unmistakable, the gleam of head-lights on the water from a vehicle rounding a corner somewhere up the coast.

'OK. This is it.' Farrell scrambled to his feet. 'Now remember what I said. No matter where the truck stops, you're to stay by the Zodiac so I know where to find you. It'll take me around twenty-five seconds to reach the truck, arm the Maverick and make it back to the beach. If anything goes wrong, your job is to scare the living shit out of the guards and keep them pinned down while I get the Zodiac launched.'

'If I see them, you wish me to kill Rajavi and Bozorgian?' Ali-Khaleefa checked the magazine on his rifle.

'You might not have the time. You'll be up against combat-trained soldiers. They won't mess around.'

'So Miss Almira has been wrong? You are not here for revenge?'

'What the hell do you think this is?' Farrell held up the Maverick. 'If I run into trouble we'll see what happens. You do what you like.'

The Omani spat out his cigarette. 'I shall pick my targets well, but my hands are not so steady. Instead of feeling like a young Dhofari again, I can taste only fear. It is the same for you?'

'Yeah.' Farrell nodded. 'But it's going to be over real quick. Ten minutes from now we'll be back on board the *Seawraith* and all we'll be tasting is cold beer.'

'The truck draws near so it is best we prepare ourselves. Allah be with you.' Ali-Khaleefa eased himself off the edge of the road, waving his farewell before he limped away to disappear amongst the boulders and the clumps of seaweed on the beach.

Alone now, gripping the Maverick hard enough to break it, Farrell crouched down, his head level with the road surface, waiting for his first real glimpse of headlights.

As well as travelling too fast the truck driver saw the rock-fall only at the last minute. He slammed on his brakes and fought to control a thirty-foot slide across the rubble, finally coming to rest with his front bumper hard against the cliff face.

Farrell hadn't bargained on the dust. A huge cloud of it was obscuring his view of the men spilling out of the truck. But it was the right truck. Already Rajavi was climbing down from the cab, caught in the headlights as he hurried to check for damage. And Bozorgian was there too. The Iranian

Brigadier was standing by himself, speaking into a hand-held radio transmitter.

Although the dust was dispersing, Farrell wasn't certain all the men were out. So far he had counted five; Rajavi, Bozorgian and three soldiers in full battledress, clutching assault rifles while they picked their way between the rocks and headed off towards the bridge.

Six men altogether, Farrell decided, one more than there was supposed to be, either because Rebecca had overlooked the driver, or because the intelligence from Tehran had been faulty.

Responding to shouted instructions from Bozorgian, the driver extricated his truck from the larger rocks at the base of the cliff, but, once he had done so, he seemed to be at a loss. He endeavoured unsuccessfully to straddle some of the rubble, allowing one of his front wheels to become jammed against a lump of clay that refused to break when he gunned the engine in an effort to use force instead of brains.

The truck was the same model as those Farrell had seen this morning, a twin rear axle Mercedes painted in desert camouflage with the cargo area covered in canvas. Which meant access would be easy, he thought, but impossible to attempt unless Rajavi and the brigadier joined forces with the soldiers to help clear away the rocks.

All three soldiers were returning, keeping close to the cliff with their rifles levelled as though they were half expecting trouble.

Farrell kept his eyes on them, wondering if something had made them suspicious or whether they were simply following orders. He didn't know. Nor could he waste any more time. Slithering down on to the beach, he crawled along the shore for what he estimated to be twice the length of the truck before climbing a weed-covered boulder and cautiously raising his head to confirm that he was in the correct position.

What he saw was what he'd hoped to see. To his right, twenty yards away, the truck was stationary in the centre of the road, engine running, headlights on full beam. In front of it, under the guidance of Bozorgian, Rajavi and the soldiers were using shovels and an iron bar to clear a pathway.

With nothing to prevent him from making his run, Farrell froze. Drenched in sweat, a miniature flashlight clamped between his teeth and the Maverick slippery in his hand, he tried to regain his nerve, waiting for the right instant to start his run.

The opportunity came soon enough — after the truck driver created an accidental diversion by dropping his clutch too quickly and nearly running over one of the soldiers.

Farrell counted under his breath. Then, suddenly, he was up on the road, gulping in dust on a heart-stopping rush to the truck.

He reached the back of it in under five seconds. In another three he had loosened the tie-downs and had wormed his way up under the canvas.

Inside, the darkness provided an illusion of security, but he could see very little. Holding his fingers over the lens, he switched on the flashlight, allowing only a glimmer of light to escape while he explored his surroundings.

The truck was empty except for a thick layer of grit and what appeared to be a giant egg-crate strapped to the floor by lengths of nylon webbing. Nearly four feet long and more than two feet wide, it was a purpose-built container supporting row upon row of flasks in hollow blocks of plastic foam.

Knowing the seconds were ticking away, he extinguished his light and worked by feel, ramming his hand between the plastic lining and the side of the crate to lever open a gap for the Maverick. When he had enlarged the gap sufficiently, he armed the detonator by wrenching out the pin and used all his strength to force the case downwards until he was certain it was out of sight.

He used the flashlight to make a final

check, then returned to the rear of the truck, wasting more precious seconds to make sure he had disguised his footprints in the grit.

The delay was fatal.

Before he could locate the opening in the canvas there was the roar of another engine and the night became ablaze with light.

He didn't hesitate. Tearing at the canvas, he threw himself out headfirst on to the road. Less than fifty feet away, the second truck was closing on him quickly, blinding him with its headlights as the driver tried to run him down.

Scrambling to his feet, Farrell spun round, changing his direction just before the truck's bumper smashed in to a rock beside him.

Caught between the two vehicles and the cliff, he took the only option open to him. He ran, sprinting for the beach and the Zodiac, praying the bullets would be slow to come. At the same time Ali-Khaleefa opened fire.

Farrell didn't make it. There were soldiers on the beach, two of them crouching under cover to return the Omani's fire, another appearing from nowhere to slam a rifle butt against the side of Farrell's head.

For a moment he believed he might still be able to escape. Dazed from the blow, but fully conscious, he seized the barrel of the rifle, attempting to wrest it from the soldier's hands. For his trouble he received a kick in the stomach that was savage enough to drive him to his knees.

Unable to breathe, he started to crawl away before collapsing face-down on the sand.

He lay there for a long time, fighting for air, aware only vaguely of the gunfire and the shouting, but already knowing he had been betrayed.

Rough hands pulled him back on to the road, dragged him stumbling over the rock-fall and thrust him in to a glare of head-lights where Rajavi was standing.

Farrell leaned against a mudguard, sickened more by the knowledge that he had been deceived and outmanoeuvred than by the pain and the taste of his vomit. He could see the men from the second truck now, nearly a dozen heavily armed soldiers from the Revolutionary Guards who had come to help close the trap. Some were busy clearing away the rocks, but the majority had joined in a deadly hunt for Ali-Khaleefa.

The worst and cruellest way to fail, Farrell thought bitterly. After all the planning and all his hopes, there had not been the remotest chance of success because the odds had been stacked against them so thoroughly that failure had been guaranteed.

From somewhere along the beach the cry

of a wounded man was drowned out by three prolonged bursts of gunfire interspersed with the sound of single shots and someone shouting.

Rajavi displayed no interest in the proceedings. After ordering the truck engines to be switched off he came to inspect his prisoner.

'So, Englishman, you think you will surprise us,' he said. 'But instead we have the surprise for you. By coming to steal from us some red mercury, you understand now you have risked your life for nothing.'

Farrell kept quiet, hardly daring to believe that his reason for being here had been misunderstood.

Rajavi slid back the bolt on his machine pistol. 'First you will tell me if it is the American Travers who pays you for this.'

'Not unless you bring your men back. You don't have to kill anyone.'

'For the old Omani it is too late.' Rajavi pointed into the distance. 'Already the soldiers deal with him.'

Even if Farrell could have yelled a warning it would have been of no consequence. On the centre span of the bridge the unearthly, moonlit figure of Ali-Khaleefa had appeared.

Ignoring a hail of bullets ricocheting off the steel-work, he began to limp towards the trucks, firing his M16 from the hip as if to

357

demonstrate his contempt for the men who had been searching for him.

Farrell waited for the inevitable, watching in horror until he realized he was witnessing something immeasurably more profound than an exhibition of contempt. This was defiance — a means for Ali-Khaleefa to cheat fate, the act of a man who had the spirit to confront death head-on, and who had chosen his own way and his own time to die.

The end was mercifully swift. Shortly before the Omani reached the approach to the bridge, the soldiers of the Jerusalem Force granted him his wish. And, as silence descended on the roadside and the river-mouth, so a shadow from the crumpled body of Ali-Khaleefa fused with other shadows to form a pool of darkness where a brave man once had stood.

14

A hundred years ago, after the third
hand-grenade had gone off inside the hull of
the stricken *Stingray*, Farrell had been
prepared to die. Somehow, then, in the warm
waters of the Gulf of Oman, he had been able
to accept the idea. But this wasn't Oman and,
because instead of being about to drown he
was facing the likelihood of a roadside
execution, his courage had all but deserted
him.

Under Bozorgian's orders the soldiers had
brought back their dead and wounded, four
injured men who had managed to survive
Ali-Khaleefa's bullets, and three who had
been less lucky, killed outright, all of them by
shots to the head.

One by one the bodies of the dead were
being thrown unceremoniously into the rear
of the second truck, leaving the wounded
either to help themselves, or to seek
assistance from their companions.

The body of Ali-Khaleefa had not been
retrieved, nor was there any indication that it
would be. Instead, Bozorgian came over to
discuss something with Rajavi, waving his

hands and kicking at the rubble with his boots.

The two men were conversing in Farsi. Farrell could recognize several words, but not enough of them to understand what was being said.

Rajavi returned his attention to Farrell. 'Answer the question about the American,' he said.

'Why the hell should I? You murdered Tony Nelson, and those soldiers just killed an old man for no damn reason at all. Go and screw yourself.'

'You believe now we will also kill you?'

'Have you got something else in mind?'

'Perhaps we put you on television in Tehran so the world will understand how the Americans try to undermine the security of Iran. But first I think we shall see what you have to say here. You are paid to do this job?'

'Yeah.' Despite the hint of a reprieve, Farrell had no illusions whatever about his future. His only chance, he knew, lay in reaching the beach — a sprint for safety that he couldn't even begin to make until he'd recovered some of his strength.

'It is the Americans and the British who send you to obtain a sample of the red mercury?' Rajavi enquired.

'Right. Travers offered me two hundred

thousand dollars for one flask.' With nothing to lose, Farrell decided to embellish the lies. 'The US are shit scared about you selling red mercury to the Middle East. So are the British. They've got military scientists standing by to evaluate the stuff. You ought to have done a deal with the West at the same time.'

Rajavi shrugged. 'Tehran would not be pleased with such an arrangement. Now you will explain how the man Travers has come by the information about our shipment to the Khvormuj Mugharet.'

'Sure, as long as we can do a deal. If you want to know how to crack open the People's Mujahedin in Tehran I can give you names. All I need is one of your flasks and a guarantee of safe passage, and they're yours.'

'You think we are fools?' Rajavi muttered something to Bozorgian who nodded and spoke again into his radio.

Although Farrell's mouth was so dry that his lips were sticking together, he could no longer avoid asking the question that had to be asked. 'How did you know I'd show up here?' He looked directly at Rajavi.

'Because we are careful. Last week, after a phone call comes to say you have returned to Oman and that the girl with the twisted arm catches a plane with you to Kuwait, we arrange for a man to see what you do there.

Once we learn of your chartered boat, we believe soon you will come to find us in Esfahan or Shiraz, or perhaps here by the bridge where it is quiet and where you think it will be simple to deceive us.'

Any other explanation would have been bearable. This one was not. Farrell was no more able to come to terms with the possibility of his worst fears proving to be true than he could accept the prospect of a bullet to the head.

He clenched his teeth. 'Who phoned you?'

'The call is from Muscat — from the home of your friend Mr Muammar.'

'Almira?'

Rajavi's face was impassive. 'While she lies in your bed waiting for you in Kuwait, I think you are not so sure about her. When I tell you of the little game she has played with her brother, perhaps you will understand why it is she opens her legs so wide for you.'

Hasan Rajavi would never tell anyone anything again.

From the roadside came the awful hammering of an automatic rifle at close range.

The bullets caught him chest high, driving him back against the cliff. Another burst reduced his body to a pulp of bloodstained flesh and splintered bone.

362

Farrell heard Almira call to him before she fired again. He saw the soldiers scrambling for cover and, as he turned to make his run for the beach, saw the muzzle of Bozorgian's gun begin to rise.

Farrell had less than ten feet to go when fragments of hot lead spattered into his legs while, only inches to his right, bullets started cutting furrows in the road surface and ricocheting off both sides of the boulder in front of him.

He jumped, smacking painfully into the boulder and sliding down feet-first over the seaweed until he hit the sand.

Almira was there, clipping a fresh magazine into the M16.

'Leave it,' Farrell yelled. 'Get to the Zodiac.'

'We can't — not without Ali-Khaleefa.'

He grabbed her, carried her kicking into the water and threw her bodily into the inflatable. 'Ali-Khaleefa's dead,' he shouted. 'Lie down and stay down.'

Disregarding the pain in his stomach and his dizziness, he used all his strength to push the Zodiac out of the shallows, diving headlong over the stern as Almira discharged the M16 towards the shore.

Half expecting to have his head blown off and blinded by muzzle flashes he pulled desperately on the outboard's starter cord, willing the engine to fire.

It coughed twice before coming to life, its propeller churning in the sand to drive the Zodiac away in a slow retreat from the beach.

Watching for submerged rocks and waiting to be strafed by a storm of bullets, Farrell saw that Almira was going to ignore his instructions.

She was kneeling, trying to keep her balance with the rifle barrel wavering around alarmingly.

This time he ducked before she fired. Simultaneously, fountains of water erupted all around them. Farrell could hear the bullets zipping past. They were dangerously close, missing the fragile, airfilled hull by the slimmest of margins or creating streaks of white foam only feet away.

But the propeller was free of the bottom now, giving him some badly needed control over the Zodiac's direction.

Holding Almira to prevent her from falling overboard, he swung the bow north, held his course for two or three seconds and then headed directly out to sea in a series of wild, evasive turns.

He kept the power on too long, realizing his mistake when she kicked his leg.

'Farrell, it's all right,' she shouted. 'We're

out of range and we'll overshoot.' She pointed. 'Look.'

The *Seawraith* was nearby, not a mile out to sea, but much closer in, floating quietly at anchor a hundred yards away. He headed straight for it, his eyes not on the boat, but on Almira. How she had survived he could not imagine. On a night so thick with bullets that neither of them should be alive, for her to be unharmed was as remarkable as finding that, by some miracle, he too had escaped with his life.

She was frightened, barefoot and wearing only a saturated T-shirt and a pair of shorts.

'How the hell did you get ashore?' he asked.

'When I saw the second truck and heard the gunshots I waited for you to flash your light at me, but you never did. So I moved the *Seawraith* to where it is now.'

'You didn't swim from this far out — not with the rifle?'

She nodded.

'Jesus.' Farrell stared back at the bridge. It was over half a mile away, illuminated by the headlights of the two trucks as they recommenced their journey south.

'Who killed Ali-Khaleefa?' she asked. 'What happened?'

'There were fourteen or fifteen soldiers.

365

Rajavi and Bozorgian had us tailed all the while we were in Kuwait.'

'How did they know we were there?'

Farrell tried to see her face, but she turned away from him. 'You know how,' he said. 'You were near enough to hear what Rajavi was saying. Someone made a phone call from your father's home.'

'Salim,' she said. 'If Salim followed us to the airport he would have seen what flight we caught, wouldn't he?'

'Sure.' Letting the Zodiac nudge up against the transom of the *Seawraith*, Farrell tossed the M16 into the cockpit and helped her climb on board, but doubled up in agony when he tried to follow.

Conscious of stabbing pain from what he guessed was a broken rib, he was more careful with his second attempt, relying on her assistance and avoiding any sudden movement.

Almira was anxious. 'What is it?' she said.

'Nothing.' He pushed the Zodiac away. 'I'm OK. Now listen — we're not out of this yet. You have to keep an eye open for anything coming from the north or from behind us.'

'Why? There's no one out here.'

'Bozorgian had a radio transmitter. For all we know he's arranged for Iranian patrol boats to intercept us. There's a naval base at

Bushehr and another one out on Khark Island.' Farrell started the *Seawraith*'s engines, letting them idle while he went to pull up the anchor.

He returned to find Almira sitting down, her face buried in her hands.

'I can't believe Ali-Khaleefa's dead,' she mumbled. 'And I've never shot anyone before.'

'Don't think.' Farrell pulled her hands away. 'Just do what I've told you to do. We're still a long way from home, and I need you.'

'No, you don't. You're not sure it was Salim, are you? You think it might have been me.'

Refusing to argue with her, he increased the engine revs and swung the *Seawraith* west towards the open sea. Although he was almost certain it was Salim who had betrayed them, because the moment of Rajavi's death had been so convenient, some of his doubt had returned. Coincidence? Farrell wondered. Or a well-timed execution to prevent him from learning how long her game with Salim had really lasted?

As though aware of his distrust she stood up, bitting her lip. 'It couldn't have been anyone except my brother,' she said. 'You know it was him, don't you?'

'Not Rebecca Harris?'

'You might as well pretend it was Travers, or my father, or Aunt Latifa. Why won't you believe anything I say?'

'Look,' Farrell said, 'you don't have to convince me; you just saved my life. I don't care why you shot Rajavi when you did. All I care about is getting back across the Gulf in one piece.'

'What about you and me? Don't you care about that?'

'For Christ's sake. Stop being so bloody stupid. Go and fetch the grenade launcher and bring back all the spare ammunition. If we're going to have visitors I want to be ready.' He checked the inshore chart and began to give the *Seawraith* its head, permitting their speed to build until they were travelling at nearly twenty-five knots on a course that would carry them well south of Khark Island, but without burning up too much diesel.

Farrell was concerned at the state of their fuel reserves. Reluctant to economise while they were still this close to the coast, but guessing their tanks would be empty before they reached Kuwait unless he slackened off soon, he began re-estimating the fuel consumption for a lower average speed. He was in the middle of his calculation when Almira shouted.

He turned quickly, expecting to see wakes

or the shadowy outlines of boats converging on them. But there were none. The *Seawraith* was alone, speeding away from the deserted coast road and the bridge on an empty, moonlit sea.

Farrell had misunderstood. The threat was coming from elsewhere.

Travelling at nearly the speed of sound, the fighter screamed across the bow, banked and went into a vertical climb on full reheat.

He was stunned, hitting the throttle levers automatically, for a second unable to believe he could have ever been so foolish. Not patrol boats. Not even a surveillance helicopter or a spotter plane. Instead, the Iranians had gone for overkill, electing to send a military combat jet to make certain the *Seawraith* would never reach shore again.

Almira was equally shaken, looking skywards, following the glow from the afterburners while she steadied the M16 on the cockpit rail.

'Forget it,' Farrell shouted.

She hesitated, but dropped the gun. 'We'll have to swim,' she said. 'There's nothing else we can do.'

Before he could reply the plane was on top of them again. It was a Russian-built MiG 29, sweeping past to starboard at an altitude of less than 500 feet, the Iranian markings clearly visible on its wings.

Identification runs, Farrell thought grimly, two of them because the pilot was being careful.

Almira began scrambling towards the stern. 'Farrell,' she cried. 'Come on.'

'No.' Hauling her back by her arm he yelled at her to watch for rocks, then pushed the Seawraith into a punishing 180 degree turn, centring the bow on an invisible point on the coastline.

He kept his attention on the shore, relying on Almira to alert him of trouble, navigating more by instinct than by his instruments.

By now the big diesels were thundering, driving the Seawraith faster and faster until the river was left behind. In another minute the bridge too was out of sight and soon, where there had been lights on the road, all Farrell could see was the sombre, receding shape of the headland.

Almira was concentrating hard, occasionally glancing over her shoulder and shouting instructions whenever she detected a tell-tale line of breakers or picked out the faint outline of a rock.

She saw the reef before he did, yelling at him at the same moment he spun the wheel, not in response to her warning, but to some sixth sense.

It was a manoeuvre that saved their lives. From a speed of nearly thirty-eight knots, in a near-suicidal turn that took them close enough to disaster for Farrell to brace himself for impact, the *Seawraith* threw up a ten-foot-high wall of spray.

There was a glimpse of the fighter, guns flickering, but moving so swiftly that it was gone before he realized that they had not only missed the reef but had somehow escaped the first attack.

Wrenching on the wheel to realign the bow with the shore, he waited for the hull to stop shuddering and gather speed again.

'You're out of your mind.' Almira was white-faced. 'What are you doing?'

'Where's the plane?'

'I don't know. Farrell, we won't get away like this. How can we?'

'Four minutes until we're directly off-shore from the valley.' He checked his watch. 'Maybe five.'

'What do you mean?'

'The Maverick. It's in the truck.'

She stared at him. Then she stared at the coast.

Less than a quarter of a mile away, the road was a thin black ribbon winding its way inland in the moonlight — the road along which 160 flasks of red mercury had already

371

passed — the only road to the underground complex of the Khvormuj Mugharet.

Farrell's estimate of four minutes might as well have been four hours.

The fighter came from nowhere. Cannons stuttering, red flashes spurting from the leading edges of its wings, it strafed the *Seawraith* with one terrible burst of fire that tore half the superstructure away. Simultaneously Farrell felt the hull smack into a hidden rock.

He fought for control and checked that Almira was all right.

Surrounded by pieces of the radar, shattered fibreglass and splintered wood she, like him, was unharmed, but with an expression of terror on her face.

Farrell too was scared witless — so scared that he almost forgot to check for leaks below the waterline. There weren't any. The hull was intact and both engines were still running. But whether or not the *Seawraith* could survive another attack, seemed doubtful. All he knew was that if the gamble of a lifetime was ever to pay off, the luck that had kept them alive this far would have to continue keeping them alive for another two and a half minutes.

He didn't tell Almira. Instead he indicated that she should lie face-down on the cockpit floor. She was unprotesting, but when he helped her to lock her hands around the frame of the galley door he could feel her trembling.

With a minute to go, before he turned the *Seawraith* back out to sea, he took a last look at the valley ahead of him. It was a dark vee set into the hills, revealing nothing of its secret. There was no glow of lights, no radio aerials that he could see, and, apart from the road, not a shred of evidence to confirm that this was the right valley.

But Farrell knew it was. It was the right valley because it had to be — because if he was wrong his subterfuge would have been in vain.

Now they were leaving the shallows he gave up watching for rocks in favour of scanning the horizon, looking out across reaches of the Gulf that were as lonely and featureless as the hills had been.

The illusion was perfect, he thought, one last deception to persuade him to make one last mistake.

With his watch registering 4.15, Farrell abandoned his search for the MiG, all but convinced that his trap had failed. What made him hurl himself sideways he never knew.

Skimming fifty feet above the water, the pilot attacked head on, raking the *Seawraith* from bow to stern with cannon fire before embarking on a climb in a premature celebration of his kill.

At precisely seven seconds after 4.15 on the morning of November 30th, over a vast area of Iran's western seaboard, dawn broke early.

From the head of the valley where a million tons of rock had burst aside, came a flash of incandescent light so intense that, for over 300 square miles, the night became brighter than the brightest day.

And with the flash came the shock wave, a nightmare of noise and boiling gas that surged upwards and outwards across the Gulf.

At sea level the fury of the blast was severe enough. The *Seawraith* became airborne as though hurled forwards by a giant hand.

At higher altitude the effect was a hundred times more violent. Like a paper aeroplane caught in a hurricane, the MiG lasted only for an instant. Wings crippled, on fire and with its back broken, the whole airframe disintegrated to be carried away in a whirlwind of sparks and burning wreckage.

On board the *Seawraith* conditions were chaotic. The remaining aft section of the superstructure was matchwood, a gaping hole had been torn in the foredeck and one of the engines had been reduced to a twisted mass of metal.

Farrell had the presence of mind to switch off the other engine before he started crawling, searching frantically through the debris for Almira.

She was lying in the galley, breathing, but curled up in a foetal position.

Insensitive to the pain in his ribs, he carried her into the cabin where he placed her on one of the bunks.

'It's my side,' she whispered.

'Hang on.' Her blood wet and sticky on his fingers, cursing his clumsiness in the dark, he tried to discover where she'd been injured.

The cabin lights were dead. So were both of the halogen lights. But one of the flashlights worked.

Once he'd peeled away her blouse he was able to see where the blood was coming from. Buried in her left side was a sliver of plexiglass from a cabin or cockpit window. The silver was protruding nearly an inch, but because there was no indication of how deeply it had penetrated he was reluctant to withdraw it.

'How bad does it hurt?' He pulled her hair away gently from her face.

'Not so much as it did. What about you? Are you all right?'

He didn't waste time checking. As long as he continued breathing and could move around, all that mattered was getting help.

'Farrell.' She endeavoured unsuccessfully to raise herself. 'Where's the plane?'

'Gone. So is Bozorgian, so is the complex. But we're still afloat and we've still got one good engine, so all you have to do is make yourself comfortable while I get us underway.' He removed his shirt and folded it into a pad. 'Can you hold this against your side until I fix up a proper bandage for you?'

'I think so.' She took it from him. 'Do we have enough fuel?'

'Don't worry about the fuel. That's my job. Let me handle everything. I'll be back as soon as we're clear of the reefs.'

She nodded.

Telling himself that her injury could not possibly be as bad as it looked, he went to inspect the hull again.

Two rows of splintered holes from cannon shells were sufficiently high above the waterline to ignore, but six feet from the stern on the starboard side a long crack was weeping water.

There was no decision to make. Cracked or not the hull would have to hold together, and with one engine or no engines, he knew he had to find a way to get her to hospital in Kuwait.

He restarted the diesel and cautiously

increased the revs. Then, after glancing over his shoulder at the dull red glow coming from the valley, and as the *Seawraith* headed westwards on its final run for home, Farrell offered up another prayer — this time not for himself, but for a girl who had risked her life for him, and for the promise he had made her — a promise for a future that had suddenly become more uncertain that it had ever been.

★ ★   ★

For the next four hours he struggled to suppress a feeling of increasing helplessness. By sunrise the true extent of her injury had become apparent, and when she had spoken to him last, she had been a good deal weaker.

Now, with Kuwait still 140 miles away, so limited were his options that even turning back to Bushehr was out of the question. Only a passing tanker would provide the chance of medical assistance, and then only if he could attract the attention of a captain who might be prepared to stop in mid-Gulf.

After checking the fuel gauge and trying once more to get the radio working, Farrell knew it was time to find out if he could summon the nerve to extract the splinter from her side.

She was pleased to see him, her eyes clearer

377

than they had been ten minutes ago, her hair gleaming in the early morning sun that was streaming through the hole in the deck above her.

'Fifteen knots,' he said. 'Not bad for one engine and no crew.'

'Help me sit up,' she said quietly. 'I want you to tell me about Greece — about all the islands you're taking me to.'

Being very careful he slid a pillow behind her so she could lean back against the bulkhead.

She smiled at him. 'Don't say we're only going for a few days.'

Drawing on his recollections of the picture in the airline brochure, Farrell described the olive groves, the beach, the colour of the sky and the sea, and told her how the summers would never be as hot and dry as they were in Oman, nor as cool and moist as they were in England.

He was reaching for her hand, when from her lips there came a bright red rush of blood. A moment later she died cradled in his arms.

15

Now the summer tourists had gone and the island had returned to normal, Farrell usually took the steep, cobblestoned street on his way to the waterfront. This morning he wished he hadn't.

From the little café by the church where someone had put a fresh cassette into the tape deck, music was drifting through an open window, triggering all the wrong memories.

In front of him, the azure blue of the Aegean was not the blue of the Gulf. Nor were the whitewashed stone villas of Myconos the villas of Muscat. But the music made them so.

It was a song called *Peaceful Easy Feeling* by the Eagles about a girl with brown skin and sparkling ear-rings — a song that Farrell fervently wished had never been recorded. In the eleven months he'd been living on the island he'd heard it twice by accident on the radio, and once right here coming from the same window. And on each occasion the result had been the same as it was going to be today.

He sat down on the church steps, knowing the morning was spoiled, letting the words do their damage. At the end of the first verse, without waiting to hear any more, he resumed his walk and, for the next two hours, made himself think about something else altogether.

It was nearly eleven o'clock when the lady from the post office came to find him on the quay. Apart from her being Greek, because of her personality and her manner she always reminded Farrell of Aunt Latifa.

'There is another letter,' she said. 'So I come to look for you.'

'Same American Travel envelope?'

She nodded. 'I shall tear it up as you have asked me to do with the others?'

'Right. Thanks for letting me know, though.'

'Mr Farrell, if you will permit me to say, it is not good for a young man who will not read his letters to be alone on the island as you are. Would it not be better for you to return to England where you have friends?'

He smiled. 'I had a friend who figured you should never go back to anywhere you've been before. I like it here.'

'Although some days you go out with the fishermen and on other days you come here to watch and to spend your time, you cannot do this forever. Why not read the letters when they may bring good news?'

'They bring trouble,' he said. 'American Travel paid me a lot of money once, and they've got some crazy idea I might want to do another job for them.'

'But this is not the reason for your sadness?'

'I'm OK.' Farrell smiled again. 'Just having a bad day.'

'Last month when you have helped my husband to repair the engine in his boat you have spoken to him about a girl you must forget.' She stopped talking. 'You will forgive me. It is not my business.'

The damn song was running through Farrell's head like an endless tape. Almost as though Almira was beside him, he could see her ear-rings, feel the warmth of her skin and smell her perfume. He looked at the woman. 'Do you want to hear a story?'

'If it is what you wish. We shall drink coffee at my house, perhaps?'

'No. Right here, right now before I change my mind.'

'Your story is about the girl?'

'Her name was Almira,' Farrell said. 'I first saw her one morning a year ago at a place called Mutrah in Oman.' He hesitated, wondering how to describe her, suddenly uncertain of himself. But once the memories became clearer he found it as easy to paint a picture of her as it was to describe the night on board the *Stingray* when everything had begun.

He spoke without stopping, omitting nothing and without worrying about how it sounded or how long he took. It was an exercise that was supposed to be cathartic, a way to eliminate the burden of the past, but no sooner had he finished than he knew the effort had been wasted. The hurt hadn't gone, and the sense of loss was still with him.

The woman touched his arm. 'You do not say if the brother of the girl tells you the truth of his bet with her.'

'I didn't ask him.'

'Then by staying on Myconos you are only running away from yourself. Am I not right?'

'Probably.'

'So perhaps today is a good day for you to telephone your wife.'

'Mary?' He didn't know whether to take the suggestion seriously.

'You may make the call from the post office.'

'Now?'

The woman smiled at him. 'Of course. You have told me these things only because I am a stranger. But only a stranger can see what

THE GREENWAY
Jane Adams

When Cassie and her twelve-year-old cousin Suzie had taken a short cut through an ancient Norfolk pathway, Suzie had simply vanished . . . Twenty years on, Cassie is still tormented by nightmares. She returns to Norfolk, determined to solve the mystery.

FORTY YEARS
ON THE WILD FRONTIER
Carl Breihan & W. Montgomery

Noted Western historian Carl Breihan has culled from the handwritten diaries of John Montgomery, grandfather of co-author Wayne Montgomery, new facts about Wyatt Earp, Doc Holliday, Bat Masterson and other famous and infamous men and women who gained notoriety when the Western Frontier was opened up.

TAKE NOW, PAY LATER
Joanna Dessau

This fiction based on fact is the love-turning-to-hate story of Robert Carr, Earl of Somerset, and his wife, Frances.

must be done if the future is to hold some happiness for you.'

The elusive future, Farrell thought. Through the dust of all his dreams, the need to search for it was still there — the need for the peaceful, easy feeling that no one but Mary had ever properly understood or ever believed he'd find.

'You are coming?' The woman turned to leave.

'Yes.' He stopped staring out to sea. 'Yes, I'm coming.'

THE END